THE
TWELVE TRIBES
OF HATTIE

Ayana Mathis

R A N D O M   H O U S E
LARGE PRINT

Copyright © 2012 by Ayana Mathis

All rights reserved.
Published in the United States of America by
Random House Large Print in association with
Alfred A. Knopf, New York.
Distributed by Random House, Inc., New York.

Grateful acknowledgment is made to Rita Dove for permission to reprint an excerpt from "Obedience" from **Thomas and Beulah: Poems** by Rita Dove, Carnegie Mellon University Press, Pittsburgh, PA. Copyright © 1986 by Rita Dove. Reprinted by permission of the author.

Cover photograph © Mark Pennington/
Millennium Images, U.K.
Cover design by Kelly Blair

The Library of Congress has established a Cataloging-in-Publication record for this title.

ISBN: 978-0-8041-2102-6

www.randomhouse.com/largeprint

FIRST LARGE PRINT EDITION

Printed in the United States of America

10 9 8 7 6 5 4 3 2

This Large Print edition published in accord with
the standards of the N.A.V.H.

For my mother,
and for Grandmom
and Grandpop

All of you came to me and said, "Let us send men ahead of us to explore the land for us and bring back a report to us regarding the route by which we should go up and the cities we will come to."

The plan seemed good to me, and I selected twelve of you, one from each tribe.

—DEUTERONOMY 1:22–23

The house, shut up like a pocket watch, those tight hearts breathing inside— she could never invent them.

—RITA DOVE, "Obedience"

THE
TWELVE TRIBES
OF HATTIE

Philadelphia and Jubilee

1925

"PHILADELPHIA AND JUBILEE!" August said when Hattie told him what she wanted to name their twins. "You cain't give them babies no crazy names like that!"

Hattie's mother, if she were still alive, would have agreed with August. She would have said Hattie had chosen vulgar names; "low and showy," she would have called them. But she was gone, and Hattie wanted to give her babies names that weren't already chiseled on a headstone in the family plots in Georgia, so she gave them names of promise and of hope, reaching forward names, not looking back ones.

The twins were born in June, during Hattie and August's first summer as husband and wife. They had rented a house on Wayne Street—it was small, but it was in a good neighborhood and was, August said, just an in-the-meanwhile house. "Until we buy a house of our own," Hattie said. "Till we sign on that dotted line," August agreed.

At the end of June robins beset the trees and roofs of Wayne Street. The neighborhood rang with birdsong. The twittering lulled the twins to sleep and put Hattie in such high spirits that she giggled all of the time. It rained every morning, but the afternoons were bright and the grass in Hattie and August's tiny square of lawn was green as the first day of the world. The ladies of the neighborhood did their baking early, and by noon the block smelled of the strawberry cakes they set on their windowsills to cool. The three of them, Hattie and her twins, dozed in the shade on the porch. The next summer Philadelphia and Jubilee would be walking; they'd totter around the porch like sweet bumbling old men.

HATTIE SHEPHERD LOOKED DOWN at her two babies in their Moses baskets. The twins were seven months old. They breathed easier sitting upright, so she had them propped with small pillows. Only just now had they quieted. The night had been bad. Pneumonia could be cured, though not easily. Better that than mumps or influenza or pleurisy. Better pneumonia than cholera or scarlet fever. Hattie sat on the bathroom floor and leaned against the toilet with her legs stretched in front of her. The window was opaque with steam that condensed into droplets and ran down the panes and over the white wooden frames to pool in the dip in the tile behind the toilet. Hattie had been running the hot water for hours. August was half the night in the basement loading coal into the hot water heater. He had not wanted to leave Hattie and the babies to go to work. Well, but . . . a day's work is a day's pay, and the coal bin was running low. Hattie reassured him: the babies will be alright now the night's passed.

The doctor had come around the day before and advised the steam cure. He'd prescribed a small dosage of ipecac and cautioned against backward country remedies like hot mustard poultices, though vapor rub was acceptable. He diluted the ipecac with a clear, oily liquid, gave Hattie two small droppers, and showed her how to hold the babies' tongues down with her finger so the medicine would flow into their throats. August paid three dollars for the visit and set to making mustard poultices the minute the doctor was out the door. Pneumonia.

Somewhere in the neighborhood, a siren wailed so keenly it could have been in front of the house. Hattie struggled up from her place on the floor to wipe a circle in the fogged bathroom window.

Nothing but white row houses across the street, crammed together like teeth, and gray patches of ice on the sidewalk and the saplings nearly dead in the frozen squares of dirt allotted to them. Here and there a light shone in an upstairs window—some of the neighborhood men worked the docks like August, some delivered milk or had postal routes; there were schoolteachers too and a slew of others about whom Hattie knew nothing. All over Philadelphia the people rose in the crackling cold to stoke the furnaces in their basements. They were united in these hardships.

A grainy dawn misted up from the bottom of the sky. Hattie closed her eyes and remembered the sunrises of her childhood—these visions were forever tugging at her; her memories of Georgia grew more urgent and pressing with each day she lived in Philadelphia. Every morning of her girlhood the work horn would sound in the bluing dawn, over the fields and the houses and the black gum trees. From her bed Hattie watched the field hands dragging down the road in front of her house. Always the laggards passed after the first horn: pregnant women, the sick and lame, those too old for picking, those with babies strapped to their backs. The horn urged them forward like a lash. Solemn the road and solemn their faces; the breaking white fields waiting, the pickers spilling across those fields like locusts.

Hattie's babies blinked at her weakly; she tickled

each one under the chin. Soon it would be time to change the mustard poultices. Steam billowed from the hot water in the bathtub. She added another handful of eucalyptus. In Georgia, there was a eucalyptus tree in the wood across from Hattie's house, but the plant had been hard to come by in the Philadelphia winter.

THREE DAYS BEFORE, the babies' coughs had worsened. Hattie threw on her coat and went to the Penn Fruit to ask the grocer where she might find eucalyptus. She was sent to a house some blocks away. Hattie was new to Germantown, and she quickly got lost in the warren of streets. When she arrived at her destination, bruised from the cold, she paid a woman fifteen cents for a bag of what she could have had for free in Georgia. "Well, you're just a little thing!" the eucalyptus woman said. "How old are you, gal?" Hattie bristled at the question but said that she was seventeen and added, so the woman would not mistake her for another newly arrived southern unfortunate, that she was married and her husband was training as an electrician and that they had just moved into a house on Wayne Street. "Well, that's nice, sugar. Where're your people?" Hattie blinked quickly and swallowed hard, "Georgia, ma'am."

"You don't have anybody up here?"

"My sister, ma'am." She did not say that her mother had died a year earlier while Hattie was pregnant. The shock of her death, and of being an orphan and a stranger in the North, had driven Hattie's younger sister, Pearl, back to Georgia. Her older sister, Marion, had gone too, though she said she'd come back once she'd birthed her child and the winter passed. Hattie did not know if she would. The woman regarded Hattie closely. "I'll come round with you now to look in on your little ones," she said. Hattie declined. She had been a fool, a silly girl too prideful to admit she needed looking in on. She went home by herself clutching the bag of eucalyptus.

The winter air was a fire around her, burning her clean of everything but the will to make her children well. Her fingers froze into claws around the curled top of the brown paper bag. She burst into the house on Wayne Street with great clarity of mind. She felt she could see into her babies, through their skin and flesh and deep into their rib cages to their weary lungs.

HATTIE MOVED Philadelphia and Jubilee closer to the tub. The additional handful of eucalyptus was too much—the babies squeezed their eyes shut against the menthol mist. Jubilee made a fist and raised her arm as if to rub her running eyes, but she was too weak and her hand dropped back to her side. Hattie kneeled and kissed her little fist. She lifted her daughter's limp arm—light as a bird bone—and wiped her tears with her hand, as Jubilee would have done if she'd had the strength. "There," Hattie said. "There, you did it all by yourself." Jubilee looked up at her mother and smiled. Again, Hattie lifted Jubilee's hand to her bleary eye. The baby thought it a game of peekaboo and laughed a feeble laugh, ragged and soft and phlegmy, but a laugh nonetheless. Hattie laughed too because her girl was so brave and so good-natured—sick as she was and still bright as a poppy. She had a dimple in one cheek. Her brother, Philadelphia, had two. They didn't look a thing alike. Jubilee's hair was black like August's, and Philadelphia was pale as milk with sandy-brown hair like Hattie's.

Philadelphia's breathing was labored. Hattie lifted him out of the basket and sat him on the rim of the tub where the steam was thickest. He was a sack of flour in her arms. His head lolled on his neck and his arms hung at his sides. Hattie shook him gently to revive him. He hadn't eaten since the evening before—both babies had coughed so violently during the night that they'd vomited the bit of vegetable broth Hattie had managed to feed them. She pushed her son's eyelid open with her finger, his eyeball rolled in the socket. Hattie didn't know if he was passed out or sleeping, and if he were passed out, he might not . . . he might not . . .

She pushed at his eyelid again. He opened it this time—there's my boy!—and his lip curled in the way it did when she fed him mashed peas, or he smelled something he didn't like. Such a fuss-budget.

The bright bathroom overwhelmed: white tub, white walls, white tile. Philadelphia coughed, a protracted exhalation of air that shook his body. Hattie took the tin of hot mustard from the radiator and slathered it on his chest. His ribs were twigs beneath her fingers; with the slightest pressure, they would snap and fall into the cavity of his chest. He had been, both had been, so fat when they were well. Philadelphia lifted his head, but he was so exhausted that it dropped; his chin bumped against Hattie's shoulder as it had when he was a newborn and just learning to hold up his head.

Hattie walked circles around the little bathroom, rubbing Philadelphia's back between his shoulder blades. When he wheezed, his foot flexed and kicked her stomach; when he breathed, it relaxed. The floor was slippery. She sang nonsense syllables—ta ta ta, dum dum, ta ta. She couldn't remember the words to anything.

Water dripped from the windows and from the faucets and down the wall into the panel around the light switch. The whole bathroom dripped like a Georgia wood after a rainstorm. Something buzzed, then fizzled inside the wall, and the overhead light went out. The bathroom was all blue and fog. My God, Hattie thought, now this. She leaned her head against the doorjamb and closed her eyes. She was three days without sleep. A recollection descended on her like a faint: Hattie and her mother and sisters walking through the woods at dawn. Mama first with two large travel bags and the three girls behind, carrying carpetbagger satchels. Through the early morning mist and the underbrush, they made their way to town, skirts snagging on branches. They snuck like thieves through the woods to catch an early morning train out of Georgia. Hattie's father was not two days dead, and at that very moment the white men were taking his name plaque from the door of his blacksmith shop and putting up their own. "Have mercy on us," Mama said when the first horn sounded from the fields.

Philadelphia's foot dug into Hattie's belly button, and she was jolted awake, back into the bathroom with her children, startled and angry with herself for drifting away from them. Both began to cry. They choked and shuddered together. The illness gathered force, first in one child and then the other, and then, as though it had been waiting for that moment to do its worst, it struck like a two-pronged bolt of lightning. Mercy, Lord. Mercy.

Hattie's babies burned brightly: their fevers spiked, their legs wheeled, their cheeks went red as suns. Hattie took the bottle of ipecac from the medicine cabinet and dosed them. They coughed too hard to swallow—the medicine dribbled from the sides of their mouths. Hattie wiped her children's faces and gave them more ipecac and massaged their heaving chests. Her hands moved expertly from task to task. Her hands were quick and capable even as Hattie wept and pleaded.

How her babies burned! How they wanted to live! Hattie had thought, when given over to such thoughts, that her children's souls were thimbles of fog; wispy and ungraspable. She was just a girl—only seventeen years longer on the earth than her children. Hattie understood them as extensions of herself and loved them because they were hers and because they were defenseless and because they needed her. But she looked at her babies now and saw that the life inside them was muscled and mighty and would not be driven from them. "Fight," Hattie urged. "Like this," she said and blew the air in and out of her own lungs, in solidarity with them, to show them it was possible. "Like this," she said again.

Hattie sat cross-legged on the floor with Jubilee balanced in the crook of one knee and Philadelphia in the other. She patted their backs to bring the phlegm up and out. The babies' feet overlapped in the triangle of space between Hattie's folded legs—their energy was flagging and they leaned against her thighs. If she lived to be one hundred, Hattie would still see, as clearly as she saw her babies slumped before her now, her father's body collapsed in the corner of his smithy, the two white men from town walking away from his shop without enough shame to quicken their pace or hide their guns. Hattie had seen that and she could not unsee it.

In Georgia the preacher had called the North a New Jerusalem. The congregation said he was a traitor to the cause of the southern Negro. He was gone the next day on a train to Chicago. Others too were going, disappearing from their shops or the fields; their seats on the church pew occupied at Sunday service and empty by Wednesday prayer meeting. All of those souls, escaped from the South, were at this very moment glowing with promise in the wretched winters of the cities of the North. Hattie knew her babies would survive. Though they were small and struggling, Philadelphia and Jubilee were already among those luminous souls, already the beginning of a new nation.

THIRTY-TWO HOURS AFTER Hattie and her mother and sisters crept through the Georgia woods to the train station, thirty-two hours on hard seats in the commotion of the Negro car, Hattie was startled from a light sleep by the train conductor's bellow, "Broad Street Station, Philadelphia!" Hattie clambered from the train, her skirt still hemmed with Georgia mud, the dream of Philadelphia round as a marble in her mouth and the fear of it a needle in her chest. Hattie and Mama, Pearl and Marion climbed the steps from the train platform up into the main hall of the station. It was dim despite the midday sun. The domed roof arched. Pigeons cooed in the rafters. Hattie was only fifteen then, slim as a finger. She stood with her mother and sisters at the crowd's edge, the four of them waiting for a break in the flow of people so they too might move toward the double doors at the far end of the station. Hattie stepped into the multitude. Mama called, "Come back! You'll be lost in all those people. You'll be lost!" Hattie looked back in panic; she thought her mother was right behind her. The crowd was too thick for her to turn back, and she was borne along on the current of people. She gained the double doors and was pushed out onto a long sidewalk that ran the length of the station.

The main thoroughfare was congested with more people than Hattie had ever seen in one place. The sun was high. Automobile exhaust hung in the air alongside the tar smell of freshly laid asphalt and the sickening odor of garbage rotting. Wheels rumbled on the paving stones, engines revved, paperboys called the headlines. Across the street a man in dirty clothes stood on the corner wailing a song, his hands at his sides, palms upturned. Hattie resisted the urge to cover her ears to block the rushing city sounds. She smelled the absence of trees before she saw it. Things were bigger in Philadelphia—that was true—and there was more of everything, too much of everything. But Hattie did not see a promised land in this tumult. It was, she thought, only Atlanta on a larger scale. She could manage it. But even as she declared herself adequate to the city, her knees knocked under her skirt and sweat rolled down her back. A hundred people had passed her in the few moments she'd been standing outside, but none of them were her mother and sisters. Hattie's eyes hurt with the effort of scanning the faces of the passersby.

A cart at the end of the sidewalk caught her eye. Hattie had never seen a flower vendor's cart. A white man sat on a stool with his shirtsleeves rolled and his hat tipped forward against the sun. Hattie set her satchel on the sidewalk and wiped her sweaty palms on her skirt. A Negro woman approached the cart. She indicated a bunch of flowers. The white man stood—he did not hesitate, his body didn't contort into a posture of menace—and took the flowers from a bucket. Before wrapping them in paper, he shook the water gently from the stems.

The Negro woman handed him the money. Had their hands brushed?

As the woman took her change and moved to put it in her purse, she upset three of the flower arrangements. Vases and blossoms tumbled from the cart and crashed on the pavement. Hattie stiffened, waiting for the inevitable explosion. She waited for the other Negroes to step back and away from the object of the violence that was surely coming. She waited for the moment in which she would have to shield her eyes from the woman and whatever horror would ensue. The vendor stooped to pick up the mess. The Negro woman gestured apologetically and reached into her purse again, presumably to pay for what she'd damaged. In a couple of minutes it was all settled, and the woman walked on down the street with her nose in the paper cone of flowers, as if nothing had happened.

Hattie looked more closely at the crowd on the sidewalk. The Negroes did not step into the gutters to let the whites pass and they did not stare doggedly at their own feet. Four Negro girls walked by, teenagers like Hattie, chatting to one another. Just girls in conversation, giggling and easy, the way only white girls walked and talked in the city streets of Georgia. Hattie leaned forward to watch their progress down the block. At last, her mother and sisters exited the station and came to stand next to her. "Mama," Hattie said. "I'll never go back. Never."

PHILADELPHIA PITCHED FORWARD and struck his forehead on Jubilee's shoulder before Hattie could catch him. He breathed in ragged wet whistles. His hands were open and limp at his sides. Hattie shook him; he flopped like a rag doll. Jubilee too was weakening. She could hold her head up, but she couldn't focus her eyes. Hattie held both babies in her arms and made an awkward lunge for the bottle of ipecac. Philadelphia made a low choking sound and looked up at his mother, bewildered. "I'm sorry," she said. "I don't understand either. I'll make it better. I'm so sorry." The ipecac slipped from her grasp and shattered against the tile. Hattie squatted next to the tub, Philadelphia in one arm and Jubilee balanced in her lap. She turned the faucet for the hot water and waited. Jubilee coughed as best she could, as best she could she pulled the air into her body. Hattie put her fingertips to the running water. It was ice cold.

There was no time to load the furnace in the basement and no time to wait for the water to heat. Philadelphia was listless, his leg kicked against Hattie's stomach involuntarily. His head lay heavy on her shoulder. Hattie crossed the bathroom. She stepped on the shards from the broken bottle and cut her foot; she bloodied the white tile and the wood floor in the hallway. In her bedroom she pulled the quilt from her bed and wrapped it around her children. In an instant she'd descended the stairs and was putting on her shoes in the small foyer. The splinter of glass in her foot pushed in more deeply. She was out the door and down the porch steps. Wisps of condensation rose from her damp housedress and bare arms and faded into the cold, clear air. The sun was fully risen.

Hattie banged on a neighbor's door. "They have pneumonia!" she said to the woman who answered. "Please help me." Hattie didn't know her name. Inside, the neighbor pulled back the quilt to reveal Jubilee and Philadelphia inert against their mother's chest. "Oh sweet Lord," she said. A young boy, the woman's son, came into the living room. "Go for the doctor!" the woman shouted. She took Philadelphia from Hattie and ran up the stairs with him in her arms. Hattie followed, Jubilee limp against her.

"He's still breathing," the woman said. "Long as he's still breathing."

In the bathroom she plugged the tub. Hattie stood in the doorway, bouncing Jubilee, her hope waning as she watched the woman turn the hot water to full blast.

"I already did this!" Hattie cried. "Isn't there anything else?"

The woman gave Philadelphia back to Hattie and rooted around in the medicine cabinet. She came away with a tin of camphor rub that she unscrewed and waved under the babies' noses like smelling salts. Only Jubilee jerked her head away from the odor. Hattie was overwhelmed with futility—all this time she'd been fighting to save her babies, only to end up in another bathroom just like her own, with a woman as helpless against their illness as she was.

"What can I do?" Hattie looked at the woman through the steam. "Please tell me what to do."

The neighbor found a glass tube with a bulb at the end; she used it to suction mucus from the babies' noses and mouths. She kneeled in front of Hattie, near tears. "Dear Lord. Please, dear Lord, help us." The woman suctioned and prayed.

Both babies' eyelids were swollen and red with broken capillaries. Their breathing was shallow. Their chests rose and fell too quickly. Hattie did not know if Philadelphia and Jubilee were scared or if they understood what was happening to them. She didn't know how to comfort them, but she wanted her voice to be the last in their ears, her face the last in their eyes. Hattie kissed her babies' foreheads and cheeks. Their heads fell back against her arms. Between breaths, their eyes opened wide in panic.

She heard a wet gurgling deep in their chests. They were drowning. Hattie could not bear their suffering, but she wanted them to go in peace, so she didn't scream. She called them precious, she called them light and promise and cloud. The neighbor woman prayed in a steady murmur. She kept her hand on Hattie's knee. The woman wouldn't let go, even when Hattie tried to shake her off. It wasn't much, but she tried to make it so the girl didn't live this alone.

Jubilee fought the longest. She reached feebly for Philadelphia, but she was too weak to straighten her arm. Hattie put his hand into hers. She squeezed her babies. She rocked them. She pressed her cheeks to the tops of their heads. Oh, their velvet skin! She felt their deaths like a ripping in her body.

Hattie's children died in the order in which they were born: first Philadelphia, then Jubilee.

Floyd

1948

THE BOARDINGHOUSE WAS cleaner than most. The colored places, ones Floyd could afford, were generally in need of fumigation and a paint job. Floyd scratched the welts on his back. The last place had bedbugs. But he was in the South in summer . . . what could you do. Everything down here was overgrown and lousy with crawling, biting things. He walked into his room—hot, sure enough, despite the fan whirring in the window. The sheets were a little faded and threadbare, but the floors shone from a recent waxing, and there were some pretty white flowers in a vase on the nightstand.

"Ain't that nice? My mamma used to put out cut flowers," Darla said.

Damned if Darla wasn't a loud woman. Even

when she called herself talking softly, it was like she was shouting at you from across the street. She stepped around Floyd and put her carryall on the floor next to the bed. She didn't travel well, either. That is to say that her dress was wrinkled and her hair had napped around her forehead. She hadn't stopped smoking during the five-hour drive—even when Floyd pulled over for her to go to the bathroom, a plume of smoke rose up from behind the bush where she squatted. All that smoke made her eyes red and her fingers yellow at the tips.

"I guess you know I might not come back here tonight. But you can stay in the room until you get yourself settled somewhere," Floyd said.

"Ain't no telling who's gon' be where by this evening."

Darla was an easy, roll-with-the-punches type, even if she was a little cheap. The orange dress she was wearing was bright enough to give a body sunburn. Of course, Floyd had never met a concert-hall girl who wasn't rough: they picked their teeth with their pinky nails or talked like they just walked out of a cotton field. He never held on to one for more than the night or two that he played a gig in any given town. This morning he'd dressed, grabbed his horn, and had a good start on creeping out of the door when Darla hopped out of bed and said, "Baby boy, I'm coming right along with you to the next place. I'm sick of this old town." Must have been his hangover that made him say yes. Stupid. But there wasn't anything to do about it now.

"You ought to take me out for something to eat," she said, sitting on the boardinghouse bed.

Floyd frowned down at his shoes.

"What you pulling faces for? I know we ain't going steady, don't mean you can't buy me a tomato sandwich." Floyd smiled. "Shoot—a goddamn can of sardines. I never saw somebody so stiff."

Darla's shoe dangled from her toe. She kicked it playfully toward Floyd. "What you got to be so serious about? You need to learn to relax."

"I know what I need," Floyd said, shutting the door.

His shirt was off by the time he reached the bed, his pants a minute later. He unzipped Darla's dress, and that was all there was as far as undressing. Nasty girl, she didn't have a thing on underneath. Darla called him Daddy and Big Boy and yelled her head off, and they both had a good time. It was marred only by a photograph on the dresser—a sepia tone of a muscled hayseed on a horse. It seemed to Floyd that the young man's gaze followed him around the room. He stared as Floyd ran his hand over Darla's hips and stared as Floyd orgasmed. When they finished, Floyd rested his cheek against the sheet just close enough to feel the humid heat rising from Darla's body.

The smell of sex filled the little room. When

Darla got up to fiddle with the window fan, she didn't wrap the sheet around her like a nicer girl would. She had a high, round behind and her thighs tapered down to her thin legs. They were, perhaps, a little too thin, but there was an efficiency about her body that Floyd liked.

He'd had a lot of bodies. Floyd was good-looking, and if he wasn't as light skinned as some, he did have wavy black hair that curled at the temples. After a gig, he had his pick of women. In Philadelphia they called him Lady Boy Floyd. He'd had two women in a single night, three in the course of a full day. This was more easily accomplished in the South than it had been in Philadelphia. Never mind that at home he had taken women in bathrooms and the backseats of cars, he was convinced that in Georgia the women were loose. Maybe it was in the way they walked. Half of them—not the nice girls, of course—didn't even wear girdles. And in the smaller towns some didn't carry purses! They just switched down the street, hands swaying at their sides; you could do anything you wanted with that kind of free in a woman.

The women at home Floyd knew were mannered and proper like his mother and sisters. Hattie wanted him to stop playing and to marry. She'd forbidden him to practice in the house, and when he'd gotten a job as a janitor at the Downbeat Club, where he could meet the musicians who played there, she said only, "I don't know why you'd want to clean up other people's dirt." When he met Hawkins and Pres, she didn't comment at all. But it happened that a few nights a week, when he got back to the house on Wayne Street after a gig at a corn liquor bar or from scrubbing the bathrooms at the Downbeat, he found his mother awake and sitting in the window seat in her nightgown. Hattie was bleary with insomnia but she'd smile at him, and they would sit together for a while in the silence of the hour.

When Floyd was a child, in the years right after the twins died, it had been just he and Cassie and Hattie. Hattie didn't rise from her bed until afternoon. Some days, after hours of leaning against the footboard waiting for his mother to get up, Floyd would put his hand in front of her mouth to make sure she was breathing. She wore her white nightgown all day and floated through the rooms of the house, pale and silent as an iceberg. Floyd and Cassie ate the odd things their mother thought to feed them—cold rice with milk and sugar or a plate of buttered crackers or baked beans still in the can—at whatever hour she managed to prepare the food. When August came home in the evenings, there was music and whistling, and his voice, sad or angry but always insistent, telling Hattie to get dressed, bathe the children, comb her hair. Sometimes Aunt Marion came—she too was strident and bullying, or so it seemed to Floyd. But at some point the house emptied and silence returned. Though Hattie's grief suffocated, though Floyd and Cassie were untended as strays, the cold, cloistered rooms of Wayne Street took on a kind of beauty in Floyd's memory. Hattie rarely managed more than a wan smile, but she allowed Floyd and Cassie to climb into her lap, plait her hair, kiss her forehead, as though she were a living doll. They were companions, mother and children, equally vulnerable and yearning, drifting through the days together. Even now that Floyd was a grown man, there was an understanding between him and his mother, and Hattie was the only person in this world with whom Floyd was serene. He missed her stillness. He was so often sunk in a loud, internal confusion that threatened to overwhelm him.

Floyd felt it most on the long drives between gigs, when he was alone in the car with the rotting-jasmine smell of the South pouring through the windows. His heart pinging in his chest from the bennies that kept him awake from one gig to the next, he'd fly along the roads, pressing the accelerator and feeling himself unhinged from reasonable desires. He stopped to refuel in towns composed of nothing but a clapboard church and a gas pump. There he would be directed to a house down the road where he could buy a plate of food for a dollar. If the lady of the house was alone, if she was willing, they might go to the bedroom before Floyd got on the highway again. There had been too a big buck of a gas station attendant in Mississippi and a man working a general store in Kentucky. They had gone round back in the high heat of the afternoon when road and store were deserted.

Floyd's tour was his first time away from home for any significant period. The longer he was away, the more he indulged the urges he had managed, for the most part, to suppress in Philadelphia. They'd grown more insistent in the months he'd been on the road, more reckless and more difficult to reconcile with the man he understood himself to be.

AND NOW HERE he was in another boarding-house with another stranger in a town where he didn't even know which way to go for a cup of coffee. This South. What was he doing, after all, wandering in this wilderness with only his trumpet and a few dollars in his pockets? Floyd had wanted to leave Philadelphia. He was twenty-two and eager to make a name for himself as a musician. He'd come down here to play the jukes and jazz joints, but he was three months into this shabby little tour and felt like a kite broken off from its string.

He stood in front of the dresser fidgeting with the knobs on the drawers.

"Lord, sugar. Ain't you tired after all that?" Darla winked. "You need some more?"

"I'll take some," he said halfheartedly.

"Well, you got to come over here to get it."

She watched him rifle through the pile of clothes on the floor.

"Oh, I wish you'd stop all that moving around! You making me nervous."

Floyd fished a pack of cigarettes from the breast pocket of his jacket.

"Let me ask you something, sugar. What you doing down here? You look like them young fellas goes to Morehouse or somewhere."

"Playing gigs," Floyd said.

"They ain't got jukes up north? You ain't have to come all the way down here. You must got some reason for wanting to live two days here and three days there. Most folks don't."

"I just told you the reason," Floyd said.

Darla shrugged. "It ain't none of my business no how."

The sun was going down. It was a dull sunset, a hazy band of orange low in the sky, the sun a red ball shrouded in clouds.

"I guess I'll take a bath," Floyd said.

He wrapped himself in a sheet and went down the hall toward the bathroom. His bath soothed him. When he returned to the room, Darla was fast asleep, nude and spread-eagled, her hair mashed against her head on one side and her mouth open. Floyd laughed. He felt an odd tenderness for Darla's rough ways—she didn't try to impress him. He fit himself around her on the bed and slept.

FLOYD WOKE to voices in the street below. The room was dark aside from the lights coming in through the window and beneath the door. His mouth was gauzy with thirst, and he felt a kind of general, undirected irritation.

Darla woke and squinted at Floyd.

"What's that ruckus?" she asked.

He didn't answer. The voices in the street grew louder. From the window, Floyd saw a crowd moving down the boulevard in front of the boarding-house. He turned on the overhead light.

"You trying to blind me?" Darla asked.

The last of Floyd's clean clothes were wrinkled at the bottom of his suitcase. He kicked the dirty things into the corner and dressed quickly. The room was small around him, the scent of sweat and Darla's cheap perfume cloying. And that damn hayseed farmer still looking out at him from the picture frame on the dresser.

"I'm just about ready to go," Floyd said.

"Looks like it." Darla stood and stretched, then

bent to take another loud dress from her bag. Floyd tapped his foot, but Darla didn't move any faster. He flipped his lighter open and closed. He sighed.

"Baby Boy, you got something you want to say?"

"I'll head out, I guess."

"You gone through all that huffing and puffing 'stead of just saying you was leaving?" Darla shook her head and turned back to her travel bag. "You a funny one," she said.

Downstairs, the front door of the boardinghouse stood open, as though the proprietor had run off in a hurry. Outside, a crowd spread from curb to curb and spilled up onto the sidewalk. In place of street-lights, torches burned in tall stands at the corners. A man head to toe in vibrant green—green hat and shoes, green pants and shirt—beckoned for Floyd to join the parade. A woman draped in yards of puffing and billowing white fabric walked next to a man with symbols drawn in coal on his cheeks. Others carried a simple something in their hands: a branch in full flower, a stalk of sugar cane, a yellow bird in a cage.

The people beat tambourines and cowbells and two-stepped down the boulevard. It was not a dance that Floyd had ever seen, all thrusting pelvis and a low kind of chicken walk that made the women's skirts ride up their thighs. A man dropped to a squat, then somersaulted to standing. The people whooped. He danced harder, and the yellow paint on his chest streaked with sweat. The smell of burning pitch filled the air, and another sweet smoky smell Floyd could not identify. A boy carrying small metal pails on a tray came toward him.

"Myrrh? You want myrrh, mister?" he asked, gesturing toward the pails and the sweet smoke wafting from them.

"What is this?" Floyd asked.

"Seven Days!"

The boy darted back into the crowd.

When Floyd took the gig, no one told him there would be a party. And I'm all buttoned up like somebody's grandfather, he thought, loosening the knot in his tie. A brass band played somewhere up ahead. This was the kind of night where anything might happen and damned if he hadn't left his whiskey upstairs with Darla.

He leaned against the doorjamb of the boardinghouse and smoked a cigarette. You couldn't see who was who in this craziness—everybody was up for everything, the men and the women, all sashay and switch and swagger. His fingers twitched in anticipation as they did right before his first song at a gig. After the host announced him, Floyd would take the stage and wait; he let the audience fidget and slurp their drinks and whisper until their anticipation swelled to yearning. Only then would he lift the horn to his lips. He always knew when the crowd was ripe.

Two women in blue dresses and blue-feathered hats approached him on the sidewalk. The dimpled one smiled at him. She was a pretty thing, the color of peanut brittle, so he allowed her to take his elbow and guide him into the crowd. "What's this all about?" he asked. She did not answer. It occurred to him that the people in the crowd were dressed as things in nature, clouds or flowers or animals; his companions were two little bluebirds. The pretty one sipped from a mason jar that she held out to him—corn liquor strong enough to polish his horn mixed with something sweet Floyd didn't recognize. She gestured for him to drink slowly, but he ignored her and took three long pulls. The drink aroused him. This bluebird girl might offer him some relief, perhaps in one of the side streets or in the Packard. Floyd slid his hand to her lower back and rested it there.

The main boulevard curved and led into a park. Floyd was in the thick of the crowd; bodies pressed him from every direction. He stood on tiptoe to see if there was somewhere he might take his bluebird, but sweaty backs and shoulders walled him in. We should get out of this crowd, he whispered in her ear, and isn't it hot, and surely there's a place from which we can see everything but not be quite so sardined. She smiled at him and cocked her head to the side. Man, those dimples were something. He roped his arm around her waist and pulled her toward what he thought was the corner, but blue-bird waggled her index finger at him and slipped from his grasp.

The crowd heaved around him. Talcum powder and hair grease and smoke fouled the air. Floyd unfastened the first few buttons of his shirt. He couldn't breathe. It's only a parade, he told himself, when he felt panic scudding in his chest—nothing more than a bunch of drunken country folk. But all of these bodies! The liquor coated Floyd's tongue with a sweet-sick taste. He barreled blindly past the thickest part of the throng and broke, at last, through the outermost ring of people and into a clearing where he bent next to a tree and vomited violently.

When he was able to stand, Floyd found he was near a church in a woodsy cul-de-sac some distance from the revelers. A twig snapped. Something jangled in the woods in front of him. Sounds like chains, Floyd thought. Not quite loud enough, but anything was possible in this bogeyman night—a man in chains could walk right out of those woods. They had chain gangs in Georgia, didn't they? Could be one of those poor souls haunted the place. Floyd picked up a tree branch and held it in one hand like a sword. The jangling drew nearer. Floyd widened his stance and brandished his branch.

A young man emerged from the wood. His scarlet neckerchief shone in the moonlight like a jewel. In one cupped hand he shook a few coins and with the other he tipped his hat at Floyd.

"Whoa now," he said. "I'm just passing by."

"I . . . sorry. I just didn't know what was . . ." Floyd dropped his stick.

The man couldn't have been more than eighteen. But he was not a boy, that is to say his lips were red and voluptuous, plush as pillows, and he held them slightly apart. It was a mouth as ripe as a strawberry; the young man was not unaware of this.

"Seem like you a little agitated," the boy said and chuckled.

A firecracker popped.

Floyd jumped. "I'm not. I ain't . . . I've never seen anything like this."

The boy studied the cut of Floyd's jacket and the silk of his tie. He studied his haircut and his shoes.

"Yeah," he said. "I can see you not from around here."

His voice was reedy and low like a clarinet.

"Just in town to play a gig," Floyd said.

"Uh-huh," the young man answered, ready to take his leave.

"What's this parade?" Floyd blurted, because he wanted to know and because he didn't want him to go.

"Seven Days."

The boy waved dismissively in the direction of the crowd. "They put on this juju mess every year. I don't believe in it myself."

Floyd smelled wood smoke, as if from a bonfire. "It's some kind of magic festival?"

The young man sighed. "I guess you might call it that. Hoodoo folk celebrating how they figure God made the world," he paused and smiled at Floyd. "They say God made the world, case you ain't heard where you from."

"I didn't see any crosses or preachers," Floyd said.

"Every day's crosses and preachers around here. These people," he said, as though he were not one of them, "call the conjure man soon's they come out the church. Seven Days they get to be heathens out in the open."

"Kind of spooky," Floyd said. The boy shrugged.

"You know if there's somewhere around here to get a drink of water?" Floyd asked.

The young man led Floyd around the side of the church. When they reached the pump, Floyd drank deeply and splashed his neck and face. He wondered how the water could be so cool and pure in this humid and muddled place. The water dripped onto his shirt and splattered his polished shoes. He must look like a barbarian. But then, coiffed though he was, the young man was just a country boy, and there was no need to try to impress him. Floyd had not tried to impress any of the others he had met in this way. The boy stood a few feet from Floyd with his arms folded cross his chest. Beneath his scarlet ascot, a triangle of clover honey skin glowed in the floodlights.

Floyd wiped his wet hands on his pants and introduced himself. The boy shook Floyd's hand like a man not accustomed to doing so.

"Name of Lafayette," he said.

They sat on a bench at the farthest edge of the church lawn. Floyd talked to Lafayette as he would a woman he had his eye on: where was he from and what did he do and did he live here in town? Lafayette responded to these attempts at conversation in monosyllables: from here, he cut heads, no, he didn't live in town. He was unfazed when Floyd told him he played the trumpet and was from Philadelphia. Lafayette's indifference made Floyd angry; a man from a nowhere town like this one ought to be fascinated by the great cities of the North. He continued, speaking quickly, embellishing the details of his life: he'd seen Monk at Minton's in New York—Lafayette might have heard of Minton's, it was very famous—and he'd had a drink with Duke. As he talked, Floyd realized it was not just his pride and his vanity at stake. He wanted Lafayette to like him.

Floyd did not remember when he was so bumbling and amateur. He abandoned his attempts at small talk. The thing to do was sit a little closer and gaze at Lafayette to make his intentions clear. But Floyd was too nervous, so he rubbed his palms against his pant leg and worried the ground with the toe of his shoe. Lafayette shifted toward him on the bench. He traced the nape of Floyd's neck with his fingers. His breath was quick but steady. He slid his hand inside Floyd's shirt where the two top buttons were undone. The boy's cool hand warmed against Floyd's chest, fingers twitching slightly. Floyd leaned into him. With these small gestures they were agreed. They had reached an accord. Floyd followed Lafayette into an opening in the trees. He looked back and saw a bit of orange flash round the side of the church. Could have been anything—firecracker, a Seven Days reveler dressed up like the sun. Floyd quickened his pace to keep up with Lafayette.

The moon was full, but the light struggled to reach the two men beneath the leafy canopy. Lafayette knew the way and moved quickly. Soon he was several paces ahead. Could be, Floyd thought, I'm a fool, and this cat is luring me into trouble. Floyd had been in bars or at filling stations when men turned on him for no reason, and he wondered now if they had known, as Lafayette knew, and they had wanted to beat it out of him.

They came to a small clearing bright with moonlight. Lafayette was urgent; he unbuttoned Floyd's shirt and unbuckled his belt. Floyd—how like a boy

Lafayette had made him, how compliant—stood naked in the moonlight shaking with desire and with fear. Lafayette patiently, teasingly, undressed himself. He was the same clover honey shade all over, with a hairless chest and a belly with a hint of a paunch. His thighs were hard and powerful and did not yield to Floyd's squeezes. The boy was practiced in a way that made Floyd self-conscious. He groaned and stepped away from Lafayette.

"I don't know . . . I mean I haven't . . ." he began.

"That's alright," Lafayette murmured, putting his lips to Floyd's ear.

"That's alright."

IT BEGAN to rain. Floyd's and Lafayette's sweat mixed with the raindrops and beaded on their skin. Floyd could not stop looking at Lafayette's penis lolling against his thigh. He imagined the curve of it pressing against the fabric of Lafayette's pants when they dressed and walked out of the woods later.

At the edge of the clearing a tree stump, as large around as two men standing together, was covered with black slashes and squiggles.

"What's that?" Floyd asked, pointing at the stump.

"Some like to leave they mark."

Floyd came up onto his haunches. "Their names?"

"Names? Heh, why don't you write yours on there? No names, just a mark."

The top was scored with knife scratchings. There were several hearts, some letters that could have been initials, the outline of someone's hand.

"Lot of people come here?" Floyd asked.

"Ain't nowhere else to go where you can take your time," Lafayette replied.

"I guess it's different in Macon or Atlanta maybe?"

"Is it different where you come from?" Lafayettte asked sharply.

"I don't know anything about that."

"Oh, you don't?" He smirked. "Well, I don't reckon it's no different nowhere."

"I mean, I'm not a . . . I go with women."

"Folks like to think that about theyselves."

"It's a fact."

"I ain't said it wasn't. Seem like you go with men too though, don't it?"

Floyd had not known anything about the few men he'd been with. Their encounters were quick and furtive, only the slightest attempt had been made at conversation. Afterward, Floyd pushed the experiences from his mind, as he might a night of excessive drinking or losing all his money at dice or any other debauchery. He could not dwell on these breaches of his willpower, lest he indulge them more often. Lest he become like Lafayette. Lafayette, who was not decent enough to leave Floyd with his honor. Lady Boy Floyd, they called him. Who was Lafayette to say anything different? He was the kind you'd see swishing around Greenwich Village. Why they didn't have sense enough to act normal, to protect themselves from scorn, Floyd did not know. He glanced at Lafayette. The boy's eyes were on him, a challenging, flinty gaze that Floyd wouldn't have expected in a man like him. Something in it made Floyd ashamed of himself.

"You don't ever think about leaving here?" he asked softly.

Lafayette cut his eyes and crossed his arms over his chest. He was naked as the day he was born, with his paunchy little stomach sticking out and his lips pressed into a frown. Floyd wanted to laugh. If he knew Lafayette better, if he knew him very well, he might say, "Aww, come on," and kiss him on the cheek.

"I'm not trying to be any kind of way. I'm just asking," Floyd said.

"My sister lives in New Orleans."

"You been there?"

"Naw. I ain't never been nowhere."

"Well, you're mighty worldly for somebody that's never been anywhere."

"You think so?" Lafayette asked. His smile was the most genuine, the most guileless, he'd allowed himself that evening.

If only Lafayette would not be so . . . if he would not wear that scarlet scarf, Floyd might take him somewhere. They would be just two men traveling together. No one would be any the wiser. They could be together night after night. Floyd had never considered the possibility of continued acquaintance with a man.

The rain fell in fat droplets. The two sought shelter beneath a tree at the edge of the clearing. For a long time they sat together looking out at the broad leaves of the elephant ears swaying under the downpour. Floyd thought to reach for Lafayette's hand, but he might push him away. And if he did not reject him and they sat holding hands in the rain, what would that mean? It would be best to get up and leave that clearing. But Floyd inched toward Lafayette until their thighs were touching, until his thigh leaned against Lafayette's and Lafayette's leaned back.

After they had been together a second time, Floyd began to hope they might spend the night in the clearing beneath the sheltering tree, but Lafayette stood and said abruptly, "I got to be going."

He dressed quickly and led the way out. The path, which had taken so long to traverse earlier, was no more than two city blocks. In an instant they were back in the little yard behind the church.

"Alright, then," Lafayette said.

Floyd was reminded of the way he had dismissed

Darla just a few hours earlier. Lafayette was prepared to leave him in that park with nothing.

"Okay," he said.

"Alright," Lafayette repeated. The men stood
facing each other, not more than a foot apart. "See
you around, then," he said.

"Wait!" Floyd cried. "I mean to say I'm playing
Cleota's tomorrow night."

"You asking me to come?"

"If you want to."

"You asking or not?"

"I'm asking. Ten o'clock."

"I be there at eleven." Lafayette winked. Quickly,
head down, he crossed the park beyond the churchyard and was gone.

Floyd was desperate for a cigarette. His clothes
were wet and mussed and who knows how he
smelled. The rain had made a muddy puddle near
the bench where he and Lafayette had sat together.
Gnats swarmed the bulb of the floodlight above
the church door. In Lafayette's absence the place
was wilted and derelict.

I have a date with a man, Floyd thought. And
he had been glad about it, overjoyed about it. But
now he was alone, and it was as though a light had
gone out, exactly like that, the way a child is dis-
oriented and frightened in the dark and nothing is
recognizable. For instance, what did it mean that
he had felt more in three hours with Lafayette than

he ever had with any of his women? That would make him . . . What he needed was a walk. He would go to the boardinghouse and get his horn, and from there he would find a secluded place and play until his fingers hurt and his mouth could not hold the embouchure.

He left the churchyard. The Seven Days crowd had all but dispersed. Pails of the burning stuff the boy had called myrrh, extinguished now, rolled down the middle of the street. A couple pawed each other drunkenly against a tree, the woman's top had fallen from her shoulders. The festival had degenerated into depravity. Maybe everyone had been drinking the liquor the bluebird gave Floyd, and it had made them lusty and indiscriminate. Under the most normal circumstances Floyd was a man who liked sex more than was in his best interest; surely it was his appetites and the Seven Days that had caused this trouble with Lafayette. And trouble could be undone or ignored. He had ignored it for years, for as long as he could remember. There was no reason anything had to change now. No reason at all. Even as he lied to himself, Floyd knew that after he played the next night, he would tell Lafayette he had a gig in New Orleans, though it was not true, and if Lafayette said yes, they would drive away together in the deepest part of the night.

It was not true either that he had never considered

the possibility of involvement with a man. There was Carl. Of course, Floyd was only thirteen at the time and sexually excitable—he could understand it in that way. He had, in fact, made many attempts to understand it that way. The boys were best friends. They spent winter afternoons at Carl's house. Their last afternoon was at Carl's. They sat on his bed with blankets around their shoulders. It was very cold and the daylight was waning. They were doing something, drawing or playing checkers or doing homework. The boys sat very close in the chilly room, warming themselves in a narrowing shaft of sunlight that slanted in through the window. Carl put his cold hand on Floyd's knee. At first he'd had the urge to swat it like a fly, but he didn't say anything, and they were still for a time. Carl's hand warmed, the half moons at the nail bed went from bluish to pink. He rubbed Floyd's thigh, and everywhere he touched him, Floyd burned. The boys sat cross-legged, knee to knee, panting and trembling.

The bedroom door opened. They had not heard footsteps—how had they not heard the footsteps? Carl's mother looked from one boy to the other, and then one to the other again. As she understood what she saw, her face twisted until it was a not a face but a rage. Floyd jumped from the bed, but she blocked the doorway. No one had ever looked at him with such revulsion; he had never done anything so terrible that it made him less than human. Get out get out get out she screamed, even as her slapping and jabbing made it all but impossible for Floyd to pass her. He ran down the steps and to the front door, where he rooted through the closet for his coat. Upstairs, Carl's mother hit him again and again; the slaps rang through the empty house.

Now Floyd ran down the emptying boulevard, as though he could outrun the memory of Carl's beating or of the pained shock on his face. Floyd rounded the corner. His heart beat too quickly in his chest, and his legs were wobbly. Amber light spilled onto the sidewalk from an open door in the middle of the block. A woman in a cotton house-dress stood fanning herself just inside the doorway. The light drew him, and the butter smell of the bread baking. Another woman kneaded dough on a long table, her forearms covered in flour up to the elbow. There was dough all around her: rising in loaf pans and puffing out of muffin tins.

The woman in the doorway narrowed her eyes and said, "We don't sell no kind of liquor." A couple of Seven Days stragglers weaved down the boulevard on the opposite side of the street.

The kneading woman stepped forward. The girls were sisters, he thought, barely out of their teens. "That's right," she said. "Ain't nothing here but butter rolls."

"I . . . ," Floyd did not know how to tell them

that he only wanted to step inside of the amber glow and smell the baking bread, that they seemed like nice girls and he was in need of a moment's shelter.

"Do you all have a phone in here?" he asked. He felt his pockets for a handkerchief and, not finding one, wiped his tears with the back of his hand.

"I'll pay a dollar if you let me make a call," he said. He took out his wallet and held the limp dollar bills out to the girls. "Two dollars for a phone call and one of those rolls."

The sisters glanced at each other. The one who'd been kneading shrugged, and the other said, "Come on through here." She led him through a set of double doors into a little bakery with bright yellow walls and a vase of lavender on the counter. She pointed to a phone on the wall, and while Floyd waited for the operator to connect him, the girl set three hot-to-the-touch rolls on the counter. She was gone before he could thank her.

He didn't hear a ring, just crackling static and the operator telling him to hold awhile longer. He bit into his roll and began to weep again. There was a click and then a voice faint on the other end.

"Mother," Floyd said. "Mother?"

"Floyd?" Hattie said.

"I hope I didn't . . . I guess I woke you up." He hoped the crackling hid the tears in his voice.

"Is that you, Floyd? What's the matter? Are you alright?"

"I'm fine, Mother. I'm fine. I just wanted to . . . I haven't called in a while."

"You never have called," Hattie said in that way that would have been an accusation in anyone else's mouth but was a simple statement of fact in hers. "Are you hurt?"

"No, Mother. I'm not hurt. I just wanted to say hello. I'm coming back in about two weeks."

"You got some mail from this colored musician's association," Hattie said.

"Two weeks, Mother."

"I heard you." She sighed. "You're in one piece?"

"I'm fine."

"Fine doesn't call before dawn." The line buzzed between them.

"I guess I'll hang up. I just wanted to say hello. I guess . . . how you keeping?"

"I'm alright, Floyd. Same as always."

"Daddy? How's Daddy?"

"He's fine too. Everybody's fine. Floyd, what's going on?"

"I'm going to hang up now, Mother. I know it's late. I thought . . . I figured you might have been sitting down there in the living room like you do."

"I was."

"So I didn't wake you up."

"No, you didn't."

"Well, I guess I'll hang up."

"Alright."

"Mother?"

"Yes?"

"Do you remember Carl? What happened to Carl?"

Hattie paused a long while before answering. "I don't know what happened to him. The family moved away."

"But he's alright, don't you think? I mean, you never heard of anything bad happening to him."

"I don't know. I have no idea. Why are you asking me about that boy, Floyd?"

"No reason. He just came to mind is all. I'll hang up now. It was nice talking to you, Mother. I'll see you soon."

"Good-bye, Floyd."

"I'll see you soon!"

The line died. He put the receiver back into its cradle and sniffed the butter rolls a good long time before finishing them off. Floyd put another dollar on the counter and left the bakery through the front door.

FLOYD'S CONCERT BEGAN promptly at ten the next night, before the drunks got too loud and all the respectable women had gone home for the evening. Women were good at a gig: the more there were, the less the chances of a fight. Floyd took the stage, horn in hand. The place was packed. Cleota's, Floyd had learned, was the only music club in three counties that allowed colored people.

Floyd felt the weight of the audience's expectations and of their weariness and their circumstance, which he could not ever know, not quite. Hattie referred to Georgia as, "that place." She wouldn't call the state by its name. Floyd didn't know what had happened to her there. Hattie and August were refugees from the South; Floyd's knowledge of it was comprised of their terror and nostalgia and rage. Not so infrequently, news of a lynching or a murdering white mob traveled up from "that place" and invaded the houses of Wayne Street, leaving the residents of the block hushed and grateful for their asylum in the North. Looking out at his audience, Floyd felt an irremediable gap of experience about which he was at turns defensive and at turns humble. He owed these people something, of that much he was sure. Music was the only way he could step into the current of their experience. There was some condescension in this, but he knew no other way to go about it.

Floyd rubbed the bowl of his trumpet, for luck and in homage to the songs he was going to play. Cleota's was too poor for proper house lights, so the proprietor turned off a few of the overheads in the back, but Floyd could still see the people. The piano man played and the drummer tapped the snare, easy, just enough to prime the crowd. Darla was in a dress as red as a drop of blood. Floyd hadn't seen her since the night before. He waited. Lafayette was not in the club. The piano man grew impatient with dragging out his intro. Floyd told himself it wasn't the boy's arrival he was waiting for. Still, it was not until a moment later when Lafayette slipped into the crowd that Floyd lifted the horn to his lips.

Now the piano man played in earnest and the drummer pixied the cymbals with the drum brush. The crowd leaned forward. Floyd's horn flashed in the light. He blew " 'Round Midnight." A man in the front called out, "Goddamn!" Floyd made the horn stutter, then played it smooth. It keened and it wailed. It asked the people what their troubles were and blew them back to them. Floyd got out of the way and let his horn carry him out to the edges of himself. There wasn't anything that horn couldn't say. "Not in this world or the next!" shouted the man in front.

In the midst of these ecstasies, a ruckus in the center of the crowd. Floyd looked over the bowl of his trumpet to see a motorcar of a man swaying drunkenly on his heels in the center of the confusion. He shoved Lafayette mightily with one fat arm. Lafayette stumbled backward but did not fall. He regained his footing—he was quick—and advanced on the man, fists up. The pianist stopped playing, as did the drummer. Only Floyd went on blowing one endless note, his chest tightening.

The drunken man swung and missed, the force of his wild punch destabilizing him. Lafayette was on him in an instant, jabbing at him double time, a punch to the gut and another to the throat. He would have kept hitting him had a couple of guys not grabbed him from either side and held his arms behind his back. The big man was bent over with the wind knocked out of him. He pointed at Lafayette and tried to say something. The men who'd intervened muscled Lafayette toward the door.

It was not the fat man they'd decided to remove but Lafayette. No one protested. Floyd held his horn at his side. Some of the people in the crowd jeered as Lafayette passed them. Most did nothing, but Floyd couldn't find any sympathy in their faces. Even if it had been worse, if the big man had beat Lafayette bloody, the people would not have protected him. In this place, or in New Orleans, or wherever they might go, now and always, Lafayette would be a thing too awful to be tolerated.

He wrenched himself free from his captors long enough to spin on his heels and fix Floyd with that flinty gaze from the night before. Floyd almost jumped down from the stage. He'd punch his way through the crowd and bash the men with his trumpet until they released Lafayette. Floyd stepped to the edge of the stage. Lafayette scuffled at the door with the two men. The audience, no longer interested in the disturbance, looked up at Floyd expectantly. He nodded to the piano man and lifted the horn to his mouth once again.

The crowd loved him. He played three encores. The band that went onstage after Floyd invited him to share their last set. When the show was over, the man in front, who'd hooped like he was in church, wouldn't be denied the chance to buy Floyd a whiskey, and then another and then a third. Darla came to the bar too but was soon whisked off to the dance floor. The whiskies made Floyd nauseous. He didn't take his eyes from the door. As if Lafayette would come back after Floyd had denied him. The hooping man said, "That's some mess they started in the middle of your song. That boy ought to know better than to come in here."

Floyd sat on the barstool surrounded by admirers. All at once, his cowardice and his heartbreak caught up to him. He steadied himself against the onslaught, though he felt like crying, and tried to finish his drink. The glass slipped from his hand. The men who were huddled around him slapped him on the back and ordered shots, "Little glass, easy to hold on to!" the hooping man said. Floyd laughed louder than anybody and put back three shots so fast the bartender could barely keep up. When he careened from his barstool and stumbled outside, his group of fans must have thought he'd gone to vomit.

Floyd hid in an alcove a few doors down from Cleota's. It was late and the street was quiet. The men from the club came outside to look for him, their shouts covered the sound of his sobbing. He didn't know where Lafayette lived. He didn't know his last name or where he worked. Floyd bent at the waist, hands on his thighs for balance. The night was cooler than the previous one had been, and the breeze calmed him. Lafayette had mentioned that his mother's house was on the outskirts of town. It was not much to go on, but the town was small; he could find Lafayette and ask his forgiveness, and they could leave that very night as Floyd had imagined. He had parked on one of the side streets, though he didn't recall which one. He walked quickly to the corner.

"What you rushing for?" a man called, a bottle in his hand. He crossed the street toward Floyd. "I said, where's the fire?" He looked Floyd up and down.

"You know that boy?" he asked.

Floyd walked on.

"You ain't got time to speak? Guess you got to get where you going?"

The man's footsteps quickened behind him.

"I seen that boy look at you. You going to see about him?"

Floyd turned. The man held the bottle by the neck.

"I don't know what you mean."

"You don't know what I mean? You got the nerve to be proper too? I mean your friend."

"I don't know him."

Floyd balled his fists for the fight. Just then, a woman's voice called from the other side of the street. "Sam! Come on now! Jim gonna ride us in his truck." The man gave Floyd another once-over and walked away.

Floyd hung his head like a whipped dog. He told himself he had done the right thing; it would not have been prudent to admit he knew Lafayette. What could have been gained but a fight that would delay his search? He rounded the corner and leaned against the façade of a building to catch his breath. The car, he remembered, was just off the main drag. To hell with these people. To hell with them. Action was required. He would do this one thing; he didn't know what would happen after that, but he could do this one thing that was right. As Floyd jogged toward the car, he noticed a hint of dawn, just a sigh of pink at the bottom of the sky.

"Hey! That you, Floyd?"

Darla stood in the middle of the street.

"Lot of fools around here, ain't it?" she said, walking toward him. "You got a cigarette?"

Floyd shook his head.

"Ain't nobody got a cigarette in this whole town, and the store's closed. This a funny little place, that's sure." Darla rummaged through her handbag. "I always keep one in my purse for emergencies. You sure you ain't got one?"

"I'm sure."

Darla cocked her head to the side and considered Floyd for a few seconds.

"Ain't that your car?" she asked.

"Uh, yeah. I guess it is."

"You skipping town?" Darla chuckled.

"No, just going for a walk."

"Is that right?"

She sidled closer to him. "You want to get in the backseat?" Floyd shoved his hands in his pockets and looked down at his feet.

"No, you don't. I wonder if you ever really did." She paused, "Maybe it's a cigarette in the car?"

Darla walked to the Packard and looked in the windows. "Now I know why you keep going from place to place every two and three days."

Floyd wanted to slap her.

"I saw you go in them woods with that boy last night," she said. "Is that why you in a dash for the car?"

"I don't know what you're talking about," Floyd replied.

"I saw you."

"It wasn't me."

"Ain't nothing to me. I mean, I think it's nasty but I can't say as I really give a damn."

"It wasn't me."

"It ain't nothing new. Though I reckon you ought to play it close. You seen what happened to that boy."

"I don't know him."

"Aww, come on, Floyd."

"It wasn't me you saw."

Darla bent to fiddle with the door handles. "You got the keys?" she asked.

Floyd smelled his cowardice; he was all rot inside. If he saw Lafayette in the street at that moment, he wouldn't be able to meet his eye. He unlocked the car door and sat in the driver's seat. He put his hand on his thigh to steady the twitch in the muscle. Darla climbed in next to him. "Get out," Floyd wanted to say. She searched the glove compartment for cigarettes, and finding none, she moved to exit the car, but Floyd reached for her arm and pulled her back inside. "If we leave now," he said, "I can just make the next gig. Two hundred miles."

"You must think God made me a fool," Darla replied, wriggling free of him and getting out of the car. She took a few steps away, then turned to face him and said more softly, "You better get yourself together if you gon' drive all that way."

Floyd watched her tip tap down the street in her run-down heels. The sun rose in an angry orange ball. Could be another earth, another earth just like this one all up in flames. The upper sky was still a dark layer of purple clouds. Floyd turned the key in the ignition and thought, I should hang myself like Judas.

Six

1950

THE REVIVAL TENT WAS smaller than Six had imagined. Fewer than thirty people stood inside and already it was crowded. Six, seated with two other men on folding chairs in the front, looked past the crowd, through the unfastened tent flap, to the yard beyond. A steady rain pelted the trees; the tender green leaves bobbed on their boughs. A family came in, saw Six behind the pulpit, and went out again. They left because of Six, because he was only fifteen, and a northerner, and no one had ever heard of him. The other preachers sitting with him were unknowns too, but they were middle-aged and looked the part. When he first met them earlier that day, they had called Six green. They chucked him under the chin and joked that he was still wet behind the ears. They rubbed his head playfully with their wide hands. Six felt their palms—dry or clammy, steady or trembling—through the fuzz of his close-shaven scalp. He distrusted their kindness.

Six's was the tent of lesser lights. That was fine with him. He'd preach and the people who'd brought him there would see they'd made a mistake and send him back home to Philadelphia.

A few hundred feet away, in another, larger tent, the pages of the hymnals rustled and a piano played. The crowd had already started singing. Six's audience looked tired—too worn out for good preaching, too worn out to feel anything.

Six returned his gaze to the trees. A woman in a bright yellow dress stood beneath them, soaked to the bone. Her skirt clung to her thighs and her blouse was slick against her breasts. Six thought it peculiar that she didn't use an umbrella. Most of these people didn't, he'd noticed. They entered the tent shaking the rain off of themselves, a sign, surely, of their backward country ways. He recalled an image of his mother, stepping out of the back door and into the rain, her umbrella held high. Two of Hattie's long strides and she was halfway down the alley. Hattie walks like a train comin', August would say. Six always knew where his mother was in the house, which room she would charge into next. He was home too often. Hattie didn't like that he was such a homebody; she thought he ought to be out with his brothers. To avoid her displeasure, he skulked around the corners of the house and spent most of his time in the bedroom he shared with Franklin and Billups. His favorite hiding spot was a recess under the stairs, though he was too big to fit there comfortably and had to curl himself into a ball with his knees touching his chin.

He felt best in the cubby, hidden from view, the house and its inhabitants bustling around him like so many bees. He could hear Hattie in the hallways and his brothers calling to one another quietly—Hattie would not have shouting in the house—his father whistling, his sisters whispering. His scars didn't bother him when he was under the stairs. He couldn't feel the keloids pulling across his neck and curving around his torso and back. Though they were years healed, they itched and burned as intensely as they had when Six was a child and the wounds first scabbed.

Six kept his constant discomfort a secret, not because of stoicism or bravery, but out of bitterness. His pain and weakness made him special—especially wronged and especially indignant—exceptional because he had suffered. His pain was his most precious and secret possession, and Six held on to it as fiercely as a jewel robbed from a corpse.

The tent flap blew open again. The woman in the yellow dress darted out from under the trees into the rain. Six could not see her well enough to know if she was pretty, but his pulse quickened at the way her skirt clung to her thighs. She was young, he knew that much. He wished she would come into his tent. She would be disappointed at hearing him preach—they all would—but his scars itched powerfully in the steamy close tent, and she might distract him from his suffering and homesickness.

Six had preached four times before at Mount Pleasant Baptist church near his house in Philadelphia. The Word had come over him like a fit; it hijacked him utterly. The first time was nearly two years before, during the evening service one Sunday. Just before the call to prayer, Six heard a low flat whistle, like the sound of air blowing through a hollow bone. He felt something—spirit? demon?—coming toward him. When it reached Six, it entered him, not like the dove of the Holy Spirit that the Bible talked about, but like a thunderclap that wakes the neighborhood in the middle of the night. The force of it bent him double. He squeezed his throat with his hand, but that did nothing to stop the Word rising in him. He was so afraid he thought he might vomit. The Word collected in his mouth like a pile of pebbles and pushed itself out through his lips.

Afterward, the parishioners told him he'd preached like God's anointed for nearly thirty minutes. Six remembered very little of what he'd said or done. There remained only a lingering euphoria that faded quickly and whose departure left him depleted and confused. At home in his hiding place under the stairs, Six squeezed his eyes shut and tried to summon God, or whatever had come to him, but it was like trying to remember a dream—the longer he thought about it, the further it receded. The preacher had said it was grace. But what was grace if it came on him like a seizure and then left him as frail and hurting as he had been before its visit? There wasn't anyone to ask about it: Hattie said it was just the same as when the church ladies caught the spirit and spoke in tongues, which only showed they were excitable. August said there were some odd things you just couldn't explain in this world, and Six's fits were one of them.

Six wasn't sure religion was any more than a lot of people caught up in a collective delirium that disappeared the minute they stepped out of the church doors and onto the street. And who could blame them? Who would not want to be carried away by something bright and exalted? But Six wasn't like the other church people. His experience of God was a violent surge he couldn't control. He came to believe that, like everything else in his life, his preaching had something to do with his poor health. He could not see that perhaps there was a blessing in it, that some help was being extended to him. In the middle of the night while his family slept and Six was insomniac with body aches and bouts of itching, he knew his Jesus spells were another indicator that he was a freak, not merely of body but of spirit. His soul was susceptible to God's whimsy, just as his body was susceptible to any opportunistic thing that might hurt it. If he'd known how to pray, Six would have asked God to take his gift away.

The people in the tent settled for the service. Six hadn't any idea what he'd preach. The congregants watched him. He didn't want them to see him squirm, but in his agitation his skin had ignited like a match head. He looked at the other preachers: one held a dog-eared Bible with a brown leather cover crisscrossed with creases and the other read his notes, stopping every now and again to glance heavenward and mouth a prayer. Most of what Six knew of the Bible he'd learned in Sunday school or from snippets of sermons he'd heard when his aunt Marion took him to church. August and Hattie went to services only at Christmas and Easter or for christenings and funerals. Aunt Marion said they'd suffered because of it. "If you don't come to the Lord's house, he won't come to yours," she was fond of saying.

Six had not said good-bye to his brothers before he left Philadelphia to come to the revival. He'd been bundled into a car in the predawn before anyone on the block was awake to see him leave. Six had beaten a neighborhood boy badly the day before. From the depths of him emerged a violence he had not known was there. The boy's relatives wanted revenge, and the neighbors said he was crazy.

The journey to Alabama took two days. Six slept in the car one night and was hosted on the other by a church-going lady in Tennessee. They stopped in the dead of night on a country road with no streetlights. The moon was a sliver. It was so dark Six could not see the borders of his own body, and he and the darkness were one indivisible thing. An old woman holding a lantern opened the door to the house and told them the electricity was irregular. Hers was the only house on the road; inside it smelled of grass and dew and the rooms buzzed with mosquitoes. It seemed to Six that the walls didn't serve much purpose other than to keep people from seeing inside. He didn't sleep at all for the vertigo caused by the darkness and the bugs and the silence. In the morning he saw that the house was little more than a wooden shack, leaning under the weight of its roof, the window frames too slanted to accommodate a pane of glass.

Now, Bible in his lap, he thought of John 3:16 and Jesus walking on water and Daniel in the lion's den. He tried to feel something about these stories, to reproduce his religious fervor, but his heart kept its steady beat; he was lucid as could be, and frightened. Six closed his eyes and his Bible and decided to open it at random and preach about whatever he found there. Leviticus 14:20, the rituals for cleaning a leper. Genesis 49:9, "Judah is a lion's whelp." He didn't know what a whelp was. The tambourines stopped, and a man approached the card table that served as a pulpit.

Two days earlier Hattie shook him awake at dawn. "Shhh," she'd said and held her fingers to her lips. She laid out a jacket and tie that he had never seen before and indicated that he should dress quickly in the bathroom. It was barely light. He descended the stairs, and they were all there, Hattie and August and their old friend Reverend Grist, assembled in the vestibule by the front door. Reverend Grist said they were leaving right then, at that very moment. Tent revivals in Alabama were starting in two days' time; they could make a circuit around the state and be gone for two weeks.

"Two weeks!" Six said.

"Boy, after all this mess you done caused you lucky it ain't two years," August said.

"You think that's long enough?" Hattie asked.

"I guess we gon' find out," August answered.

Six had never been away from home. He looked toward the second floor, where his brothers and sisters were sleeping.

"No time for good-byes," Hattie said.

She opened the front door, and the four of them moved toward a car parked at the curb. Reverend Grist carried the travel bag Hattie had packed for Six. She lagged behind the group, stiff and inscrutable. At the very last minute, when he was settled in the backseat and the car's motor choked to life and Six had given up hope for a farewell from his mother, Hattie rushed forward and held a Bible out to him. She squeezed his hand when he took it, then turned her back to him and walked into the house.

THE CROWD FIDGETED. Six opened his Bible again and his finger fell on the Beatitudes: "Blessed are the poor in spirit . . . Blessed are they who mourn . . ." And the meek and the merciful and so on. Six did not want to be meek. Sickly and scarred as he was, people mistook his physical limitations for humility. Six thought mercy and weakness were the same thing and was as revolted by them as he was by his own frail body. He wanted to punish, not forgive. He wanted to be a sword, not a lamb.

The story of Joshua came to mind. Six vaguely recalled a wall and a city whose name he could not remember. He had trouble finding it in his Bible. The man behind the pulpit led the congregants in prayer. It was a long and passionate supplication. Someone in the tired-looking assembly even let out a shout. Six's hands were slick; the pages of his Bible clung together in the humidity, and the pads of his fingers left smudges on the corners of the pages. He wanted to loosen his tie and unbutton the collar of his shirt. Jericho! He remembered the name of the city.

"Amen," said the man leading the prayer. "Amen," the congregation said in response.

"We gon' bring you the Lord's Word three ways tonight," he said. "He done blessed us with three of his servants."

Six found the passage. There was no battle as he had hoped, only a few trumpets and the Israelites walking around the city walls. The man who'd led the prayer said, "We got Six Shepherd all the way from Philadelphia." Six kept his head bowed so he could finish reading.

"Look like our young Brother Shepherd done lost hisself in the Word." A pause followed, but Six did not raise his head. "I say," the man said, clearing his throat. "This gon' be a sermon to remember!"

When Six stood, the crowd leaned forward expectantly. They whispered to one another. Someone said, "He ain't no bigger than a minute." He walked to the pulpit and made a show of placing his Bible on the table and turning the pages back and forth, careful not to lose his place. His eyes teared. They probably already knew the story of

Jericho. Everyone knew that story. He ought not to be here, he ought to be sitting on the ledge in his bedroom window in Philadelphia watching his mother make her way down the alley.

"I'm gonna talk to you about Joshua," he said. "If you could . . . if you could turn your Bibles to the book of Joshua."

The assembly looked at him. There was none of the flutter and fidget that usually followed the announcement of the scripture. The man who'd led the opening prayer came up behind him and whispered, "Lot of these folks ain't got they Bibles with them. You gon' have to read it."

"Oh! I . . . Excuse me. I can just . . . I'll read . . ." He lost his place, and the words moved around on the page so he couldn't find the verse he'd chosen.

"Cain't hear you!" someone shouted from the back.

"I'm sorry. It's, er . . ." Six took a deep breath. "Joshua 6:15," he shouted at them. His voice was artificially loud and deep, like a child imitating a man. He read aloud in his false baritone. He dared not look up. He could feel their boredom. But as he read, the scene took shape in his mind. Six saw a man leading a mighty army dressed in white; the hundred followed the bearded Joshua astride his black horse. In front of him, other men carried horns and trumpets shining so fiercely in the sunlight that their glinting could be seen from across the desert. They marched around a high, thick wall beyond which nothing could be seen. Once, twice, a third time, a fourth, Joshua's army marched around the wall. Nothing happened. The army of the Lord began to doubt its leader.

Six looked out at the congregation; the people were as skeptical and exhausted as Joshua's men. Joshua's army circled the city a seventh time. The trumpeters lifted their horns in unison, as though they were one many-handed organism. Joshua raised his arm and his army shouted, "Hurrah! Hurrah! Hurrah!" They shook their swords in the air. "Hurrah! Hurrah! Hurrah!" A wall of sound pressed against the city's wall of stone. Jericho quivered. The gray boulders in its walls split in half and then in quarters until they were nothing and there was the city of Jericho, naked.

"Those walls crumble into dust, brothers and sisters, into nothing. Can you see it? Close your eyes, brothers and sisters, and picture what the Lord has done!"

"Amen!" someone shouted. The spirit came on Six now. He couldn't see the faces in front of him; his anxiety was replaced with an ecstasy that spun in his chest like a ball of fire.

Six remembered a song from his childhood and sang it in the reedy, cracking tenor of boys his age. **Joshua fought the battle of Jericho, Jericho, Jericho. Joshua fought the battle of Jericho and**

the walls came a-tumbling down. The people sang it with him. He raised his Bible heavenward, and the crowd was on its feet. The women in the front row shook their tambourines. The assembly clapped and stomped. Six held out his hand to silence them.

" 'Then they devoted to destruction by the edge of the sword all in the city, both men and women, young and old, oxen, sheep and donkeys,' " he read. "Seems a little extreme, doesn't it, brothers and sisters? But you know what, the Lord doesn't do things halfway. He doesn't come to sit on the porch and sip lemonade, does he? He doesn't come to take the scene in. He comes to take over!"

"I know that's right!" a woman shouted.

"Brothers and sisters, let me tell you what our Lord can do. When I was a little boy, I got hurt bad. They had me at the hospital, a whole hospital full of doctors couldn't do anything for me. You know what the doctors told my mama, brothers and sisters?"

Six paused a beat.

"They told her I wouldn't see the morning. They said call the funeral home. Call the undertaker. They didn't give me any more of their medicine. Those doctors just went on home. But the Lord stretched out His hand."

"Tell it!"

"The Lord stretched out His hand and said, 'It's not his time. My servant has some work to do before I call him home.' "

"Amen!"

"You know what, brothers and sisters? He saved me for this ministry. I don't have much experience. But what I do have—Amen!—what I do have is the Lord's hand to guide me. Sure as I am standing here He led me to you tonight. He saved me so I could be here tonight to tell you that if we ask Him, the Lord will make our tribulations and strife fall down just like that wall in Jericho."

"Praise Him!"

"Make a joyful noise unto the Lord tonight!"

They shouted.

"I said a joyful noise. You all don't have anything more for Jesus?"

The congregation roared. Six paused to catch his breath and wipe the sweat from his forehead. The people clapped and shouted. The ladies in the front raised their arms over their heads and shook their tambourines.

"Let's bow our heads and pray together. Father God, tonight we ask that you reveal what you have laid on our hearts, and give us the strength to do what you require of us. Tell us Lord, how to march around our Jericho. Give us your instructions tonight, Jesus, and we will follow them to victory."

Six looked out at the assembly. A woman wept in the front row. Her shoulders heaved with the force of her sobbing; her arms hung limp at her sides. Six stepped from behind the makeshift pulpit and walked toward her. He wasn't sure why. His feet carried him to her though he didn't know what he'd say. He touched her arm with his fingertips.

"Ma'am?" he said.

She opened her eyes.

"Ma'am, what has Jesus laid on your heart tonight?"

He spoke quietly, as though they were the only two people in the tent. Looking at her closely, he saw that this woman was utterly defeated. She had been kicked until she'd fallen down and then kicked some more. A thin scar ran from the corner of her eye to the corner of her mouth. She wasn't young, but she wasn't old either. Six wanted to touch the tip of his tongue to the raised welt of the scar.

"I didn't know about coming here tonight, on account of I been away so long. I was saved when I was young but I backslid. I come because I wanted—I don't know—I just wanted to be back near Jesus."

"The Lord always welcomes his sheep back to the fold. What's your name, sister?"

"Coral."

"Sister Coral, His arms are always open."

She nodded her head. Her dress was a light-colored cotton, maybe it had been pink once. Its white collar was yellowed and frayed at the edges.

"I believe that's true, Reverend," she said.

Coral stood with her hands clasped in front her, pressed together so tightly that her knuckles reddened. She tried, in great shuddering gasps, to stop crying.

"I can see you have a sincere spirit," Six said. He could feel her troubled heart and see that she meant well. That scar, he thought, ought to be avenged.

The crowd formed a semicircle around them.

"I ain't been . . . I ain't been married. Lord forgive me for saying this to a young fella like you. I ain't been married, but I lived with a man, and he went on his way. I had a child by him, but she passed when she was a little thing, and I come to live with my sister. She been through a hard time too."

"God bless her," Six said.

"She sick now. Doc been round, and he say he don't know what's wrong with her. She been in her bed a month and she fadin' away. Look like a haint, ain't nothing to her. She the only living person on this earth ever been kind to me."

She looked at Six with such eyes, such a look she gave him, with all that's futile and unspeakable in this world.

"Let's pray, Sister Coral. You and me and all these souls the Lord has brought together this evening. We're all going to pray."

Six took Coral's hand, and they kneeled together on the packed dirt floor. It was only in church that he felt compassion for anyone beside himself. Something happened to him when he looked at Sister Coral. When he was preaching about Jericho, strength built in his body, rising in Six until it spilled over the edges of him. He had so much power that he could afford to share it, had to share it, or it would explode in him. He could be kind, if only for that hour, because he was, if only for that single hour, strong.

Six put his hand in the dip between Coral's shoulder blades and put his other hand on her forehead. He had seen the minister do this at Mount Pleasant. Six felt the Word pass from his body into Sister Coral's, and her faith and grief passed into him. He felt the ridges of her spine and the hot, damp skin on her forehead. She looked like such a rough woman; he had not expected her skin to be soft. His fingers twitched. Six had never been so aware of another person; Coral's soul whirred inside of her like a motor. They were one organism in that moment. Six could not feel his body itching or his pulling, pinching skin.

"Let's lay hands on our sister," he said.

A dozen hands trembled on Sister Coral. Six wept as the assembly groaned and called to Jesus.

After some time, he didn't know how long, Six returned to himself. His knees were damp and stiff from kneeling in the dirt, his throat was raw, and Coral's blouse was wet beneath his hand. He was seized with a powerful urge to urinate. He rubbed his knees and stood facing the assembly. Some were exhilarated, some exhausted, their faces oily and streaked with tears. Coral was still on her knees. Two women helped her to her feet and led her to a folding chair where she sat with her hands in her lap. Six didn't know how to end the service. He couldn't imagine how to make a neat finish to what had happened to them. He was suddenly shy, as though he had been doing something private and everyone had seen him.

"Amen," he said and walked out of the tent and into the stand of trees outside.

Someone called his name, but Six didn't turn back. Behind him the tambourines jangled; the strains of a hymn floated out to him on the chill, wet air. The rain had stopped. The wind shook the leaves, and droplets fell onto his head and shoulders. There was still some daylight left. Six knew he should go back to the tent, but he wanted to climb into the trees. The last rays of sun caught in the drops of water on the leaves, and for a few moments the trees were all quivering gold. He was quiet inside, not peaceful but hushed, spellbound. He thought, I'm not just anybody. I'm not just any sick boy.

With great difficulty Six climbed into a tree and straddled one of the lower boughs. He heard a bell in the distance, a baritone clanging from somewhere down the dirt road that led to the revival site. Red-dirt road—nothing but trees on either side and a few cars parked in the clearing in front of the tents. A ghosted quarter moon appeared. How rarely he saw the moon over Wayne Street. The sun dipped below the horizon. Far off in the distance, a string of lights went on along the road. Beyond them, a larger illuminated cluster indicated the town. Reverend Grist told him its name, but Six had forgotten it. He hadn't any desire to go there.

Six's moment with Coral was already receding. He didn't know where he would sleep that night or what he would eat or who would feed him. Hattie had given him five dollars when he left. He knew that wasn't enough to get him back to Philadelphia.

Beneath Six's perch in the oak, two men relieved themselves against the trunks of the trees.

"That boy, what's his name?"

"Six, name of Six."

"He ain't old enough to have no hairs."

"You seen how he run outta there when he finish?"

"That's that Coral. She got so much heathen in her she scare a young boy."

"She come up here repenting tonight."

"Sho' that's right, but she have somebody behind a shed tomorrow."

"You wish it was you!"

"Naw, I ain't got my mind on nothing but Jesus."

They laughed.

They're laughing at me, Six thought. Maybe they were all in the tent laughing at him. Stupid country folk. If August had stayed in Georgia, he might have been like these men. He might have driven a truck or hitched a ride from town to a Friday night tent revival and had a conversation like the one Six was overhearing. He thought of the South as a single undifferentiated mass of states where the people talked too slow, like August, and left because of the whites, only to spend the rest of their lives being nostalgic for the most banal and backwoods things: paper shell pecans, sweet gum trees, gigantic peaches. August could recite the names of the people who lived in the town in which he grew up. In Georgia, he said, the old people never went untended. The North was cold and colorless—the food was awful and the people were desperate. When he talked that way, Hattie would fold her arms and press her lips together into a thin line.

Floodlights came on—the soft indigo evening

was swallowed in an ugly circle of light. A few people trickled out of the small tent. A man holding a young boy's hand ambled into the brightness and crossed out of it again. Six watched them walk down the road until he couldn't see them anymore. He couldn't remember holding August's hand that way. Other boys went fishing with their fathers or to ball games. Perhaps the man and boy he'd just seen had been fishing that very day. No matter, the bait would have made Six nauseous. His schoolmates called him a prissy boy and teased him relentlessly.

The men below Six's tree continued to talk. "He fifteen, huh? Ain't much to him."

"He awful small."

"He done alright, though."

"He can preach, sure, but it's something peculiar about him."

"You just saying that 'cause he so proper."

"Naw, it ain't that. He put me in mind of a boll weevil."

"That's a shame. It ain't his fault he small and skinched-up looking."

Six didn't know what a boll weevil was, but he guessed it was something little and ugly. He shifted on his tree branch; how he wanted to return to his brothers and to his cubby under the stairs.

One of the men under the tree said, "Ain't that he look like a weevil, it's that he kinda act like one."

There was another boy like Six at school, pinched

and delicate. His name was Avery, but the other boys called him Ava. He was runty and effeminate but healthy, so, unlike Six, he was not spared physical abuse. One afternoon, Six saw a group of boys chase him down the street. Avery was slow moving; he knew they'd catch him, so he stood in the middle of the block waiting for them. They surrounded him and shoved him to the ground. He fell to his knees. Avery refused to stand. He just kneeled there on the sidewalk while they called him sissy and faggot. When they were finished with him, he stood and brushed the dirt from his knees. Six sneered at him. He wanted the bullying boys to see that he hated Avery too; in this way they would understand that Six was only infirm, not pathetic and not deserving of their scorn.

Perhaps there was some other way to understand the world, but Six couldn't imagine what that could be. It seemed to him that his own father was disgusted by his frailty. After Six recovered from his accident, August stopped spending time with him—of course, it was also true that he wasn't often home. Six once overheard his aunt Marion tell Hattie it was the babies' deaths that sent August catting, that he had been a decent-enough man before that. Six didn't know what she meant exactly, but he did know that his father's presence in his life was peripheral at best. August had never taught Six any of the things fathers were supposed to teach their sons. The night before Six was sent to the revival, August had said, "I didn't think you had that kind of hurtin' in you, boy." How would you know what I have in me? Six thought. All you do is make jokes and tell useless stories about a town in Georgia nobody ever heard of. How could you know what hurt I have?

Footsteps approached the stand of trees.

"Evening, Reverend," the two men said.

"Praise the Lord, brothers," Reverend Grist replied.

"That's your young man preached?"

"That's right. First time preaching away from home," said Reverend Grist.

"Got the spirit in him, that's sho'."

"Have you all seen him? They said he came this way."

"Naw, sir, ain't seen not hide nor hair."

"He turn up, surely. He run out to get some air, maybe. It's hot in there."

"Well, if you see him, tell him to meet me at the big tent. His mama left him in my charge," Grist said. The two men walked away.

At the mention of Hattie, Six's throat tightened. He sighed, then sat still as he could for fear he'd been heard.

"If there was a boy round here somewhere he'd like as not be tired. He might go on out to the car and take a nap in the back," Reverend Grist said.

He paused, listening. "Such a boy might say yessir or some such so I'd know he was alright."

"Yessir." Six's voice was soft and breathy, barely audible over the cicadas and the soft shirring of the leaves and the drip-drip-drip of raindrops falling through the oaks.

When Six was certain he was alone, he climbed out of the tree and, keeping to the darkness beyond the floodlights, found his way to the reverend's car, where he fell asleep stretched across the backseat.

Six woke once deep in the night, well past midnight and far from dawn, to the sound of the car's motor stopping. He got out and was led into a house, down a corridor, and into a room that smelled of fried fish. He undressed in a half sleep, too tired to be concerned with whether the reverend saw his scars. A cot had been prepared for him. He climbed in, and the canvas sagged under his weight. Six dreamed he was swinging in a hammock on a porch in front of a big white house with a trellis, and his father came up the porch steps, saying, "I knew you'd like it here. I knew you'd want to stay forever."

IN THE MORNING there was no sign of Reverend Grist. The room Six had slept in was drab and cheerless, with yellow walls that had dingied over time. Sunlight streamed in from a window near his cot. The light was clouded somehow and grainy. The window was sheeted with a thin gauzy material through which the light filtered. Voices murmured somewhere in the house—the sound was menacing, as though someone were whispering against him. Six swung his legs over the side of the cot and looked for his pants, keenly aware that he didn't know where he was or whose house he was in and that he couldn't recall the name of the town. The only person he knew in this foreign, faraway place was Reverend Grist. Tears welled in his throat. Baby. Baby boy crying. He would not snivel, he thought, and he kneeled to look for his clothes under the cot. He found only his shoes.

"Damn!" he said. Reverend Grist opened the bedroom door.

"The Lord doesn't like that kind of talk, boy."

Six, dressed only in his briefs, whirled around to face him, shamed by his scars and his nakedness. He covered himself with his hands.

"Excuse me, sir," Six said.

"It's not fitting of a boy who preached so fine last night."

The reverend walked farther into the room and laid Six's clothes on the cot.

"The lady of the house washed and pressed them for you," Grist said. "She prepared a breakfast for you too. These sisters are real kind. Most of them hardly have enough for themselves, but they put us up and feed us. Just like the widow in the temple. You know that story, boy?" the reverend said.

Six shook his head.

"You have a lot of fire in you, and the Lord does bless you with his spirit, but you don't know the Word like you need to if you keep on preaching." He gave Six a hard look. "You want to keep on preaching?"

Six did not want to keep on preaching. It was true that the night before he'd felt something with Coral that he'd never experienced and that, unlike the other times, he could recall it. But Six wanted to go home. The reverend would think him ungrateful, so Six replied, "I don't know, sir. I guess so."

"Preacher has to be called, young man!" Grist said sharply. He gestured toward Six's clothes. "The Lord brings us into this world naked, but I don't suppose he means us to stay that way."

Reverend Grist had been kind to Six during the trip from Philadelphia. "It's Jim Crow now," he said, when they crossed the Mason-Dixon. "You ever been down south?" he asked. Six shook his head. "Well, when there are white folks about, make yourself scarce, and if you can't, smile and don't ever look them in the eye."

The reverend rocked on his heels as Six dressed.

"The Lord gives us breath and life," he said. "And He gives us flowers and the moon and eyes to see them with and a heart and mind to appreciate their beauty. That's something only we can do. You know that? A cow in the field doesn't have appreciation of beauty. That's a gift He gave us, just to make life a little sweeter. Isn't that something?"

Reverend Grist paused, then asked, "What happened to you, boy?"

"Sir?"

"I . . . I wondered what happened."

"Burned, sir."

"Must have happened a good while ago, healed over now, like it is."

"Yes, sir."

"Must have been real painful—and you were just a little fella at the time, I imagine."

"Yes, sir."

"Must have given your mama a real scare."

"I guess so."

SIX REMEMBERED the ambulance ride to the hospital and Hattie weeping beside him. He had not seen her cry before or since. He was only nine at the time, but he remembered the heaving sobs that pulled her body to and fro and how she kept touching the parts of him that weren't burned. "Please, not this one too," she said. She shook and rocked, but her hands were calm and steady on him, as though they weren't attached to the rest of her body.

He stayed in the hospital for two months. Each

time he woke from the painkillers, Hattie was there, face white as chalk—sitting straight backed in the chair or standing at the window or pacing at the foot of his bed. August came too. He whistled Six a tune or brought him odd presents: a wooden recorder that he played very softly until a nurse came along and told him to stop, cherries that he peeled with a small knife and cut into pieces so Six could taste the sweetness on his tongue without having to chew with his burned jaws.

His sisters visited. He woke one afternoon to find Cassie standing behind Hattie. "I'm so sorry, Mother. I'm so sorry. I'm sorry," she said. Hattie turned to face her and nodded. Cassie left the room in tears.

The sun filtered through the heavy curtains in the hospital room. Six felt as though he had been asleep for a long time and that perhaps he was still sleeping and everything he saw or heard was a dream. In the dream he got up from his bed, put his arm around Cassie, and said, "See, I'm fine. It was just a little accident, and I'm just fine."

The burns covered 50 percent of his body. The doctors told Hattie they didn't know if Six would live, and so in his sleeping and sleeping he was dying, or almost.

Bell and Cassie thought they had killed him. After he was better and had gone back to school, and even now, six years later, they blamed themselves. Either would do anything for Six if he asked. When he was short with them or cold or looked at them in anger, it hurt them deeply. Six sniped at them purposely when he wanted to inflict pain or when he wanted someone to remember that night with him and to suffer.

On the evening of his accident Cassie was getting dressed for a prom to which an older boy had invited her. Hattie had given her permission because he was, as she said, the right sort, college bound. Hattie had managed to pay for most of the dress, and Cassie cleaned houses to pay the rest. Cassie was the first Shepherd to attend a prom. Hattie didn't say much, but she spent a long time pressing the dress and then laid it out on Cassie's bed as gently as she would a newborn baby. It was pale green and softly shining. Layers of chiffon frothed around the skirt when it moved. Six kept going into his sisters' room to look at it lying on the bed. The dress was so delicate and pretty it could have taken flight and floated out of the window.

Cassie and Bell were in the bathroom rolling Cassie's hair into curlers. "Six," one or the other called, "bring us some more bobby pins." Or, "Six, tell Mother we'll need the hot comb in twenty minutes." He came when summoned and hung around the bathroom door watching his sisters. When she wasn't busy with Cassie's hair, Bell stood behind him with her hands on either side of his face rubbing his cheeks absentmindedly, the way she would a cat. His sisters were prettier than anyone Six knew. They gabbled to each other like bright birds. Bell went downstairs to light the hot water heater. By the time she returned, Cassie had put the stopper into the tub, and the hot water rushed out of the faucet in a loud steaming torrent. The water was hot enough to cook an egg. Six sat on the edge of the tub. One of them, maybe Cassie, asked him to get a clean towel from the hall closet, and the other had made a joke that he was their butler, and they'd laughed. Six was just about to stand for an exaggerated pretend bow when he lost his balance and fell into the tub. Hot enough to cook an egg. So hot that for a long while Six couldn't breathe or cry out. He felt as though his flesh was sliding off of his bones. Cassie screamed. She screamed as she pulled him out and screamed as she laid him on the floor and screamed as he convulsed on the tile. He heard Hattie shouting and footsteps, many footsteps, coming down the hallway, and then, mercifully, he blacked out. He woke in the ambulance to his mother's hands moving on his feet and legs, fluttering over him as though her fingers had become butterflies.

"THE SCARS DON'T LOOK so bad, you know," Reverend Grist said. "And glory to Jesus you still here."

"Glory be, sir," Six replied.

Six dressed and breakfasted, and he and Reverend Grist got in the car and drove through the town—the Reverend wanted Six to see a genuine southern municipality. Down at the revival site the ministers would be praying and studying their Bibles in preparation for the afternoon service. It was Saturday, and they would start at four.

"There's gonna be a crowd this evening like you never saw."

"Everybody here is so church going as all that?" Six asked.

"The revival's the only game in town, so to speak. Not much round here for folks to do, save the pool halls and the drinking places, but they can go to those anytime. The revival's entertainment. But that's alright—they come for whatever reason they want to, then it's the Lord that occupies Himself with their souls. Amen."

The town was five blocks of storefronts and a five and dime. The reverend pointed out the post office and a little place where a woman he called Aunt Baby Sugar made the best sweet potato pie in the state of Alabama. "They have an entrance round back for Negroes to buy something and take it home," Reverend Grist said.

The white people looked almost as badly off as the Negroes. The women Six saw wore faded dresses and their hair was stringy, or they were fat and red-faced. The men were sweaty and their shoes weren't polished. Negroes skirted the white people on the sidewalk; one man nearly fell into the gutter as he hopped off the curb to avoid colliding with a white woman who was walking toward him. The town seemed to be comprised of equal numbers of each race. In Philadelphia, Six rarely saw white people aside from the teachers at his school. At home they thought of white people as a vague but powerful entity—like the forces that control the weather, that capable of destruction, that hidden from view.

The Negroes and whites in the town knew one another. For all of the shucking and ducking, they greeted each other frequently, often by name. There was something almost intimate in their knowledge of one another, and it was this intimacy that disturbed Six most. These people had probably known each other all their lives, and still one had the power to demand that the other step into the gutter, and that other was cowed enough to do it.

They arrived at the end of the main strip. The sidewalks disappeared, and the street widened into a highway. As Grist drove farther from the town, the whites disappeared too. A mile or so down they passed a Negro woman driving a mule with a stick. She wore a man's hat pushed down over her forehead. Despite the previous night's rain, the ground was dry; red dust clouds whirled around the woman's feet as she walked. Her mule had a bell attached. Six recognized it as the source of the clanging he'd heard the night before, and he wondered if this same woman drove her mule day and night along these roads, never coming from anywhere and never having anywhere to go.

The red-dirt road was lined on either side by trees with long fronds that hung like hair and grazed the ground. A white clapboard structure came into view. The church was surrounded with stumps and browning tufts of flattened grass, not so much a parking lot as a widening of the road. Even the plain wooden cross in front had the air of the makeshift. The church didn't have steps like a church ought to so that the members could stand on them after service and be seen by the neighborhood in their Sunday best.

A few women stood in front of the doors; their voices floated into the car's open windows along with a nutty, oily smell. The women turned, squinting into the sun, toward the sound of the engine.

"That's him! That's him!" one woman cried, waving both arms over her head to flag the car.

Reverend Grist pulled into the church lot.

"Praise the Lord! Praise Jesus! That's you in there?" she said.

"What can we do for you, sister?" Reverend Grist said as he climbed out of the car.

In the daylight Coral didn't look like the woman

Six had prayed with the night before. Her hair was streaked with gray and plaited into four braids, two on either side of her head. She was missing a tooth on the right side of her mouth. Three thick wrinkles creased her forehead.

"Reverend Six," she said. "You come on out here and let me see you!"

The other women, murmuring among themselves, approached the car.

"Y'all was in that big tent, so you ain't seen him. Step out here and let my friends see you!" Coral said.

Six didn't want to step into the throng of raggedy women who were bending at the waist to peer into the car.

"Good morning, ma'am," Six said. He wished Reverend Grist would make them go away. Coral reached into the car window to take Six's hands in her own. Her damp hands made him want to wipe his palms on his pant legs.

"Thank you, Reverend Six. Thank you!"

"Now you calm yourself, sister. What's this all about?" Reverend Grist asked. He gestured for Six to get out of the car. "Give the boy a little room, now."

Six took a deep breath and closed his hand around the door handle. Sister Coral cried, "He healed my sister!"

Coral's friends joined in. "I seen it with my own

eyes. She up and sitting round back at Baby Sugar's!" one said.

"Ain't set so much as a toe out the bed in a month!"

"She walking round fit to run a foot race!"

"And I told everybody it was you that healed her, Reverend Six," Coral added. "They said, 'How Regina come to be out the house?' And I told 'em, I said it was you. I just took her home now to rest up a little, but she be at the service this evening. God bless you, Reverend Six. God bless you!"

"Praise the Lord, sister. Don't you forget to thank Him, from whence all miracles come," Grist said.

"I been thanking Jesus and rejoicing all night and all morning. I come home last night, and there's Regina sitting up in the bed! Just sitting there asking me where I been and was there anything to eat. She ain't ate nothing that wasn't forced down her throat since I don't remember when."

"Let's say a prayer of thanks together," Grist said and bowed his head.

Six said nothing, though he knew they expected him to. He couldn't be sure if the older man believed in his miracle. It was true that he had felt Sister Coral in his body, that he had felt the depth and breadth of her pain as though it were a tangible thing that he could hold in his hand. And it was true too that when he was deep in his prayer for her he had an inkling of a sickbed, not a vision, but an intimation of sweaty sheets and languor and the claustrophobia of being in a room with an ill person. He had assumed it was his own convalescence that he was remembering. The intimation was fleeting, but . . . Could be, he thought, that the lady just felt better. Six had been near death yet here he was, and there wasn't any miracle in it.

He was so absorbed in his thoughts that he didn't notice the reverend's prayer had ended. One of the women said, "Look at that. Reverend Six just taken up with the Lord. He don't take no notice of this world."

"Bless him," another replied.

He kept his head bowed because he wouldn't have to say anything if they thought he was praying and because it had occurred to him that he might want to be what they thought he was. All his life, women had been giving him their attention because they pitied him. Now it was because they respected him.

"Alright, sisters, we'll see you all later, the Lord willing," Reverend Grist said.

They drove away from the church.

"Smell that?" Grist asked.

Six nodded.

"Cotton makes that smell. Ripe cotton," he said.

An expanse of white-tipped stalks swayed in the fields up ahead.

"Sir?" Six asked. "What's a boll weevil?"

"Boll weevil? Where'd you hear that? It's a bug, nasty as the locusts in the Bible. Eats up all the cotton. Why do you want to know that?"

Six shrugged.

"Your mama was of mixed mind about sending you down here. Did you know that?"

"No, sir."

"I don't see her at the church much," Grist said. "When she does come and folks get to talking in tongues, she looks at them like they have two heads."

They rode in silence for a time.

"I hope she finds the Lord one day," the reverend said.

"I do too," Six replied.

"Have you found the Lord, Six?"

"I don't know," he answered softly.

"Well," the reverend said, "you'd know if you had. It's not a thing you can mistake." Then, "I don't think you ought to preach this evening."

"Sir?" Six asked.

"We only have tonight and tomorrow at this revival. You come to the big tent and listen, maybe the Lord'll find you."

"Yes, sir."

THE REVEREND WAS RIGHT about the numbers of people that came to the revival on a Saturday. Soon after three o'clock, people began to arrive on foot or crowded onto the beds of pickup trucks. They carried baskets of fried chicken, bags with corn fritters and apples and peaches and jugs of water and iced tea. Before the tents opened, the people sat in the grass and spread their dinners out on squares of cloth. Now and again, a cry went up and two women walked toward each other with their arms outstretched.

Six watched the picnickers through a gap between the drawn flaps of the big tent. Coral had told half the town about his miracle. In a few hours the news spread to the houses where the visiting preachers were staying. All eight convened before the evening service to discuss their plan of action. Six had been elated to hear that he was to attend. The ministers could tell him whether he had healed Coral. They could tell him why these holy fits came on him—maybe they could pray them out of him.

Six sat next to Reverend Grist as the lead minister began the meeting.

"T'ain't for us to decide who and how the Lord calls his servants," he said.

"Amen. That's true," one minister agreed. The others were silent until a young preacher said, "Y'all know this boy ain't healed nobody!"

"Regina claims he did. I went to see her myself. She looks pretty good," the lead minister responded.

"One thing's sure, that boy ain't getting up in the pulpit tonight."

The ministers, mostly of an accord, looked at Six and nodded.

"Hold on now. I think a whole lot of folks might come tonight after hearing about Regina," the lead man said.

"You need to send the boy on home. He just causing trouble!"

More nods.

"That's right, send him on home! All this confusion!"

"There's no place for bitterness in the Lord's house, brothers," the head preacher said.

"Bitterness! Ain't nobody bitter over a little . . ."

"The fact is," Reverend Grist interrupted, "the boy isn't sure of his own calling."

The lead minister fixed his gaze on Reverend Grist. "You brought the boy up here, and he ain't sure?" he said.

"I didn't know. Don't think he did either."

One of the men jumped from his seat. "Put him on the next bus north!"

The preachers' faces contorted with rage. Reverend Grist put his arm around Six's shoulders. Six feared they would drive him from the tent. He had not considered the possibility of the ministers' wrath. He didn't think that one healing, one not-for-certain healing, could make them hate him.

"What's he even doing here!" the angry preacher

shouted. He stood up so abruptly that his chair tipped backward and fell onto the dirt floor. "This boy's messing up our thing!" Six understood in that instant that he had something the ministers wanted, and it had given him power among them. He had never been powerful among men.

In the end it was decided that Reverend Grist would take Six back to Philadelphia when the revival ended. The boy was sequestered, first in Reverend Grist's car, where his scars itched painfully and it was so hot he thought he might faint. Later, the ministers hid Six behind the big tent. At 5:00 the revival began, and the people poured in. The tent filled with the smell of Nu Nile and sun and homemade soap. Six wanted to cry with loneliness. The people were skittish as colts. They hummed with anticipation. The children jostled each other, and their mothers shrieked at them to keep still. Through an opening at the back of the tent, Six could see a section of the crowd and the backs of the ministers' fat necks. An announcer took the platform to lead the crowd in prayer and announce the speakers. A woman followed him and sang "Great Is Thy Faithfulness" in a rich alto.

She was a pillar of a woman, so thick and round a car couldn't knock her down. The song came out of her like a foghorn blast from the ships down at the Navy Yard in Philadelphia—that big and that effortless. A tambourine shook, but the woman's voice dwarfed all other sound. It flowed out of the tent and rumbled down the red-dirt road and through the trees, it roused the birds and made the stones tremble. She slowed the tempo and drew out the notes, and the people, in reverence, stopped clapping, stopped breathing, and let the song take them.

Six squatted in the dirt. All he could see of the congregants were their shoes. Most were worn, the leather scuffed at the toes and repolished. Some were caked with mud, a layer of dust covered the wearer's ankles. A white loafer tapped in time to the music. There was a smudge of something dark at the toe, something reddish and slick that recalled another pair of stained loafers Six had seen the afternoon he'd hurt that boy back in Philadelphia.

"**STOP IT,** Six! Stop it!"

Six remembered a man's voice, deep and strained with shouting.

"Stop it! Get up off him!"

The voice had brought him back to himself. Six came back into his mind with a jolt, all the strength gone out of him. He was slumped with his head hanging limp, chin almost touching his chest. He looked to his left, toward the voice, and saw a white shoe with a smear of something dark on it.

There was a great commotion around him. Six's arms hurt, his knuckles were sore, and there was a sharp pain across his upper back, as though his muscles had been tensed for a long time. His heart fired inside his chest. The beating took up the whole of his insides; his ribs could not contain a heart that beat like that. Gravel pressed into his knees through his pants. It was as though Six had vacated his body and returned to find it vandalized.

Two strong arms hooked under his armpits and yanked him to standing. The white loafers were wrenched from his view, and there was nowhere for him to rest his eyes, so he looked down, and there was Avery with a pulpy mess of a face and a tooth lying next to him in a little puddle of blood. His eyes were closed and his head turned so that one cheek rested on the pavement. The other was split so deeply a sliver of bone showed white through the slick, red flesh. Six looked at his feet and saw that they straddled Avery. He looked at his hands—his left fist was balled, and in his right hand he clutched a bloodied piece of concrete the size of an orange.

The gathered crowd shouted and jostled each other. A man knelt next to Avery, and a crying woman came out of the throng. She looked at Six with such hatred that he staggered backward. She pointed at him, and two older boys rushed forward, lunging at Six like rabid dogs. Some men pulled them away. The woman was Avery's mother, and the boys were his cousins come to his rescue, though they had never before defended him in all his years of being bullied.

Six was on Greene Street, two blocks from home. The man who'd pulled him off of Avery and another bystander, both neighborhood men Six had seen on the block for years, flanked him and led him home.

"Boy, what were you thinking?" one said.

"You done some damage," the other added.

They spoke to each other, "That Avery boy is just a slight thing."

"So's this one."

Six's neighbors stared. It occurred to him that Avery might die. One of the men knocked at the front door, and Six realized he was home. Hattie's mouth dropped open when she saw him.

"What happened to my son?"

"It's the other way round, Mrs. Shepherd."

They explained what he'd done. Hattie took in his bloody hands, sweat-shiny face, and the rip in the knee of his pants. She crossed her arms and her mouth tightened. The concern in her eyes faded, but the fear stayed and the anger grew, that low simmering anger that exploded like a thunder-cloud and sent all the Shepherds scurrying. Hattie thanked the men and led Six into the house.

"Is this all true?" she asked.

"I don't . . . I'm not sure what happened exactly," Six replied.

"There's blood on you."

Six looked at his hand and began to cry.

"So help me if I see one tear on your face . . . You hear me? Don't you cry one tear."

Six stood shaking in front of his mother. "I didn't mean to do it," he said.

Hattie slapped Six across the face with all of her strength. He fell against the wall. She advanced on him, her fists balled with rage.

"You could go to jail. They could come and arrest you right now! And you want to stand here and tell me you didn't mean it? As if a fit came on you out of nowhere and the next thing you know . . ."

Hattie gasped, her hand flew to her mouth. "Oh!" she said. "Oh, Lord. What happens to you?" Hattie looked into her son's face. "You can't stop it, can you?" Six shook his head. His mother reached toward him, her fingertips lingered on the scarring just visible above his shirt collar. "I don't know how to help you," she whispered.

Six thought Hattie might cry, but she inhaled deeply and turned away from him to take her purse and hat from the closet.

"Go clean yourself up," she said. "Stay here. Lock the door behind me and don't let anyone in."

When Hattie returned, along with August, it

was nearly dark. Six had hidden in the crawl space under the stairs. He heard kitchen sounds: water running, something sizzling in a frying pan. Then the clatter of forks against plates. Hattie's legs appeared.

"You going to come out and eat or not?" she asked, brusque and angry as ever.

He didn't respond. He expected her to reach down and drag him out. Instead she pushed a plate of fried eggs into the cubby. In the dining room Six's family ate in near silence. Hattie ordered them to bed as soon as they finished. He heard his siblings' footsteps overhead as they climbed the stairs. Hattie would do something terrible to him, he was sure.

"Hey!" Six jumped. Bell squatted in front of him. "Lemme see your hands," she whispered.

"I said everybody in bed now!" Hattie shouted from the dining room.

Bell ran up the stairs behind the others.

"That's it, Six," Hattie called. "You have to come out now."

"Come on out, boy," August said.

Six crawled out slowly. His muscles ached from the fight and from crouching in the cubby. He was more tired than he'd ever been. He wondered if he'd have the strength to stand. The dining room light was too bright. Hattie sat at one end of the table and August at the other.

"This a mess of trouble," August said. "They took that boy to the hospital. His mama like to come over here and cut you herself, if them two cousins of his don't get you first."

Six shivered with relief. All afternoon he'd been afraid he was a murderer—Avery dead on the street and his mother screaming over his body.

"We got to pay that boy's hospital, Six. But they ain't gon' call the police. That's something," August said. "And that's only on account of his father runs so many numbers that if the Man come round they like to put him in jail and throw away the key."

Hattie was rigid as stone in her chair.

"We gon' have to think something up 'cause them cousins out to get you and maybe that boy's daddy too, and he got a lot of the wrong kind of friends. I reckon we ought to send you somewhere for a minute." August turned to Hattie, "Maybe we send him down to Pearl. She got a house big as this whole block."

Hattie gave August a look that would have stopped a train. He leaned back in his chair.

"Well, we got to do something," he said.

"I sent for Reverend Grist."

"Hattie, we ain't been to church since Easter."

"Six has," Hattie snarled.

Hattie sent Six to bed when the reverend arrived. On his way up the stairs, she stopped him. "What set you off?" she asked.

Six looked at his feet and shook his head. He didn't want to tell her what Avery had said. Six walked past him on his way home from school. The boy was gathering the schoolbooks that a group of bullies had knocked out of his arms. Six didn't know why he'd paused in front of Avery and kicked away a book that the boy was reaching for, but it had scudded across the pavement and landed in a puddle by the curb.

"Your mama Hattie's a whore," Avery said, watching his book sink into the murky water. He used her first name. He said he'd seen her with a man that she had kissed on the corner in plain sight and that the neighborhood was talking about how she had become an easy woman because August wasn't shit. That's what Avery said, that his mother was a whore and his father wasn't shit. How could Six let that feeble runt of a boy, that little nothing of a boy, talk about Hattie that way?

Six had intended to give him one good punch in the jaw, but when he hit Avery, the boy fell and wouldn't get up. He lay in the middle of the side-walk looking up at Six with something nasty and reptilian in his eyes. And he kept taunting him. He was laid out on the sidewalk, but he kept whis-pering, "Whore, whore." A lump of concrete lay on the ground near Avery's head. Six picked it up and leapt on the boy. He hit him with that rock as though Avery was every bad thing that ever was.

He beat him like he was the scalding water that had burned him, as though he was every pitying glance, every cruelty inflicted on him by his schoolmates. The harder Six hit Avery, the more powerful he felt. His arm came down again and again like a part of a machine. His body moved like normal boys' bodies did; he was invincible and perfect.

Hattie sighed. She raised her hand, as if to squeeze his shoulder or to hit him again—Six didn't know which—but she thought better of it, and it dropped to her side.

"Go on to bed," she said.

August and Reverend Grist came into the living room. They watched Six climb the stairs.

"Come back here, boy," August said.

Six stopped walking but didn't turn to face his father.

"Let him go, August," Hattie said. "Just let him go."

THE SINGER FINISHED her song. Six kneeled in the dirt behind the tent. He recognized that reptilian thing in Avery's eyes as a reflection of his own ugliness. He wished he were different. His weak body housed a weak, mean spirit. While Six beat him, Avery looked up at him until he couldn't keep his eyes open any longer. They were two cruel souls in a violence together. It just so happened, Six told himself, that he'd had the upper hand that time. They were frail inconsequential boys and that made them the way they were.

"Dear Lord," Six said aloud. "I ought to ask forgiveness for what I did to Avery, but I'm not sure what sorry feels like." Six—sobbing and praying and feeling the weight of his small cruel heart—walked toward the stand of trees where he'd hidden the night before.

A woman stepped out of the shadows. "You the one healed Coral's sister?" she asked.

She wore the same yellow dress he'd seen her in the previous evening—canary yellow, bright and loud as cymbals crashing together. Her legs were thin, delicately ankled and softly curved at the calf. Six looked at her and blinked.

"You is him, ain't you? Reverend Six?" she asked again.

"I'm no reverend," he said quietly.

"What's that?"

The woman in yellow took a step toward him. She was so small, the top of her head would have barely touched his chin. The fabric of her dress moved as she walked, pressing briefly against her to reveal the swell of her hips and the length of her thighs.

"How come you ain't in there preaching?" she asked, looking up at him. "I been to Coral's place.

I ain't seen Regina so spry in the longest." She took another step toward him. "I heard you ain't even touched her."

The dress was cut high enough in the collar to be respectable, but there was a hint of the round of her breasts just below the neckline. Her collarbones arched toward one another.

"She healed for sure," she said.

"I don't know if that had anything to do with me. Just luck, maybe," he said.

"You sure is soft-spoke outside of the pulpit. I'm Rose," she said. "I come tonight on account of my mama's been poorly. She ain't been goin' to work these last weeks, just lay about the house. Every day she say she got a pain somewhere different. You might can pray on her? You wasn't nowhere near Regina and she better. If you lay hands on my mama, I know she be good as gold after."

Six swallowed and blinked again.

"It ain't far," she said.

Rose turned and walked quickly toward the road. He stood in the shadows and thought to call after her, "I don't think I can do anything for your mama!" But she was far ahead of him by the time he made up his mind to say something.

In twenty minutes they arrived at a small, unpainted wooden house. The woman in the yellow dress, a girl really, only a couple of years older than Six, left him on the porch.

"Wait here," she said. "I'ma see if my mama's awake."

I shouldn't be here, Six thought. There's a woman in that house who needs help, real help. But who could counsel her? The ministers were jealous and squabbling, no closer to God than Six. Rose came out onto the porch. She gazed at him with such expectation and such reverence—he wanted to please her, to be what she thought he was. She led him through a darkened main room and into a bedroom that smelled more of sadness than of disease. A woman lay on a pallet on the floor with the moonlight shining silver on her. Six saw her skepticism and her exhaustion.

"This him?" she said to her daughter.

"Yes, ma'am," the girl answered.

The woman turned away. Six did not feel the power in him, but he remembered the chaplains who came to see him when he was in the hospital and how they kneeled next to his bed. He sat on the floor next to the woman's pallet. Rose watched from the doorway.

"What's troubling you, ma'am?" he asked.

"Nothing a young lick like you could understand."

"God understands everything, ma'am. Doesn't matter if I do or not," he said. "Your daughter says you have some pains."

She didn't answer. Six took a better look around

the room. There were plants everywhere, spilling out of their pots, hanging from the ceiling, crowding the windowsills.

"Looks like you have a green thumb," he said.

The woman turned her head to a blooming plant near her pallet. White flowers glowed in the silver light. Hattie had houseplants. She was not a singing woman, but she hummed when she tended her plants. Six wondered if this woman did too. He reached toward one of the blossoms, and Rose's mother sat up quickly and said in a strong voice, "Don't touch that one. It's delicate." She was not as ill as she thought she was. The realization emboldened Six.

"You must love these plants or they wouldn't grow like they do. I bet you got them when they were just little things and raised them up with your love and attention."

"I guess so," Rose's mother said.

"That's how the Lord does us. The plants are there in the field, like we're here on this earth. He reaches out His hand and makes them grow."

She looked Six in the face for the first time since he'd arrived.

Maybe, Six thought, there wasn't anything purely good or holy. Maybe good was only accomplished indirectly and through unlikely channels: fake healings or a room full of jealous angry men with Bibles who nonetheless drew these sad people and lifted their spirits for a few days. It could be that Six was one of these—a bad thing used for good purposes. Maybe he could be a sword after all.

"Don't you think the Lord cares for you at least as much as he does a little bitty dandelion?"

"I don't know if he do or don't."

"Sister, I'm not going to try to convince you that God loves you. Though we see his miracles all around us, and if miracles aren't love, well, I don't know what is. I know you believe God made these plants, don't you?"

"Course I do."

"Then let me pray with you. That's all I ask. Let's pray together, and let Him show you His mercy."

Six took her hand and prayed. He prayed though he was aware of his intentions in a way he hadn't been with Sister Coral, though he felt only the faintest inkling of the divine. The townspeople said Six had the gift, and now he tried to direct it, to wield it over Rose's mother like a magic wand. He wanted Rose to see him heal her. He wanted to be an instrument of God, even a ruined one.

Like the night before, when Six finished praying, he didn't know what to do, so he stood abruptly and left the room. He went around to the back of the house and paced the small yard. After a few minutes, Rose came out.

"You want something to eat?" she asked.

"No, thank you," he said.

"My mama in there a boo-hooing like the day she was born."

In the moonlight Rose's skin looked like liquid caramel.

"You ought to have some lemonade, at least, 'fore you go back," she said.

She took his hand and led him into the main room. The porch light shined in through the window. Rose sat close to him on the low sofa. Six could smell the clean clothes smell of her skin. She kissed him. Her lips were dry and pillowy. Six pursed his mouth stiffly, as if blowing on a spoonful of hot soup. He put one hand on her shoulder and the other on the back of the sofa. He was awkward. She leaned into him and parted her lips and breathed into his mouth. "Just be easy," she said. He thought of her as he'd first seen her, with her wet yellow dress slick against her thighs. He reached under her skirt. Her skin was soft as spring sunlight. The muscles in her legs shifted under his fingers as she took off her dress and straddled him.

Earlier that day, Six had overheard the preachers talking about an assistant pastorship opening in the town. He would offer to fill it, and they would take him because the people would believe in him after word got around that he'd healed Rose's mother. He would stay in that little town and he would preach on Sundays, and the congregation would say God had anointed him to heal. He would be what they wanted him to be. Maybe it didn't matter whether Six's gift was real or not. It was like Reverend Grist had said, "They come for whatever reason, and then it's the Lord that occupies Himself with their souls."

"Reverend Six," Rose whispered, stretching alongside him on the sofa, her body damp with sweat and glistening in the light from the porch. "Reverend Six, Reverend Six, Reverend Six."

Ruthie

_____

1951

LAWRENCE HAD JUST GIVEN the last of his money to the numbers man when Hattie called him from a public telephone a few blocks from her house on Wayne Street. Her voice was just audible over the street traffic and the baby's high wail. "It's Hattie," she said, as though he would not recognize her voice. And then, "Ruthie and I left home." Lawrence thought for a moment that she meant she had a free hour unexpectedly, and he might come and meet them at the park where they usually saw each other.

"No," she'd said. "I packed my things. We can't . . . we're not going back."

They met an hour later at a diner on Germantown Avenue. The lunch rush was over, and Hattie was the lone customer. She sat with Ruthie propped in her lap, a menu closed on the table in front of her. Hattie did not look up as Lawrence approached. He had the impression that she'd seen him walk in and had turned her head so as not to appear to be looking for him. A cloth satchel sat on the floor next to her: embroidered, somber hued, faded. A bit of white fabric stuck up through the latch. He felt a rush of tenderness at the sight of the bag flopping on the linoleum.

Lawrence lifted the satchel onto the seat as he slid into the booth. He reached across and tickled Ruthie's cheek with his finger. He and Hattie had never discussed a future seriously. Oh, there had been plenty of sighs and wishes in the afternoon hours after they made love: they had invented an entire life out of what-ifs and wouldn't-it-be-nices. He looked at her now and realized their daydreams were more real to him than he'd allowed himself to believe.

Lawrence wasn't a man who got hung up on ideals or lofty sentiment; he had lived pragmatically as far as his emotions were concerned. He had a car and nice suits, and he had only infrequently worked for white men. He left his family behind in Baltimore when he was sixteen, and he had built himself up from nothing without any help from anyone. And if he had not been able to save his mother from becoming a mule, at least he had never been one himself. For most of his life, this had seemed like the most important thing, not to be anybody's mule. Then

Hattie came along with all of those children, that multitude of children, and she didn't have a mark of them on her. She spoke like she'd gone to one of those finishing schools for society Negro girls that they have down south. It was as though she'd been dropped into a life of squalor and indignities that should not have been hers. With such a woman, if he would only try a bit harder, he might become a family man. It is true that he had not met Hattie's children, but their names—Billups and Six and Bell—were seductive as the names of foreign cities. In his imagination they were not so much children as they were small docile copies of Hattie.

"What happened?" he asked Hattie. Ruthie kicked at her swaddling. She looked very like him. The old wives' tale says babies look like their fathers when they are new to the world. Ruthie was light-skinned like him and Hattie, lighter than August. Of course, Lawrence had not seen Hattie's other children and could not know that most of them were this same milky tea color.

"Did August put his hands on you?" Lawrence asked.

"He's not that kind of man," she answered sharply.

"Anybody is, if his manhood is wounded enough."

Hattie looked at him in alarm.

"A lot of men, I mean," Lawrence said.

Hattie turned her face to the window. She would need money—that was certain—and they would be able to spend more time together now that August knew the truth. Lawrence could put her up somewhere. It occurred to him now that his choices were two: run from the diner and never see her again or become, all at once, a man of substance and commitment.

"I'm so ashamed," Hattie said. "I'm so ashamed."

"Hattie, listen to me. Our little baby isn't anything to be ashamed of."

She shook her head. Later that evening, and for years to come, he would wonder if he had misunderstood her, if her shame wasn't at having a child with him but something larger that he didn't understand, and if it wasn't his failure to grasp this that had doomed them. But in that moment, he thought she only needed convincing, so he talked about renting her a house in Baltimore, where he'd grown up, and how they'd bring her children from Philadelphia and what it would all be like.

Hattie's eyes were red-rimmed, and she kept glancing over Lawrence's shoulder. He had never seen her so skittish, so in need of him. For the first time, Lawrence felt Hattie was his. This was not proprietary but something all together more profound—he was accountable to her, wonderfully and honorably obliged to take care of her. Lawrence was forty years old. He realized that whatever he'd experienced with other women—lust? infatuation?—had not been love.

Hattie was incredulous. She refused him.

"This is our chance," Lawrence said. "I'm telling you, we won't ever get over it, we won't ever forgive ourselves if we don't do this. Baby."

"But do you still . . . ?" she asked.

Lawrence had discussed his gambling in passing. He had told Hattie he made his living for the most part as a porter on the trains, which had been true for a few months many years ago. Hattie's uncertainty made Lawrence understand that she did not take his gambling as lightly as he had supposed.

"I'll stop," he said. "I already have, really. It's just a game or two when it's slow with the trains."

Hattie wept in heavy wracking sobs that shook her shoulders and upset Ruthie.

"I'll stop," he said again.

Lawrence slid next to Hattie on the banquette. He leaned down and kissed his daughter's forehead. He kissed Hattie's temple and her tears and the corner of her mouth. When she calmed, Hattie rested her head on his shoulder.

"I couldn't stand to be a fool a second time," Hattie said. "I couldn't stand it."

HATTIE HAD HARDLY SPOKEN during the four-hour drive to Baltimore. Lawrence's was the only car on the highway—his high beams tunneled along the black road. Such a dark and quiet night, the moon was slim as a fingernail clipping and offered no light. Lawrence accelerated to fifty miles per hour, just to hear the engine rev and feel the car shoot forward. Hattie tensed in the passenger seat.

"We're not too far now." He reached over and squeezed Ruthie's fat little leg. "I love you," Lawrence said. "I love you both."

"She's a good baby," Hattie replied.

August had named the baby Margaret, but Hattie and Lawrence had decided before her birth that they'd call her Ruth after Lawrence's mother. When Ruth was nine days old, Hattie brought her to meet Lawrence in a park in his neighborhood.

"This is your father," Hattie said, handing her to Lawrence. The baby fussed—Lawrence was a stranger to her—but he held her until she quieted. "Hush, hush, little Ruthie girl, hush, hush," he said. Tears rose in his throat when the visit ended and Hattie took the baby back to Wayne Street. In the hours and days until he next saw her, Lawrence thought of Ruthie every instant: now she is hungry, now she is asleep. Now she is cooing in the arms of the man who is not her father. It was possible, of course, that Hattie was mistaken and Ruthie was August's baby, but Lawrence knew, he knew in a way that was not logical and could not be explained, that she was his child.

Lawrence tightened his grip on the steering wheel until his fingers ached. "They never made a car better than the '44 Buick. I told you it was a smooth ride," he said. "Didn't I tell you? I drove this car all the way to Chicago once to see my cousin."

"You told me," Hattie said.

A car passed in the opposite direction. Hattie put her hand over Ruthie's eyes to shield her from the headlight glare.

"You'll like Baltimore," Lawrence said. "You'll see."

He did not know if she would. They were to live in a couple of rooms in a boardinghouse until he could get the money together to rent a house. A place large enough for all Hattie's children would cost twenty-five dollars a week. Lawrence could make that money easily; he could pull six months' rent in a single night with a couple of good hands. It wasn't the money that made him nervous, though he was skinned at the moment.

" 'As the sparks fly upward . . . ,' " Hattie said. "It's from the Bible," she added.

"Well, that's dismal. Don't you remember anything else?"

Hattie shrugged.

"Guess not," Lawrence said.

He reached over and tapped her playfully on the knee with the back of his hand. She stiffened.

"Come on, baby. Come on, let's try and be a little bit happy. This is a happy occasion, isn't it?"

"I like that verse. It makes me feel like I'm not alone," Hattie said. She shifted away from him in her seat. "You're going to pick up more shifts on the railroads, right?" she asked.

"We talked about this. You know I will."

Lawrence felt Hattie's gaze on him, uncertain and frightened. Her shine was going, Lawrence thought. There was something used and gray about her these days. Lawrence did not want Hattie to be a normal woman, just any old downtrodden colored woman. Hadn't he left Maryland to be free of them? And hadn't he married his ex-wife because she was glamorous as a rhinestone? It did not occur to him that he contributed to the fear and apprehension that had worn Hattie down.

He missed the Hattie he'd found so irresistible when they met—a little steely, a little inaccessible, angry enough to put a spring in her step and a light in her eye. Just angry enough to keep her going, like Lawrence. And there was another side of her, the one that yearned and longed for something she wouldn't ever have—the two of them had that in common too. Lawrence took Hattie to New York a few months before she got pregnant. The trip had required elaborate lies—Hattie told August and her sister Marion that she'd been hired to cook for a party at a white woman's place way out

on the Main Line and that she had to stay over-
night. Marion kept the children. Lawrence had not
anticipated Hattie's guilt, but it had cast a pall over
their trip, and over New York City itself—or so
Lawrence thought until the next day when they
were driving back to Philadelphia. As they drove
out of the Holland Tunnel, Hattie turned for one
last glimpse of the city's ramparts glowing in the
setting sun. Then she slumped in her seat. "Well,
that's gone," she said. Something in the New York
streets was familiar to her. More than familiar, she
said, she felt she belonged there. Lawrence understood. It seemed to him that every time he made
one choice in his life, he said no to another. All
of those things he could not do or be were huddled inside of him; they might spring up at any
moment, and he would be hobbled with regret. He
pulled to the shoulder of the road and held her. She
was a beating heart in his hand.

Lawrence hardly recognized the distant, dis-
traught woman next to him now.

"You act like your whole life was one long January afternoon," Lawrence said. "The trees are
always barren and there's not a flower on the vine."

"It wouldn't do any good to go around with my
head in the clouds."

"It would sometimes, Hattie. It sure would."

He was responsible for her now. She might, he
thought, at least try to be a little more . . . Well,

after all they were starting a life together that very day, that very moment. Lawrence needed her steeliness. He needed her resolve to bolster his own. More was required than his charms and his sex and a bit of laughter and forgetting. He had to be better than August.

That bum. August was always out at nightclubs or at the jukes. Lawrence saw him once at a supper club where all the dicty Negroes went. August was on a date; he was all dressed up like the mayor of Philadelphia while Hattie was at home on Wayne Street elbow deep in dishwater. August could have gotten a decent job, but he chose to work catch as catch can at the Navy Yard out of pure laziness. A man had to be responsible. Lawrence was responsible. Whatever else he might be, he took care of his own. He had this Buick, didn't he? Free and clear. And a house in a decent neighborhood. He'd kept his ex-wife in nice dresses while they were married and was still keeping her in them now that they were divorced. He saw his daughter once a week—didn't miss a visit unless there was something really important, no, something damn near unavoidable. She was the picture of good health, didn't want for anything. There were all kinds of ways to be responsible. Maybe he hadn't made his money in the way most people would approve of, but none of his had ever gone without.

"You have to take some joy from the little things, baby. Look at this—fireworks!"

A gold flare rose above the treetops and pea-cocked into a fan of light over the highway. "Isn't that something?" he said. "We must be closer to Baltimore than I thought."

Hattie barely glanced at the lights bursting over-head.

"Hey," Lawrence said, after a few moments, "do you plait your hair at night?"

"What?"

"Your hair. Do you plait it at night and tie it down with a scarf?"

"What kind of a thing is that to ask?"

"I just . . . I guess I just realized I didn't know."

"Oh, Lawrence," Hattie said. Her voice quiv-ered. After a long pause, she said, "I tie it down."

How little they knew of each other's habits. Law-rence was suddenly apprehensive about seeing Hat-tie brush her teeth and take off her girdle and roll her hair in curlers. He had rented rooms for them in a nice boardinghouse. The landlady hooked the braided rugs herself and kept the windows so clean you'd think you could put your hands right through them. But the bathroom was across the hall. It might be awkward if Hattie had to leave their rooms to relieve herself in the middle of the night. She might be embarrassed at her breath in the morning or repulsed by his. Ruthie might cry all night, and Hattie would be irritable, or Lawrence would be. What if he went to the bathroom first and then she followed to wash her face and she smelled his smells? They would be stripped to their odors and sounds and habits. Lawrence sighed. But I'm a fool. I was married for ten years! These intimacies are nothing new, nothing new at all.

Ruthie whimpered.

"We need to stop so I can feed her," Hattie said.

"Now?"

"Soon."

"We're almost there. Can we wait?" Lawrence asked.

Ruthie's whimper rose to a wail.

"Doesn't sound like it."

Lawrence pulled over to the shoulder of the road.

"Alright then," Hattie said.

"Alright," Lawrence replied.

"Well, I can't . . ."

"Oh!" Lawrence climbed out of the car and stood next to it.

"Lawrence!"

"Oh!" he said again and walked a few paces down the highway.

He was angry. Was Hattie going to send him out of their rooms whenever Ruthie was hungry? He was sure that she had fed her other children in front of August. These were things a man and woman shared after a time.

"Hattie," he said as he climbed back into the car when she'd finished, "there's no reason I should have to walk to the next county every time you want to feed our daughter."

As he spoke, Lawrence remembered his ex-wife getting up in the middle of the night to feed their daughter when she was a baby. She'd taken her out of her crib and brought her back to bed. In the light from the bedside lamp, Lawrence watched her unbutton her nightgown. Her breast flopped to the side like a bag of water. He saw the green veins under her skin. Delia put her nipple in the baby's mouth. She reminded him of a possum or a sheep or some other teated thing. She never looked the same to him after that; even when she was dressed to go out for an evening, he would look at her and think of that huge lolling breast. Lawrence hoped that he was a better man now.

"Our daughter," Hattie repeated.

Ruthie slept after her feeding. Lawrence hadn't spent much time with her. She was usually sleeping during those few afternoons that Hattie was able to take her to see him. She might hold his gaze for a few seconds, then she'd nuzzle against his chest and fall asleep. August held her every night. August sang to her and rocked her. On the night that she was born, August smoked cigars and held her swaddled body. Lawrence got the news by telephone two days after the fact and didn't see her until she was nine days old.

"She's going to have a fine life," Lawrence said, pulling onto the highway. "You'll have a fine life, Ruthie. They'll say, 'There's Ruthie, the prettiest girl in Baltimore'!"

A police siren wailed somewhere behind them. Hattie started and squeezed Ruthie so hard that the baby murmured in her sleep. Red and blue lights flashed across the highway and lit the trees along the shoulder of the road.

"State police," Lawrence said.

He slowed and pulled to the side as the police car gained on them.

"What do they want?"

Her voice was high and thin. She twisted to look out of the rear window.

"Hattie?" Lawrence said. As the car passed, the siren wailed over his voice. Ruthie began to cry. Hattie bounced her nervously. Her shoulders shook when she hunched over to kiss Ruthie's forehead.

"I thought . . . I thought they were coming for us," she said.

"Hattie! Nobody's coming, baby. Nobody's coming. This is our daughter. We haven't done anything to bring the law," Lawrence said.

He put his arm around her shoulder.

"What am I doing here?" she said. "What am I doing here without my children?"

THE CHILDREN WEREN'T just scared because Hattie was gone but because they were left alone with August. Out in the living room, his sons and daughters were shrill with hunger. He had been hiding in the kitchen for hours. "You all leave me be so I can think for a minute," he'd said. None of them had come in to bother him, but it was nearly seven and by that hour, they'd usually eaten supper and put up the dishes.

Alice appeared in the doorway.

"Daddy?" she said.

"What, girl? I'm trying to set here in the quiet."

"What are we going to do about Sunday school tomorrow?" she asked.

"Sunday sch—" It was the last thing August expected her to say, but then she was a busy, grown-acting little thing. "Well," he said, "I guess y'all should go."

"The Sunday clothes aren't clean."

"So wash them."

"There's no soap. Today is Mother's shopping day."

"Use bath soap."

"You can't use bath soap! It doesn't get stains out and makes the clothes all stiff."

"Well, I guess they can be stiff for one Sunday."

"Itchy, too."

"Awww, Alice. I guess you ain't going then."

"Aunt Marion says if we don't go, we'll go to hell."

"Alice, you like a woodpecker on my skull. You ain't going to hell if you miss one Sunday."

Alice stood in the doorway looking indignant, her back straight as a pole. August turned his back to her and bent to examine the contents of the Frigidaire, though he'd been peering at the near empty shelves most of the afternoon. There wasn't much: a little butter, a bowl of sliced peaches, some fatback. August hoped Alice would go back into the living room. Instead she put her hands on her hips and said, "Everybody's hungry.

"It's Mother's shopping day," she repeated.

August was all set to ask her if she knew where Hattie kept the canned goods when Franklin started crying in the living room. August and Alice found him at the bottom of the stairs with a bloody lip and a lump coming up on one knee. Where the hell had the rest of them disappeared to while this boy was falling down the steps? Alice felt it necessary to tell August that Franklin could have broken his neck. As if August didn't know these children were liable to kill themselves with their mama gone. He took a handkerchief from his back pocket and dabbed at the blood on Franklin's face. He left a smear on the boy's cheek, but all of his teeth were in his head and nothing seemed broken, so the three of them went back into the kitchen.

August said, as brightly as he could manage, "What y'all want for supper?"

Alice suggested they use the fatback to make a pot of string beans, but when August asked her to help him, she blanched.

"I don't know how," she said. "And besides we don't have any string beans."

"What you mean you don't know how?"

"I mean I don't know how."

"What you been doing every evening of your life while your mama makes supper?"

Alice shrugged.

"Your mama don't teach y'all to cook?" August whistled between his teeth.

"You know she doesn't like anybody in the kitchen."

Hattie had made it so nobody in that house knew how to do anything besides her. And worse, he hadn't known that until this very moment. Must be a whole lot of stuff he didn't know.

"Go on outta here and take Frank with you. And don't lose sight of him. Next thing you know, he out the front door and running in traffic."

After Alice left the room, August went through his pockets for change. Empty. That's alright, he thought. Hattie kept a tin of emergency money—if this ain't an emergency I don't know what is—on the high shelf next to the stove. August pried off the lid. One penny sliding around in there on its own. He thought of places in the house where he might find money—his suit jackets or pants' pockets, but he'd spent his last dime on cigarettes the night before. He could go into the living room and search under the seat cushions on the sofa. In front of all of his hungry children, he could rifle the furniture hoping for a couple of nickels.

"Floyd," he yelled into the living room. "Floyd!"

August searched the kitchen drawers, just in case a coin had fallen behind the forks. That boy sure was taking his time. "Floyd!" he called again. August took the contents of the cabinets—a sack of flour and some salt and a bag of dried beans that would take hours to prepare even if August knew how to cook them—and set them on the counter as if they might magically combine into a meal for his children.

Floyd came in and leaned against the doorjamb. "You wasn't in a hurry to get here, was you?" August's tone was sharp.

"Alice said you were calling me," he replied.

"Go round Aunt Marion's and see if she cain't come over here, or if she ain't got some chicken cooked up or something. And don't tell nobody," August said. Floyd eyed his father and the bags of flour and salt, then left the room without a word. The noises from the living room were louder. August pondered the food on the countertop until his children's shouting grew so urgent that he couldn't ignore it.

He charged into the living room to find Alice and Billups shoving each other. The children rushed at him as soon as he entered the room: Billups had pushed Alice. Who was supposed to be taking care of Franklin? He had fallen again because nobody was paying him any mind. Where was supper? And did August know that Floyd went off somewhere even though he's the oldest and grown and should be watching us? August looked from one face to another. Alice, her voice louder than the others, shouted, "Where's Mother?"

The children fell silent.

August couldn't think of a lie they would believe, so he settled for the first one that came to mind.

"She went round to help Aunt Marion because she ain't feeling so good."

"But Floyd just went . . . ," Alice said.

August gave her a look like a knife in the chest. That shut her up. Bell sat on the window seat with her knees pulled up to her chin. She looked right at August and started to cry. Big, silent tears streamed down her cheeks, and he knew right then that she must have overheard something—you can't hide anything from a house full of children.

He should have done something for her but he couldn't. He didn't have it in him to look into those big eyes with all of that sadness in them. Lord, that was a sad child. August ignored her and felt like a coward.

"How come Mother took the baby with her?" Billups asked.

Bell looked at her father when he didn't answer right away. She wiped her tears and said, "Because Margaret's a little baby, and Mother has to feed her."

"Why don't you just tell us if we aren't going to have supper tonight?" Alice said.

"That's how you talk to grown folks? I'll slap you into yesterday!" August had never hit any of his children. The words sounded odd coming out of his mouth. Alice didn't move. She didn't even flinch. "You hear me? You hear what I'm saying!" August shouted. "I don't want not one more word out of none of y'all. Shut up! All y'all shut up!"

August took the stairs two at a time and slammed the bedroom door behind him. He pulled the drawers out of the dresser and overturned them onto the floor. Surely Hattie had another stash of emergency money, a few dollar bills stuffed in a sock, maybe. He lifted the mattress and looked underneath. He pulled the shoe boxes from the closet and turned the pockets of Hattie's dresses inside out. When he finished, every surface in the room was strewn with clothes and shoes, the pillows were on the floor, and the mattress was hanging off the box spring. August sat on the floor on a pile of Hattie's slips. He rubbed his finger against the material and lifted it to his nose. It smelled like her: Murphy Oil Soap and butter and her skin. Jesus, Hattie, he thought, I never brought a woman home, and I don't do nothing other men don't. And I ain't never once gone away out of this house. I never would've. August threw her slip to the floor and stomped out of the room.

The scene in the living room had degenerated. Lord, but if Alice wasn't every inch her mother's daughter, eight going on forty, with those pursed lips and accusing eyes. The floor was littered with candy wrappers; the dish on the side table was empty. Franklin sat on the floor licking a butterscotch he held between his fingers. August had intended to tell them that there was no supper and he was sorry, but they'd have a good breakfast. And he was going to tell them that Hattie wouldn't be back that night, so they wouldn't keep staring at the front door. But he lost his nerve and stood silently in the middle of the room, his gazed fixed on the opposite wall so he wouldn't have to look at them. They waited for him to speak, but August, head down, stepped around Franklin, made a wide circle around the couch where Alice sat, and walked toward the dining room. "You all go on to bed," he muttered.

August went outside and sat on the back step. The noises of the house came through the screen door. He heard Bell rounding up the young ones for bed. He smoked a couple of cigarettes. After the third, Bell called, "Mr. Greer's at the door for you!" August squinted at his watch in the light coming through the screen door. Nine. Just the right time to leave for the nightclub.

"Tell him I ain't coming."

"He says he wants—"

"Send him on!"

August had planned to go to the Latin Casino that evening. The big band would play; he and his friends would dress sharp and hang out near the bar at the back of the club. After, they'd go to that juke where the bartender kept a stash of Tennessee corn liquor in a tub of ice. August didn't drink much, but he liked the feel of the glass in his hand. He liked to sip at something over the course of the evening. Of course, he'd meet a woman who would make him laugh. She would dance with him until her shoulders were dewy with sweat. He'd see her home, give her a little kiss on the cheek, and leave her at her doorstep already primed for the next date. When he saw her again, he'd kiss her some more, and in this way a new affair would begin. These women didn't mean anything. They just made his life a little more livable from one day to the next.

The house was quiet. The children were probably crying in their beds—if they had gone to bed. August couldn't muster the courage to go upstairs and check on them. What if they were still awake? It would be equally terrible if they were in bed with dirty faces and their pajamas buttoned wrong, things that wouldn't happen if Hattie were here.

She'll be on the road now, August thought. **They'll** be on the road. She said they were going to Baltimore. That man Lawrence had some people there. Hattie intended to send for the children as soon as she got herself settled. August cursed her when she said that. He said he'd set the house on fire before he'd let even one of his children go and live with her and some no account nigger.

A tune came to his mind, a little jingle Cassie used to play on the piano at Marion's house years ago. She told him it was Russian. His girls knew all kinds of things he and Hattie had never heard of. Bell was always reading something. She left her schoolbooks in the living room sometimes, and late at night when August came home from a nightclub or a woman, he would read them. He came across a poem he liked so much that he read it night after night: **This is the hour of lead / Remembered if outlived.** He couldn't recall the title or any more than those two lines. It seemed to him that he could never get a proper grip on any of the beauty in this world.

He lit a fresh cigarette from the butt of the one he'd just smoked. Floyd hadn't returned. He probably hadn't even gone to Marion's. Just as well, August thought, she would have come over here acting like I was something stuck to the bottom of her shoe.

Fool woman, and stingy. She should have given him and Hattie the piano—nobody knew how to play it besides Cassie; since she stopped going over there to practice, it was just collecting dust. Cassie had a gift with that piano. August went to Marion's to pick her up after school one day and damned if Cassie wasn't trying to pick out "Take the 'A' Train." She said she heard it on the radio—ain't that something! It wasn't long after that Hattie said she couldn't take lessons anymore even though the woman around the corner thought Cassie was so good she taught her for free. Hattie said it wasn't practical for a Negro girl to fill her head with music. "What's she going to do with that?" she said.

There was no call to mash up the child's dreams that way. So what if it wasn't practical? Cassie was only twelve at the time. Look at all this trouble August had gone through to live up here in Philadelphia and have a better life. At the very least, a better life ought to mean a child could have something that didn't have any purpose except to make her smile. He told Hattie to let her be. Hattie said she didn't think nights at the juke and good taste in suit jackets qualified August to make decisions about her children.

August tiptoed into the house and got the holiday cordial from the credenza. He stood in the dining room swigging from the bottle and listening for signs that any of the children were still awake. If they had gone to bed, it wasn't because he'd told them to but because they were too scared and confused to do anything else. Whenever he told them to do anything, they looked at Hattie to see if they had to obey him. They treated him like a dopey uncle who came around to play with them but was of no real consequence. He went out at night, sure, but why shouldn't he? He worked, when he could, and he always gave Hattie half of what he earned, or thereabouts. Lots of men August knew had a private life outside of the home. Hell, August knew men that had women and children they never saw and didn't intend on seeing.

Before August married Hattie, his friends warned him that a high yellow girl like her wouldn't do anything but step on his neck. Lord, she was pretty. She wasn't more than fifteen when they started courting, but she was already a lady. Half of the time she looked at him like he had crawled out of a swamp. She only liked August because he was a secret from her mama, and because it thrilled her to go out with a country boy she thought beneath her. If he'd had a mandolin and a piece of hay between his teeth, she'd have fallen in love with him on the spot. That mama of hers was a different story. She would have cut him down like the cedars of Lebanon. That woman didn't let Hattie and her sisters do anything. Hattie was restless. Even when she was sitting still, her foot tapped or her fingers thrummed the arm of the chair. When she managed to sneak away from her mama and go walking with August, her eyes were never steady on him for more than a few seconds. She was always looking off down the street for something. He gave her a red scarf, but she couldn't take it in the house, so she put it in a box and hid it under the porch. She loved that scarf; she said it was so soft against her cheek, it reminded her of the breeze on her face on the first day of spring. Funny that she used to be fanciful like that. Of course, the rest of the time she was so prim and proper she'd hardly let herself laugh. Still, she fascinated him, and he got her to like him a little. One night he took her to his brother's house, where she had done with him what other girls did. After his conquest, the thrill wore off for both of them. Hattie didn't mind too much when he stopped coming around as often.

Hattie told August by letter that she was in trouble. He hadn't seen her in weeks, but as soon as he read that letter, he went running to her door. He was seventeen. He didn't know what he wanted to do with his life because none of the options were any good. When Hattie said she was pregnant, August decided then and there that he wanted to be a family man. He would become an electrician and marry Hattie, who was, after all, one of the prettiest girls in Germantown. She would loosen up when she got away from her mama. They would sit on their porch on summer nights drinking buttermilk and looking at the stars. It would be an alright life. So he went over to Hattie's and spoke to her mama, who already knew, he imagined, because she looked at him like she wanted to put an ice pick through his chest. On his way out of the house he heard her tell Hattie that she had ruined her life. I ain't nobody's ruin, he thought. Now here they were twenty-eight years later, and maybe he had ruined Hattie's life, or she'd ruined his. He wondered if she would have stayed with him if her mama hadn't died a few months before the twins were born. Women did that, got sick of their husbands and went back to their mamas. Could be Hattie stayed because she didn't have anywhere to go.

It was Hattie's own fault she was so unhappy. How could she expect him not to step out a little when she was always so mad? He didn't understand her. Some nights she lay curled on her side like a fist, and other nights they were on each other until dawn—she scratched his back and bit his shoulders, and they buried their faces in the pillows so the children wouldn't hear. But the days were always the same, she didn't return his smiles, shrugged him off when he tried to touch her. She would fuck him—that's all he could think to call it—but she didn't have any tenderness for him. Didn't she know August was heartbroken too? He'd never get over Philadelphia and Jubilee either. Or that Six had been burned half to death, and it had twisted his head up so bad he put that boy Avery in the hospital. When August was a young man, he hadn't known what he wanted for his children's lives, but it surely wasn't this. He knew he should have done better by them, should do better, but he also knew the game was rigged. He couldn't figure why Hattie wouldn't admit it. She put all the blame on August. She never for one minute stopped thinking he was the cause of every bad thing that ever was, and he never stopped hoping that one morning he would wake up and prove her wrong. If she would stop hating him for one day, one hour, he'd have the strength to do the right thing by her. This was the life they had. Nobody could ever know it like they did. They owed it to each other to stay together. That was their bond.

The front door creaked open and closed again. "Hattie?" August rushed into the living room.

Bell stood by the stairs.

"What was you doing outside at this hour?" August asked.

"I took a walk."

"It's going for midnight!"

She looked down at her feet. August knew he ought to put the bottle of cordial away. He ought to ask her if she'd seen him and Hattie fighting and find a way to make her feel better.

"You go on up there to bed," he said, walking back to the dining room. "This ain't no hour for young girls." Bell followed him.

"Can I sit down here with you for a little while?" she asked.

"I think you need to get some rest."

"I don't think Mother's coming back."

August sat heavily in one of the chairs.

"Ain't no telling."

"She's not."

"Why you say that?"

"I just know," Bell said. "I saw them."

"You saw who?"

"Mother and that man."

"Where you see them?"

"On the street."

"Today?"

Bell shook her head. August could feel the liquor working in him.

"Well, hell, maybe she ain't coming back."

Bell began to cry. August thought to whistle a tune or say something to make her laugh. But what was the point?

"Let's us just set down here and have a good cry. Ain't much else to do."

Bell sat next to her father, put her head on his shoulder, and wept. He lit a cigarette and stroked her arm while he smoked. She had a mosquito bite that he worried with his index finger until she squirmed and told him to stop. Bell fell asleep.

"We in trouble for good now," he whispered to his daughter's sleeping body.

THEY WERE ONLY a few miles from Baltimore. Hattie hadn't said a word in the hour since the state trooper had passed. She held Ruthie across her lap so the baby's head rested in the crook of her elbow. She rocked her even after she had fallen asleep. Lawrence couldn't see any affection in the way Hattie dandled their daughter—like she were stirring a pot of soup. How many children could a woman really love? Lawrence was one of fifteen, and it had always seemed to him that his mother regarded him as another growling stomach, another pair of feet outgrowing last year's shoes. Lawrence shrugged his shoulders as he drove. What else could she have done? They were too many. Ruthie is one of Hattie's many, he thought. Who would she grow up to be among all of those children?

Look how Hattie was holding her—as if Ruthie were just anybody, just any baby that needed holding. What if, he thought, Hattie couldn't love any more children? Maybe we have only a finite amount of love to give. We're born with our portion, and if we love and are not loved enough in return, it's depleted. Lawrence had not loved enough. He had refused to use his allotment, and now it was spilling over, pressing at the borders of him. He might burst with it; he might pop like a balloon.

"We're almost there," Lawrence said.

So what if he was down to his last couple of dollars? He'd collect on a debt as soon as they got to town, and that would take care of them until his next game. He'd rent them a house inside of a week. Less than a week, Lawrence thought.

To Hattie he said, "We'll go down to Philly on the Pennsy and pick them up. I bet the little ones haven't even been on a train before. We'll have a house with a big yard, maybe a swing. You wouldn't believe the porches—"

"Would you stop! Please just stop talking for one minute! I can't stand it!"

"How about you start talking, Hattie? How about you stop sitting there like an icicle and act for one goddamn minute like you're glad to be here with me!"

He had not intended to raise his voice, but she was so . . . did she not understand the sacrifice he was making? Surely, if she wanted to, she could offer him a smile, some kind of encouragement.

Hattie took a deep breath. "When I was a little girl, my father took us to see some of his people near Savannah," she said. "We went to a little bitty strip of rocky beach they had for Negroes. Mama wouldn't let us swim, but she went to do something, and I lifted up my skirt and ran into the water."

Hattie cupped Ruthie's dimpled knee with her palm.

"My cousin Coleman came up behind me and splashed water all over my dress. He knew how to swim, so he went off doing tricks. He floated on his back and spit the water straight up like a fountain, and he dove down so all I could see were his legs poking out of the water like little brown sticks. Then he was floating with his arms out to his sides and his head bobbing just above the surface. I was so delighted! It was like he was pressing on the water to heave himself up and then he'd disappear again. He kept doing that and it was so funny, but then he went under and didn't come up anymore. I stood in the shallow part waiting for him to pop up and make crab claws at me, but he never did. All of a sudden everybody was screaming and running. I looked back at the shore, and Mama was holding Coleman's mother so she wouldn't go in after him. I came out and stood on the beach. A while later a man came out of the water carrying Coleman, and I knew he was drowned.

"Drowning doesn't look how you think it would. Do you understand what I'm saying to you?" Hattie looked over at Lawrence. "I told you this morning. I said I couldn't be a fool twice. "

"Nobody's drowning, Hattie. I'm here helping you."

"Helping me? It isn't help I need, Lawrence. It's a safe port in a storm."

Lawrence had lived his life attending to the immediate, the basic things necessary to his survival—food, shelter, money. Hattie was incomprehensible. There was always a drowning or a port or some big thing that couldn't be fixed and shouldn't even be thought about. It was now that mattered—this car, this highway, getting to Baltimore. He had always thought her discontent was sort of pretty, like a sad song, but maybe she was just dark and heavy. Too much for him. How was he to take care of a woman like that, who couldn't be taken care of because she was always thinking about the whys of things. But Lawrence was not a man to further complicate a complicated situation. He hadn't gotten this far by poking his nose into dark corners. Better to smooth and ease and talk his way through it.

"We're both on edge. That's all," he said. "We're just a little tense."

"Sure," Hattie said. "Just tense."

AUGUST WAS OUT LATE the night before Hattie left him. He woke the next morning to the sun beating on him with two fists. The house was quiet, and he went down to the kitchen hoping Hattie had gone out. But there she was, sitting at the kitchen table with Margaret in her lap. Hattie hardly glanced at him when he walked in.

"How she doing today?" he asked.

August loved babies—their wobbly heads and the talc and butter smell of them. Margaret wasn't fussy and she didn't cry much.

"She alright? She look good," he said.

"She's fine, August," Hattie replied.

He rummaged in the cabinets.

"Don't mess up my cabinets looking for the coffee," Hattie said.

"I'll hold her."

She ignored him and held Margaret with one arm while she reached into the cabinet with the other.

"The money for the electric bill's not in the tin," Hattie said.

"I'll put it in there next payday."

Hattie laid Margaret in the Moses basket resting on the table.

"It's a month late," she said.

"The power company can wait one more week. They ain't gonna go broke."

"They'll turn the lights off in a week."

"You ain't got some little bit put away somewhere? Just till I get paid?"

"No, August. I don't."

"I'll give it back next week."

"No you won't August. You never have. You take every nickel I save."

"It's too early for all this, Hattie."

"It's twelve o'clock in the afternoon!"

Hattie found the coffee can and slammed it onto the counter.

"I have an idea, maybe you can ask for a loan at that juke you go to," she said. "They owe you something by now. All the clothes my children aren't wearing and the shoes not on their feet are paying the juke's light bill."

"Don't start this now. I ain't in the mood."

"I **ain't** in the mood, either. And I certainly ain't in the mood to sit in the dark next week. You find a way to get that money," Hattie said.

"You couldn't wait till I so much as took a sip of water to start this mess with me, could you? You was just setting down here waiting."

He started toward the kitchen doorway. Over his shoulder he said, "Ain't no money to find, Hattie. It's next week or nothing."

Just as he reached the door, he felt a rush of air. Something large and black hurtled past him.

"You crazy, woman!"

The cast iron frying pan missed him by inches and smashed into the opposite wall. It landed on the floor with a crash as loud as a car wreck. Margaret wailed.

"You crazy? You could have bashed my brains in!" The plaster was cracked where the frying pan had hit. "What's got into you, Hattie? Calm yourself down. We got a baby in the room." He moved to lift Margaret from the basket.

"Don't touch her," Hattie said.

"Hattie, stop it now. She crying her head off."

"Don't you touch my child!"

"Goddammit Hattie, she my child too and right now she squalling to pull the roof down, and you too busy acting foolish to tend her."

"She's not your child! She's not yours, and I don't want you to touch her!"

Hattie raised her hand as if she were going to clap it over her mouth. That would've been the right thing to do, to shove those nasty words right back down her throat. But she didn't do it, and the words hung there between them. Margaret screamed. August's instinct was to pick her up;

he'd always been good with crying babies. He wanted to lift her out of the basket and rock her a while. He wanted to sing to her until she settled into sleep. Hattie's just talking, August thought. She's just mad and saying any old thing. But there were tears on his cheeks. He was so tired all of a sudden. He wanted to sit down at the table and rest his head in his hands.

"Stop now, Hattie. Stop 'fore you say something you cain't take back."

"It's already said, August."

"You don't want to talk that kind of nastiness. You don't want to talk like that."

He waited for her to take it back, for her to admit that she said it out of meanness and spite. Come on, Hattie, don't make me stand here in my own kitchen and cry like a baby.

"Hattie?"

She shook her head. She picked Margaret up and rubbed the baby's back with her palm. It seemed to August that she held her more tightly, more protectively than she had before, as if to say, "This is my child, not yours."

"Who?" August asked.

"You don't know him. It doesn't matter."

"It don't matter? You spread your legs! You was some man's whore, and it don't matter?"

"Don't talk to me like that, August."

"You been passing off this child for mine! I'm

putting clothes on her back and food in her belly, and you telling me how to talk to you?"

"Don't you judge me! I live with your womanizing and your going out every day of the week. I have saved money for down payments on two houses and ended up spending it on light bills and clothes for these children. I have been a mule, twenty-five years. From when I open my eyes in the morning to when I lie down again at night, you make me miserable. You think about that before you call me names."

"Take that baby and get out my house."

"I'll go but I'll take my children with me."

Then August said he'd sooner set fire to the house. He rushed out of the room and up the stairs. He was dressed and slamming out of the front door fifteen minutes later. He didn't expect Hattie to leave. He didn't know what was to be done about any of it, but he didn't think she'd go. He came home a few hours later to find the house empty and a note from Hattie on the bed:

His name is Lawrence Bernard. I'm only telling you that in case there's something with the children and you need to find me. I am going to Baltimore. I will come back for my children. I sent them to the park. You can leave messages for me with Marion.

August couldn't understand how Hattie had thought to send them to the park but didn't tell them she was leaving or do anything about their supper.

LAWRENCE TURNED OFF the highway onto the exit for Baltimore. The skyline was low and the lights were not as bright or as numerous as those in Philadelphia. It seemed that the dim city was a reflection of the state of things between him and Hattie. But angry and discouraged as Lawrence was, he was surprised to find himself afraid Hattie would be disappointed in Baltimore, that she wouldn't want to stay there or stay with him.

"We can take a drive around the harbor. It's pretty at night with the boats," he said. "I just need to make a quick stop at the train station."

"The station? Lawrence, I'm tired."

"Then we can go to Federal Hill. Just drive by real fast so you can get a feel for the place. It'll remind you of home maybe. We're in the South now, people are friendly."

"Jim Crow's not so friendly, as I recall," Hattie said.

Lawrence drove on calling out the street names as he passed them: Light Street and North Charles and Calvert. He was a fool jabbering about landmarks, but if he stopped talking, his and Hattie's apprehensions would fill the silence like so much rushing water.

"Lawrence," she said, "I'm so tired and Ruthie needs to lay down. Let's just get where we're going."

"You're right. Alright. We have all the time in the world."

He risked putting his hand on her knee. She didn't pull away.

"It's so quiet," Hattie said. "I never have calm at home, except in the middle of the night. Now I don't even have that." She glanced down at Ruthie. "She's up every three hours."

Lawrence heard a mounting urgency in her voice. He rubbed her thigh to steady her. Hattie swiveled to face him so abruptly that she nearly lost her hold on the baby.

"Somebody always wants something from me," she said in a near whisper. "They're eating me alive."

Lawrence stared straight ahead. He dared not look at Hattie and give away his feelings. Then, softly, hesitantly, "If you need a little break, we can wait to bring them—" He tried to keep the relief out of his voice.

"No! No," Hattie said, "I didn't mean—"

"I didn't either!" Lawrence said, though he had meant it, and he was sure that she had too.

He drove along the empty avenues, turning randomly up this street or that one. He wasn't sure why he was procrastinating. After a time he said, "We just need to make that stop at the station."

"Can't we please just get to this boardinghouse? I'm so tired."

"Just a quick minute, no time at all."

"What for?"

"I have to see a man about picking up porter work," Lawrence said.

"At this hour?"

Lawrence parked in front of Pennsylvania Station.

"We're here now," he said.

Hattie sighed.

"I guess I'll go in too," she said.

"I won't be but a minute."

"What's wrong with you, Lawrence? You wanted to come here. Now let me stretch my legs and use the restroom."

It was almost 10:00, the street was all but deserted. Lawrence walked a few paces ahead of Hattie.

"Why are you walking so fast?" she said.

What am I doing? Losing my cool, Lawrence thought.

There were a few people in the main hall: a man at the ticket window, another mopping the floor, and a woman carrying a tray loaded with a thermos and coffee cups. Hattie's eyes were bloodshot and puffy, and her hair was matted in the back. Her skirt was wrinkled. She tried to smooth it with her free hand. She looked like a little girl, all rumpled and afraid, and she was smaller somehow under the station's high ceilings. Lawrence showed her the Negro ladies room and told her to wait for him near the ticket window when she was finished.

"I thought you were just going to have a word," she said.

He was already walking away from her and pretended he hadn't heard the question. He exited the lobby and went down a small hallway where a newspaper and tobacco shop was locked up for the night. Lawrence rapped twice on the door.

"Well, look what the cat dragged in!" said the man who answered.

"What's good, Scoot?" Lawrence said.

"Game downstairs. I thought you wasn't coming till tomorrow?"

"I can't stay, Scoot. But I need that fifty you owe me."

"I ain't got it yet. We ain't started," Scoot chuckled.

"I know you have something."

"I'm playing with it. You know I ain't got no cash to part with before a big game."

Lawrence tapped his foot.

"You can tap-tap all you want. You need to get in this. Ray and all them's here," Scoot said.

Baltimore's best had come out. Lawrence could make five hundred dollars, maybe more.

"I'm telling you, I can't stay."

"You want some money so bad, you take your ass down there and see what's on the table."

"I don't have time!" Lawrence said.

"Make time. What's wrong with you?"

Scoot walked through a door at the back that opened onto a flight of stairs. Lawrence followed him into the bowels of the station. The smell of coal and cooling engines overwhelmed. Overhead, motors idled and steel wheels screeched on the tracks. Lawrence and Scoot made their way down a low-ceilinged corridor so narrow they had to walk single file. They rounded a corner, and a shaft of light stretched toward them from a half-open door down the hallway.

"Looka here!" Ray said when Lawrence and Scoot entered the room.

Eight men sat around a table piled with chips. A layer of cigarette smoke hung like a stratus cloud above the heads of the players. A woman in a tight green dress sat in the corner near a smaller table set up with food, thermoses of coffee, and a bottle of whiskey. There was always somebody's girl at these games. In a few hours she'd be dozing with her mouth slack. They'd send her upstairs for more booze or cigarettes, and all of the men would look at her backside move under the fabric of her dress.

Oil lanterns had been hung from the low ceiling, and the kerosene stink added to the closeness and the heat and the smoke.

Ray had his good-luck stone on the table next to him. He worried it absently with his thumb. Dead giveaway, Lawrence thought. He never learned to keep that thing in his pocket.

"Gentlemen," Lawrence said.

Ray had chips stacked in front of him and a glass of water. He didn't drink or smoke, and he was as thin as an alley cat. Lawrence cleared his throat and tugged at his shirt collar.

"You playing?" asked a man he had never seen before.

Lawrence looked around the room—the boy keeping the money counted a stack of twenties. Six, maybe seven hundred. Lawrence would have to get in a game eventually, but not tonight, his and Hattie's first night together. Sure, she'd have to get used to his absences and his late nights sooner or later. And it was true he'd need to start traveling again: up to New York at least once a week for the high stakes games, to D.C. for others, and he'd have to play the numbers to keep the cash flowing between big wins. Nine mouths to feed now. Lawrence eyed the money again—he could have Hattie in a house by Monday.

"You gon' play or not?" Ray said.

"Well, I didn't come to watch. But I have some business to take care of first."

The players exchanged glances.

"What you mean, you got business? We got a man traveled all the way from Boston to play in this game." Ray picked up his stone and jiggled it in his fist. "We supposed to wait on you?

"We got business too. Shit," the same unknown player said.

Ray glanced at him, and the man went back to fingering his chips. Ray stood. He took a step toward Lawrence.

"You holding up the game, and you know I don't like nobody coming in and out. This ain't the god-damn county fair. You best sit yourself down."

The woman in the green dress said, "He come in here with a high yellow gal and a baby. They waiting on him." Before Ray could ask, she added, "I seen them come in when I went to get y'alls' coffee."

"Oh, you brought your woman. Bring her down here then," Ray said.

"She's not that kind of lady."

Ray laughed. "You a sucker for the dicty ones. Fine. You got a hour. One hour."

They left the room, and Scoot pushed two twenties into Lawrence's hands.

"You remember the way out?" he asked.

"I've been coming down here since before you took your first step," Lawrence said.

"You be taking your last if you ain't back here in a hour."

He'd win hundreds tonight, enough to buy some furniture to get them started. He could make an excuse for his absence. He'd tell her something to put her off. For now Hattie needed to think Lawrence had given up gambling—for her sake, so she wouldn't be scared. She'd be angry, but the boardinghouse was nice, and Mrs. James would make Hattie a nice breakfast and fuss over Ruthie.

Lawrence took the steps two at a time. He had the tingle in his throat that he got when he was playing and knew he was going to win. It never failed—when Lawrence had that tingle everything went his way. Things would be fine with Hattie. The apprehension he felt on the drive was gone. Playing cards made him feel like himself, sharp and optimistic.

He left a matchbox in the tobacco shop's door latch so he could get back in. Hattie is waiting for me, Lawrence thought. Not for August, for me. Isn't that something!

He turned into the main hall.

"Hattie?"

She wasn't there.

"Hattie?" he called.

She wasn't near the ticket window or on any of

the benches in the waiting area. He went to the restrooms and stood at the ladies' room door listening.
A faucet turned on. Stupid, he thought. I'm running
around like an idiot and she's just freshening up.
Lawrence returned to the main hall. Hattie would
think he was crazy if she found him hanging around
outside the bathroom. He trained his eyes on the
hallway from which she would emerge. A minute
passed and then another, and finally the hall filled
with the clip-clip of heels against the marble floor.

A woman carrying a hatbox came out of the
hallway. No one followed her.

"Excuse me, ma'am," Lawrence called. "Ma'am?"

The woman looked startled.

"I'm sorry to bother you, ma'am. But my wife
and baby were waiting for me here, and I can't . . . I
wonder if you'd seen them in the restroom."

The woman looked him over, then said, "I did
see somebody a while ago. I think she went toward
the front doors."

Hattie had gone outside to wait in the car. She
was tired, poor thing. She and Ruthie had probably fallen asleep. Lawrence crossed the street and
peered into the Buick; they were not there.

He ran back into the station. The ticket agent
was asleep in his glass booth.

"Sir!" Lawrence said, rapping on the window.
The man started awake and narrowed his eyes at
Lawrence. He was sallow under the fluorescent

lights, a few strands of hair stuck to his sweaty forehead.

"What you want? No more trains tonight," he said.

"I'm sorry, sir, but did you see a woman standing here with a baby? Just a few minutes ago."

"Yeah, I seen her," the ticket man said.

"Do you know where she went?" Lawrence asked.

"Philadelphia, I reckon. Bought a ticket for the ten twenty-five."

"What platform?"

"It's ten thirty-six; that train's gone."

"What platform!" Lawrence shouted.

"You watch your tone," the man said. He leaned forward in his seat, "Track nine, but I'm telling you that train left."

Lawrence ran. There wasn't anything on track nine at all: not a porter or a janitor or an off-duty conductor. He couldn't even hear an echo of the wheels on the track or see the tiniest glimmer from the train's tail lamps. A hint of diesel perfumed the air. Lawrence knew, though he intended to search the car for a note or Hattie's carry case, that the diesel fumes were all that was left of her.

AT FOUR in the morning the front door opened and shut. August peered into the living room and saw Floyd taking his shoes off in the foyer. That boy was going the wrong way in life, a grown man, still living at home, and sneaky. Didn't nobody know where he was half the time. But August had a good idea of what he was up to. He had a vision of Floyd coming home and saying he'd gotten a girl into trouble, then he'd never make anything of his life or his horn playing. August tried to stand, but Bell had laid her head on his lap in her sleep and his legs were stiff after so many hours in the same position. "Floyd!" August hissed, trying not to wake his daughter. "Floyd!" By the time August got to his feet, Floyd had already gone up the stairs. August left Bell stretched across his chair and went into the living room. He took his last swig of cordial and smoked his last cigarette.

In his hours at the dining room table August hadn't resolved anything. He hadn't figured out what he'd feed his children for breakfast. He hadn't decided if he would let Hattie take them, or if he ought to go to Baltimore and cut Lawrence down. He imagined the confrontation, though he'd never met Lawrence. He would be handsome and high yellow, and his blood would run from his nose and mouth when August hit him. But August didn't figure a fight would really fix anything. He couldn't stand that he was unable to act, that he needed Hattie to come along and solve the problem of Hattie having left him.

The first floor of the house stank of smoke. August thought he might sit there until morning. He couldn't face the bedroom, but before dawn he'd have to go up there or risk one of the children coming down and seeing him wrinkled and drunk and helpless.

Out on the street a motor idled. The shine from the headlight panned across the living room. In those few seconds of illumination August saw the papers scattered on the floor, shoes by the door, and the rug bunched up in a corner. That was no good. The children shouldn't come down in the morning and see the house a mess. He struggled up from the armchair and began straightening the sofa cushions.

The door opened, and there was Hattie with Margaret in one arm and her travel satchel in the other. She looked like a carpetbagger.

Hattie stepped in and closed the door behind her. August reached to turn on the lamp by the sofa.

"Leave it off," Hattie said. "If you don't mind."

They stood facing each other in the near darkness, the light from a streetlamp shining through the window.

"That man drop you back here?" August asked.

"No, I came in a taxi."

"From where?"

"Train station."

"Where's he?"

"Baltimore."

The thing to do was to insult her or slap her or run her out into the night. She'd left him with all their children. She was holding another man's baby in her arms. Anyone would agree that he ought to do something terrible to her, but she had been gone fifteen hours, and in that fifteen hours his life had crumbled like a lump of dry earth.

Bell ran into the living room. "Mother!" she cried, moving to embrace Hattie.

"You'll wake the baby," she said and patted Bell's shoulder a couple of times. "Go on to bed."

"But I was so—" Bell was near tears.

"It's late," Hattie said.

When Bell was gone, Hattie turned to August. "I won't be seeing him again."

"Why you come back?" August asked.

"My children."

"He do something?"

"Don't ask me that. Don't ask me anything about him. I never asked you."

"I never went off nowhere," August said.

"You never had reason to," Hattie replied.

She sat at the edge of the sofa with the baby in her lap.

"I can go to Marion's in the morning. I just . . . . I didn't know where else to go tonight."

"These children been terrified."

"You think I don't know what a mess I've made? My God, August, I'm all done in."

"You!" He could not tell her that he had not even been able to feed them without her. "It only be worse for them if you gone tomorrow too."

"It smells like a speakeasy in here. You ought to let in some air," Hattie said.

August went around the room opening the windows as Hattie asked. The night smells came in: the dew on the grass, the neighbor's garbage cans, the marigolds in Hattie's planter on the front steps.

"You cain't think everything's alright between us. Ain't nothing alright between us," he said.

"When was it ever alright, August?"

"I don't know how I'm supposed to look at Margaret every day."

August heard a small whimpering, a quiet sniffling that could have been the baby, but it stopped so abruptly he knew it was Hattie. His stomach churned with the liquor. He stood in front of her and lifted his arms out to his sides. It was not an invite to embrace but a resignation, as if to say, here we are; this is all we have. He dropped his arms and sat, with a groan, on the sofa. There were too many disappointments to name and too much heartbreak. They were beyond punishment or forgiveness, beyond what they had inflicted on each other, beyond love.

"I've been calling her Ruthie," Hattie said.

"What for?"

"I want . . . I would like it if you would call her that too."

"Ruthie," August repeated.

"Please."

August nodded in the darkened room. He conceded, though Hattie could not see him.

Ella

1954

L ELLA WOKE UP wailing and wouldn't stop. Though Hattie rocked her and changed her and fed her, though she gave her a lump of sugar to suck and wrapped her feet in a warm cloth and rubbed her stomach in case it was colic that agitated her. Three hours passed, three hours of high-pitched shrieking that would have made a dog howl. The other children couldn't stand it. They left for school early, ran out of the house with their shirts buttoned wrong and their shoelaces untied. August bounced the baby on his knee to no avail, then left for the docks, where he'd wrangled a good shift. Of all the mornings to finally find work. "Back by twelve," he called on his way out the door.

Hattie was alone with her daughter. Ella's crying unnerved her, made her feel desperate and shabby and frightened. She went out onto the front steps hoping the morning air would calm them both. It was nearly nine o'clock and the block was quiet after the rush of children going to school and women on the way to city buses bound for the white neighborhoods, the men in their suits or their coveralls heading to a shop or a factory or an office building. Hattie thought she smelled a hint of wood smoke on the breeze, though it wasn't cold enough to light the furnaces, and besides, all of the houses on the block used coal. Autumn always made her remember the wood-burning stoves of her girlhood. A neighbor woman walked by. She nodded curtly and continued on her way.

Hattie did her morning chores with Ella bound to her in a sheet that she wound around her chest. She washed the children's breakfast bowls, wiped spilled Cream of Wheat from the table, and counted out a few coins for the milkman. It was important to do what needed doing, no matter the day or the circumstance. She took the fall and winter shoes from the hall closet and rotated them as she did each October. Shoes that had been outgrown by the older children went to their younger siblings, and the oldest child got a new pair when there was money or squeezed her feet into the pair from the year before when there wasn't. Hattie reached up to the highest shelf and pulled down the box where she kept the tiny Mary Janes and the soft leather lace-ups that Philadelphia and Jubilee had worn a few times thirty-one years earlier. Theirs were the only shoes in the house that had never been handed down or reused. Hattie meant to have them bronzed. She cleaned them with saddle soap and a soft cloth that she kept in the box for that purpose. Ella liked the smell and stopped crying.

It was ten-thirty when the chores were finished. Hattie unwrapped the baby and lay down beside her on the bed, but her legs twitched, so she hopped up to dust the dresser. Dust motes floated in the column of sunlight that angled from the window. Ella reached up and closed her fist around a tiny airborne feather from the comforter. The previous summer a storm had blown dogwood blossoms in through the bedroom window, a tumult of pink petals pirouetting through the room and landing on the bed's graying sheets and flattened pillows. Ella was too young to have shared Hattie's delight.

Hattie poured some wood soap onto the dresser, her mother's dresser, and began wiping the top. Years ago August set a cup of tea on it and stained the wood. Hattie nearly hit him when she discovered the stain, she nearly had. He'd promised to sand and refinish it. Well.

Ella sat in the center of the bed; her chin dipped into the roll of fat around her neck, that chin with its little cleft. Hattie sang to her while she polished the dresser: **Mama's little baby loves shortenin',**

shortenin'. **Mama's little baby loves shortenin' bread**. The baby extended her arm—her left arm, Hattie noted, because she wanted to remember her daughter in the smallest details. Her nails needed clipping. She'll sleep now, Hattie thought, and I will watch her sleep and file it away in my mind with her deep brown curls and her nutmeg skin and the way she makes a sound like a cat purring before she drifts off. At two o'clock Hattie's sister Pearl would arrive. At two she'd take Ella and they'd drive away, back down to Georgia, and Hattie would stand on the porch and watch her go.

IT HAD BEEN five years since Hattie last held a baby in her arms. She was forty-six years old and thought she was finished having children. When she missed her period, she hoped her change of life had come. She'd had enough of blood and milk and birthing. But then came the swollen breasts and the craving for shaved ice and cucumber slices and the familiar pulsing in her belly. She never had gotten over that pulsing, two hearts beating in her body. When she felt that, she knew, no need to go to the doctor. She told August while they were lying in bed one evening.

"You'll have to get the Moses basket out of the attic," she said.

He'd bolted upright. Hattie could feel him smiling, and she wanted to turn over and slap him. All of the years of their unhappiness hadn't diminished their physical need for each other. Days passed in which she hardly said a word to her husband, but their nights were another thing, their bodies were another thing entirely. Hattie said and did things with August she was ashamed of. In the middle of the night when they were lying in bed panting and sweaty, they would stare at each other, stunned. She didn't know what to make of this sporadic urgency with him. It had confounded and humiliated her for the thirty years of their marriage. These endless pregnancies. And worse, her body's insistence on a man who was the greatest mistake of her life. She was only fifteen when they met. Too young to understand that getting her alone at his brother's house was all August wanted from their courtship. After, when he tired of her and stopped coming around, Hattie never let on that she was heartbroken, sick-to-her-stomach couldn't-sleep-at-night heartbroken. Mama was right to call him my ruin, Hattie thought. If I had known things would turn out this way, I would have thrown myself in the river after I buried my twins.

"Maybe you can see about picking up again at the Navy Yard," Hattie said. "Mrs. Mark might not need me anymore. She's moving down to Florida to be with her grandchildren."

"You worrying already. We gon' work it out,"

August answered. "It won't be no harder than with the rest. Ain't none of them gone hungry yet."

Haven't they? Hattie thought.

Down the hall the children slept three to a bedroom; Hattie could almost hear them growing, their wrists lengthening and poking out beyond the cuffs of their sleeves, their feet outgrowing their shoes, their shoulders widening and pulling the fabric of their coats taut. For the last two weeks she had fed them navy beans with ham bones for dinner and powdered milk and oats for breakfast. They were lean; they had a hard look that was disturbing in a child's face.

Ella was born at the end of an unusually hot April. Hattie went into labor while standing over a tub of laundry she'd taken in to make extra money. Her labor was scarcely three hours, and after the doctor left the house, a few of Hattie's neighbors came, women from the block who turned up for births and funerals or an occasional glass of tea on the porch. They cleaned up the blood, looked after the other children, and brought some of whatever they'd cooked that day: a pot of string beans, a platter of chicken. The oldest of them, Willie, was from somewhere in the Carolinas. Willie had been old for as long as anyone could remember. She was a mud-colored woman with a drawl so thick it sounded as though she'd come up from Bugaloo the day before. The younger women thought Willie countrified, though most of them were from the country themselves. They were, most of them, perpetually donning and polishing their northern-city selves, molting whatever little southern town they or their families had come from five or ten or twenty years before, whatever red-dirt roads or sharecropped fields—or bragging about their families' wide porches in whatever good Negro neighborhood they'd lived in, which was just a roundabout way of demanding that Philadelphia give them their due.

Willie took Hattie's afterbirth and buried it under the oak in front of the house. The tree was a great big old thing with roots so thick and strong they broke through the squares of concrete. "So the child's spirit will stay close to home," Willie said. The neighborhood women did not want to admit they believed in such things, but they always let Willie into their birthing rooms. Later they'd cluck their tongues and shake their heads and say, "It's a shame Willie never learned any better." But they were too smart to turn their backs on the possibility of luck or fortune or a blessing, in any form it might take. If Willie's juju offered some promise that their children would prosper in Philadelphia, then so be it. Hattie thought them naïve and stupidly hopeful, though she too allowed Willie to perform her ritual. And of course the other women of Wayne Street had been wounded and chastened by the North, just as Hattie had been, but she was so insistent on the singularity of her disappointment she could not see she wasn't alone in her circumstance.

At eleven o'clock Hattie still hadn't finished dusting the dresser. Ella fussed, so Hattie picked her up. The room smelled of Murphy Oil Soap. In her distraction Hattie had poured too much, and there were quarter-sized dollops across the surface of the wood. Hattie dabbed at the soap with one hand while she bounced Ella in the other arm. Across the street a pink ribbon was tacked to the door of one of the neighbors' houses. A girl had been born there a few days before. From a distance the ribbon looked clean and new, though a closer look would have revealed frayed edges and small holes where it had been nailed to doors up and down the block. Six months before, it had been tacked to Hattie's door for Ella's birth. Hattie tried to recall where the blue one could have gotten to; it had been some time since a boy had been born.

"Look, Ella. Look at your birth ribbon." Hattie tapped the window to draw Ella's attention, and the tip of her finger left an imprint. She pressed Ella's fingertip against the glass, then her entire hand. The imprint might stay there a month, maybe longer if Hattie didn't wash it away. She had an urge to press Ella's small hand against all the windowpanes and mirrors in the house. Long after she was gone down to Georgia, the outline of her hand would ghost up through the condensation when the bathroom filled with steam.

Hattie could take Ella and run. She didn't have to give her baby to Pearl, she could escape to a remote little town where the winters were mild and they didn't know anybody. Hattie ran downstairs to the kitchen to count the emergency money in the tea tin: fourteen dollars. That wouldn't get them very far. She hadn't left Philadelphia for years, but she had a clear sense of the shape of her part of the world, at least those few states she'd seen—the Georgia of her birth and the states she, Marion, Pearl, and their mother had passed through on their way to Philadelphia when Hattie was fifteen. She had traced the route they'd taken in one of her children's geography books: up through the Carolinas, then through Virginia and Maryland and into Pennsylvania.

There were no bathrooms in the Jim Crow train cars when Hattie and her sisters and mother left Georgia in 1923, and many of the southern stations didn't have Negro restrooms, so they had to go outside. Three stood watch while the fourth relieved herself. The first time Hattie couldn't go for the shame of it. Her mama went last, and the white conductor yelled at them from a few yards up the track, "Y'all better come on if you coming!" What an outrage it was to see her mother—who was never without her hair done up in a bun, who could have passed for white but wouldn't, who was more mannered and proper than the Queen of England—squatted in the kudzu with her skirt around her waist and a white man bellowing at her. That same conductor stood waiting for them at the entrance to the Negro car a few minutes later. He had his hands in his pockets and swayed on his heels watching them walk along the track toward him. He winked at Mama. He pressed his body into theirs as they climbed up into the car. Hattie's mama said nothing, but she flushed crimson at her neck and her breath came in angry bursts. After that, they'd gone to the bathroom only when one of them was nearly doubled over from the pain of holding it.

It was a terrible trip, though something astonishing had happened. Hattie woke in the middle of the night to the clack of the wheels on the track and the rain rapping against the window, the opaque purple sky a dome against which the trees pressed. The journey had lifted her out of the plainness of her life. In Georgia she was one of many, undifferentiated from others, even in her own mind, but on the train to Philadelphia she became acutely aware of what was inviolate in her. She felt herself a single red flower in a field of green grass.

If Hattie and Ella ran away, they could be like that all of the time, two red poppies. Ella tried to fit a silver dollar into her mouth. It was 11:30. Hattie mashed up some peas and put them in a yellow bowl. She spooned the green mush into Ella's mouth while the baby trilled like a bright little bird and grabbed at the spoon. Hattie kissed the top of her baby's head and wept. She'd have to remember to tell Pearl that Ella liked peas.

PEARL FUSSED with the gold clasp on the buckle of her purse. Her husband, Benny, glanced at her from the driver's seat. She fished her compact from her bag and opened it, taking care to angle the mirror away from the sun so it wouldn't catch the light and flash in Benny's eyes while he drove. Her hair had napped a bit at the hairline despite the careful pressing she'd given it before they left Macon. She had hoped the press would hold during the two-day drive to Philadelphia. She'd packed her hot comb just in case, though Benny had said they wouldn't stop at a hotel.

"Negro hotels aren't worth a damn," he'd said when she asked where they would sleep. "Nothing but whores and bedbugs." Pearl cringed. She hated when he was vulgar.

All things considered, her hair was holding up pretty well. They had already driven through two states, and the weather had been changeable. Still, she thought, I could touch up the roots a bit. Her nose was a little shiny too, so she dabbed it with the rose-scented powder from her compact. Roses always lifted Pearl's spirits; she resolved to apply the powder every hour or so, to fight melancholy. After all, this trip ought to be a joyous occasion.

Benny frowned into the afternoon sun coming in through the windshield. Pearl noticed that his hands were curled so tightly around the steering wheel that the tendons stood out. He made a snuffling sound, a half sneeze, and said, "What's that?'

"My face powder. It's nice, don't you think?"

"It's bothering my sinuses," Benny said.

"I apologize. I don't, however, recall it bothering your sinuses on any of the other occasions that I have worn it in the last ten years."

Benny glowered. He rolled the window down and pressed the accelerator.

"Benny!" Pearl said, reaching up to keep her hair from blowing out of its coiffure. A sandy-brown strand escaped and whipped across her forehead. "Benny! The window!" she said again. But he ignored her, and they rode on for some time with the wind blowing Pearl's hair into a mess.

After a time Benny said he was hungry, and they looked for a rest stop. An hour later, they spotted a small weather-beaten sign hanging askew from a wooden post. The lettering was faded, but they could just make out the words, NEGRO REST STOP. Benny pulled off the road and drove a few feet down a gravel road to a clearing next to a pine forest. The evening was warm, there would be mosquitoes. A whiff of wildflowers gave the air a freshness that made Pearl want to breathe great lungfuls of it. It brought to mind the hint of scent left on a woman's wrist once her perfume has faded. The sun was low behind the pines, and the clearing was infused with lavender light.

There was promise in that evening. The next day Pearl would have Ella and she would take her back to Georgia and raise her as if she had been born to her. She had prayed. How she had prayed. Despite her disappointments and her illness, despite exhaustion and a depression so deep she had let her yard go to weeds and couldn't leave her bedroom, Pearl made it to the church every evening to ask the Lord to bless her with children. The women in the congregation pitied her, reduced as she was to taking her sister's child. Pearl led them to believe that taking Ella was an act of charity, though she knew it was desperation.

Pearl took the tablecloth from the backseat, and Benny lifted the wicker picnic basket out of the trunk. The silverware clanked in the bottom. It seemed to Pearl that if the two of them sat at the picnic table and ate the supper she had packed, they would have to be genial with each other. They couldn't sit in that pretty twilight—years ago she would have thought the evening romantic—and not be civil. And wasn't it true that she and Benny were on a kind of pilgrimage together and that the magnitude of their errand ought to overshadow their bickering and resentments?

Benny peeked into the basket. He took a deep breath of evening air and his shoulders relaxed. Pearl unpacked the white china plates, the forks and knives and the white cloth napkins. She brought out a covered dish with fried chicken and another with sliced tomatoes and another piled with biscuits. She set their places side by side and put a peach cobbler on the table next to her husband so he could admire it. Benny chuckled at Pearl trying to find a ladylike way to straddle the picnic bench.

Pearl said grace: "Dear Lord, thank you for this wonderful repast and for our safe journey. We thank you too"—she hesitated and looked at Benny—"for the new addition coming to our family."

Benny cleared his throat. "Amen," he said. There was no anger in his voice.

She served him first. It must have been the good air and the day's journey that gave them such appetites. Pearl's chicken had never been so tender and her tomatoes had never tasted so sweet. Benny ate three biscuits before Pearl had the chance to blink. They reached for the tomatoes at the same time and their hands brushed. Pearl smiled down at her plate and Benny shifted his body, ever so slightly, toward hers.

"It's not every woman that can make a roadside dinner into a special affair," Benny said. He had not paid her a compliment in a long time.

In the waning light they couldn't see the figures in the car rolling down the gravel path toward them. They had just heaped their plates with seconds when the driver turned on the high beams, though it was not dark enough for them, and with that Benny knew he and Pearl were not welcome. He wiped his fingers one by one on Pearl's cloth napkin and patted his lips, taking care not to leave crumbs in the corners of his mouth. It was only then that he stood and faced the headlights, one hand over his eyes to shield them from the glare. Pearl wondered if the owner of the car had jerry-rigged the lights to make them shine more powerfully. Pearl and Benny were trapped, like prisoners caught in a searchlight.

Pearl stayed seated. She stacked Benny's plate on top of her own. The clink of the china hung in the air with the sound of the car's idling engine. Benny put his hand on Pearl's forearm to signal her to be still. She sat up taller and squared her shoulders, though her palms were clammy and her stomach had soured.

The headlights went out and all of the car's doors

opened at once. Benny appraised the four men that got out. They were of average build, on the skinny side, except for the driver, who was bigger than the others. No bigger than Benny, but he looked strong. If the picnic bench could be lifted and swung, that would take care of two of them. He could throw the tablecloth over them, blinding them temporarily while he jabbed a fork into the sides of their faces or into their backs. Or he could break a plate and stab one in the gut with the shards. He could drive his fingers into their eye sockets, punch one in the throat and feel his Adam's apple give under his fist. Benny thought, as he often did when confronted with white men, how they would look laid on the embalming table of his funeral parlor. The men walked slowly toward him, purposefully menacing, the biggest in the lead. This too was a mockery—they all knew there was no need for a show of strength by four white men on a deserted stretch of Virginia highway. They all knew there was nothing Benny could do.

The big man took in Benny's leather loafers and shining cuff links and his cotton shirt with the pressed collar. His lips set in a thin line, hard and emphatic as a dash.

"Y'all lost?" he drawled. Before Benny could say anything, one of the other men said, "Answer the man. You ain't heard him ask you a question?"

"Nossuh. I mean yessuh, I heard the question, but nossuh, we ain't lost. Just havin' a bite on this here bench."

Nossuh? Yessuh? Pearl had never heard Benny talk that way.

"If there ain't no sign says colored, that means white only, don't it?" the big man said.

"And if it is one says colored, that means white too, if we say it does," the other man said.

"Well, suh, then I surely was mistaken. Me and my missus was hongry. We ain't meant no harm."

"Y'all don't know that in the state of Virginia we keep our nice places for white folks? You think we built this nice bench for you to sit on?" He paused. "Where you come from?"

"You right. You right. We from Georgia, ain't never been on no highway trip before." He grinned. "We ain't familiar with the rules a the road, yuh see."

"Out of state, is you?"

"Yessuh, yes we is."

Pearl's eyes stung. She knew that when those men looked at her, they'd see her eyes glassy with tears and they would think it was because she was afraid. And she was afraid—they could kill her husband right there and do who knows what to her, but God help her, she was angry too. Her knees knocked with rage, her toes curled with it. She wanted to take her shoes off and hurl them.

Mangy, half-starved white trash. Ruddy in the face. Liquor red was what it was, she thought. Calloused paws for hands and swollen knuckles.

One of the men stepped closer to Pearl. Her bowels dropped. He reached out and put the tips of his fingers on the edge of the picnic basket. Trash, Pearl thought again. How they must hate us! Look at my china and my good cutlery, she wanted to say. I live in a big house with a wraparound porch and fruit trees in the yard. She wanted the men to feel low and poor when they went home to their shacks and haggard wives.

He said, "Look like your missus been up to some cooking. She a good cook, boy?"

"Yessuh," Benny replied. "Yessuh, she sho' is."

The big man looked at the other one, then looked again at Benny and said, "Y'all better clear out."

"Thank you, suh. We get our things and we be going presently."

"I ain't said to take nothin' with you. I said to clear out."

Benny paused. His hands balled into fists at his side. The blood vessels in his temples jumped.

The big man continued, "Y'all done put yer stuff on white folks' table and now you gon' have to leave it here. It's a tax. Y'all pay taxes?"

Benny didn't respond. The big man stepped toward him.

"I asked you a question. You pay taxes?"

Benny swallowed hard. "Yes, we do."

"Yes what?"

Again Benny didn't answer.

The big man put his hand on Benny's chest and shoved. Benny staggered but did not fall. The cricket song roared. One of the men's boots scuffed against the gravel.

"Yessuh," Benny said. "Yessuh, we pay our taxes."

"Well, you got to pay another one. Now get, 'fore I change my mind."

Pearl put her palms on the table and pushed herself to standing. She paused, realizing she'd have to lift her leg over the bench and that trash would see her slip. She couldn't move. She shifted to the left, then the right, trying to figure the best way to maneuver off of the bench.

The big man said, "Yer missus want to stay here with us?" They laughed.

Pearl, trembling, lifted her leg; she felt the cool air against the inside of her thigh. She turned quickly so they would not see the tears on her cheeks. As she walked to the car, unsteady in her heels on the gravel, one of them wolf-whistled then said, "Maybe she ought to stay here." She heard Benny walking slowly behind her, the way one creeps away from an animal that might attack.

In the car they did not speak or look at each other for a long time. Both glanced repeatedly at the rearview mirror to check for the overbright headlights. The evening purpled into complete darkness. Theirs was the only car on the road. Pearl sat with her hands clasped in her lap, unfolding them to smooth her skirt over her thighs and pull at the hem. She felt a draft whose source she could not pinpoint, and she tugged at the hand crank that controlled the window.

"Would you please stop all that fidgeting!" Benny said. "You make me want to jump out of my skin."

"You make me want to peel mine off and throw it away," Pearl muttered.

"What's that?" Benny asked. "If you have something to say, then say it out loud."

"All of that shucking and shuffling!" she cried.

"What did you want me to do? You tell me, what else could I have done?"

"You didn't have to stoop so low. You could have kept your dignity! I've never been so humiliated!"

"Oh, yes you have. Yes you have and you know it. You've been in the house with your afternoon teas and garden club so long you think you can pretend we're not who we are, but you know just as well as I do that my dignity, my goddamned dignity, would have had us swinging from a tree."

"Those men weren't worth the dirt under my feet. I couldn't stand the satisfaction in their eyes, Benny. I couldn't stand it."

"And you think I could?"

———

MISS PRISBY, rude woman, monstrous woman, slammed the door on her way out of Wayne Street. The relief office sent her every week. Home assessments, they called them, to ensure that Hattie continued to be a suitable candidate for the benefits she received each month. Hattie thought she'd rather starve than see her again. Maybe she'd go to the relief office that very afternoon and cancel her benefits. It hardly mattered anymore, in less than two hours she would give her child away as if she were a dog. Her old-age baby, her last-born, gone away with Pearl. When Hattie saw Ella again, after three years or five, they would be strangers. Her daughter would call her Aunt Hattie or ma'am. Hattie would look into Ella's face and try not to love her. She'd have to convince herself all over again that she'd done what was necessary, that she'd saved Ella from the half-empty refrigerator and winters with no coal for the furnace. She could keep her, she still could. But. Ella was going to a bedroom of her own and hydrangeas, wide lawns and ice cream in summer and no handed-down Mary Janes. No Miss Prisby.

Miss Prisby had come for the first time four months earlier, and though Hattie hadn't told anyone—the dole was not a thing that could be told—word spread on the block. By the next morning, the neighbors, women with the same rotating pairs of handed-down shoes and mended shirts and cupboards full of canned butter beans, refused to speak to her. They greeted her with a quick nod and walked by her house as though there were a plague on it. It was acceptable not to have any money, none of them had any money, but it was quite another thing to go down to the relief office and fill out papers saying as much. The dole was too shameful, too public an admission of failure. But Hattie couldn't stand the hungry look her children had, and Ella got croup and wouldn't get better because there wasn't any money for the doctor. Marion began relaying messages from Pearl about how sorry she was to hear that things weren't going well and how much she wanted to help. Then Marion told Pearl about the dole, and Pearl wrote.

Hattie,
    Well, spring has come and gone and we've had nothing but rain. The forsythia bloomed and the dogwood, and those delicate purple things that grew around the side of the house when we were girls (remember Mama liked them?) and then a positively Biblical downpour came and mashed them all to bits. I suppose it was pretty in a way. The walkway and yard were strewn with white and purple petals. It's been quiet and sunny the last few

days. The lawn has come in and Benny says it's nicer than the Parsons' next door.

Mrs. Parsons helped me during my trouble. She's a kind woman and my fellow deaconess at the church. She's like a sister to me, such a comfort. She checked on me every day, even after the doctor stopped coming around and Benny was acting so funny. I guess men are always funny about women's things. This time I had taken the crib down from the attic and set it up in the sunny room at the back. I had planned to have the nursery back there. It's a pretty room, very airy. You've never seen it, of course. Did Marion tell you about my trouble? I don't ever hear anything from you. I suppose you are too busy and then without a telephone, such a modern convenience.

Well, I have fully recovered now but the doctor says I oughtn't to try again. Mrs. Parsons thinks that silly. What do doctors know about it, she says. Isn't it peculiar how some things run in families and others don't? You and Marion have been so blessed in that regard and here I am like Abraham's Sarah.

I talked to Marion last week. She told me her girls were doing well. She also said you've had some difficulties as of late. Well, that August never was what he ought to be.

Marion says he hasn't been working and you've been receiving relief. I'm not finding fault. I always thought northern life was full of pitfalls, but it seems some solution is needed. I thought Benny and I might be able to help. We have so much space here, you know. And this great big yard and Benny's business is doing so well. Ella would be happy here. I know she would. So much fresh air and sunshine and the Negro high school has just graduated three girls bound for Spelman College. There are so many opportunities, even here in Macon. Do you remember how Mama and Daddy joined the Negro Uplift Society all of those years ago? Well, I have kept up the dues and the society has done some very good work and I know that things will only get better. Benny says these associations can't undo laziness, but then he is so funny about things.

I told Marion I hoped to talk to you. I didn't tell her what it concerns. I know how much you value your privacy, but I know you go around to her house on Sundays and I thought I might call you there next week.

Well, I have sent twenty dollars, just to ease things a little. I hope you will accept it.

God bless and keep you,
Pearl

Hattie threw the letter away and didn't go to Marion's for over a month. But each time Miss Prisby came to the house, Hattie was forced to face how desperate things had become. Her sisters wouldn't say outright that she'd disgraced herself and their family, but it was what they thought and what Hattie knew to be true. She could bear her poverty and her disappointment, but her children could not, Ella could not. Twice a month Pearl sent an envelope with a ten-dollar bill tucked inside. Hattie kept the money. She hated herself and hated Pearl but she spent every penny.

In high summer Pearl wrote again:

I hope you are considering my proposal. I know you don't place much stock in what August says, but he is in favor.

God bless,
Pearl

Hattie put the letter into her purse and went to Marion's. When she arrived, Marion was sitting on her porch swing fanning herself in the heat.

"What do you know about this?" Hattie asked, waving the letter in Marion's face.

"I know you shouldn't be charging up my steps like one of hell's children when I haven't seen you for a month. What is that?" Marion answered, reaching for the sheet of monogrammed stationery.

"Oh," she said as she read it.

"Well?" Hattie said.

"It's just like Pearl to put things all the wrong way. It's not as bad as she makes it sound."

"What it sounds like to me is that August and Pearl have been plotting behind my back, and you too, I expect," Hattie said.

"Nobody's plotting. It just happened that August came over here to talk with Lewis—"

"Since when is August coming over here without me? He and Lewis haven't said more than ten words to each other since you all got married."

"I don't know about that, but all he said was it might not be the worst thing if Pearl took Ella, with you all having such a hard time."

Hattie put her hand over her mouth as if to stifle a scream. She took a deep breath, dropped her hand to her side, and said, "One sister is trying to steal my flesh and blood and the other's lying to cover it up. I don't have much of my dignity left, Marion. I'm asking you to tell me the truth."

"I told it to you. August was over here, he came to . . . He came to borrow some money from Lewis but he didn't want you to know about it, so we promised him we wouldn't say anything."

"He came over here begging?" Hattie asked. "What for?"

"I don't know what for, Hattie." Marion reached for Hattie's hand, but Hattie took a step backward, out of her sister's reach. "He and Lewis got to talking about things, and that's when he said he'd been thinking about Pearl."

"And?"

"And I happened to talk to Pearl the next day and I mentioned it."

"I see." Hattie took the letter and folded it back into her purse. "Thank you," she said and descended the porch steps.

"Hattie, wait!" Marion called.

"Let me be, Marion. Just let me be."

August came home that evening whistling Dixie like he always did, rain or shine, feast or famine, whistling Dixie. At dinner Hattie spooned his mashed potatoes onto his plate with such force that they spattered onto his necktie. After they ate, the children scattered like frightened cats. August was left alone with Hattie's silence and the clatter of the silverware against the plates and the rush of water filling the double sink. She whirled to face him.

"Were you going to let me know you told Pearl she could have my child or were you planning on stealing Ella and driving her down to Georgia while I was sleeping?"

August reached for his cigarettes. Hattie didn't allow him to smoke in the house, so he tapped the corner of the box against the table.

"I ain't told Pearl no such thing," he said.

"You ain't told Pearl no such thing." Hattie shook her head. "So she just made it up and wrote it to me in a letter?"

"I didn't tell her to take Ella. All I said was we was having a hard time and could be . . ."

"And could be you ought to sneak behind my back begging money from my sister's husband? And while you were at it, you thought you might say Pearl could have my child?"

"It wasn't that way, Hattie."

"What did you need that money for, August? I don't recall seeing any meat in the Frigidaire. And you certainly didn't add it to the down payment savings."

"It was just a few dollars. I already gave it back."

"I hope she was worth it."

"Wasn't no woman, Hattie. All I did was borrow fifteen dollars and tell Lewis I been thinking 'bout what Pearl said. That's all."

"You sold my baby girl for a few dollars and the money Pearl sends every week!"

"What money? I never took no money from Pearl. I didn't say she could have Ella. Hattie, listen, they got so much down there. It ain't like we wouldn't see her again. She'd just be down there with your sister. Your own blood, Hattie, just till things ease up a little."

"When will they ease up, August? When you

run out of girlfriends? Are they going to ease up when you get sick of wearing nice shirts and going out every night?" She hit the kitchen table with the palm of her hand. "And you have the nerve to come in here whistling like a fool every night."

"You think I don't know I got mouths to feed? Shoot, one of 'em ain't even mine."

"Leave Ruthie out of this!"

"I go down that yard every day, and every day they say, 'Nothin' for you.' I come home singing—you damn right I come in and bounce them children on my knee and try to make them laugh—ain't much else to give them."

"I don't want to hear your sad stories when I have Miss Prisby looking in my drawers and cupboards every week. You wonder why I don't smile at you? You're lucky I don't stab you in your sleep. A better woman would."

"You ain't never tried to understand what it is to be a man out in this world."

"Don't give me that line about how hard it is for Negroes. I'm on the dole because you spend your money in the streets. I know it's hard!"

"You know what I used that fifteen dollars for? Union dues. I thought it might get me better pay, but it ain't done nothing but buy whiskey for them white boys. I don't want Ella to go no more than you do, but cain't you see that's what's best? We poor folks, and we gon' stay that way. Pearl and Benny got lots of money. Ella will have more than we can give her."

"Well, why don't we just give them all away, August? We don't have to stop with Ella. How about Franklin? How many of our children do you think somebody else will take care of because you won't?"

"Easy, Hattie. Easy. We talking about Ella here. You know in your heart this the right thing. She goin' back where we came from, good earth, good air."

"You and I don't come from the same place," she hissed. "You came from a shack, and I came from a house on a hill. We don't have a single thing in common as far as that's concerned, and don't you forget it. You field hand. You nigger."

August rose from the table and rushed at Hattie with his hand raised. He had never hit her. She stood her ground even when he got so close she could see the sweat beading on his forehead. His raised hand trembled in the air.

"You a cold woman, Hattie." He dropped his hand and walked out of the kitchen.

As she watched him leave the room, all indignance and wounded pride, Hattie decided to give her daughter to Pearl. August wasn't ever going to do any better. He might think he was trying but he'd go on as he always had. I can't be so irresponsible, so selfish, she thought, as to subject my girl to this circumstance when there is another choice.

PEARL AND BENNY CROSSED the Mason-Dixon Line into Pennsylvania. It was safe to stop, so they pulled onto the shoulder of the highway and got out to stretch their legs and go to the bathroom. Pearl walked deep into the wood that bordered the road. It was just after dawn and the dew soaked through the ankles of her stockings. These northern forests smell different, she thought, more like tree bark and less like earth and moss. Oh, but that's silly, we only just crossed the line, it's not as though the trees changed because we left Jim Crow.

Fallen acorns pressed against the soles of Pearl's shoes and into the balls of her feet. She had an urge to take off her pumps and rub her feet in the dirt. Pearl never went into the wood near her house in Macon. She preferred cultivated places. She squatted behind a wide tree, one hand on its trunk for balance and the other pulling her girdle away from her body so she wouldn't dirty it. She squatted there so long her thighs ached and a wide puddle formed beneath her. The cool air felt nice on her backside, but she couldn't help looking around to see if anyone was there.

This is the last morning of my childlessness, Pearl thought. The closer she got to Philadelphia the more euphoric she felt—the white men at the rest stop didn't matter anymore nor Benny's scorn nor even Hattie's anger. She would come to see she'd made the right decision. Even that fool August knew it.

Pearl's knees cracked when she stood. A few feet behind her a chestnut tree was all but picked clean by squirrels; she walked farther into the forest to find another one. She wondered if Ella had ever seen a chestnut tree in full fruit. She'd probably never seen lots of things: magnolias, sugar beet fields, the horses some of the country people rode into town now and again. She hoped the baby was healthy. Marion had said Hattie was looking worn and sickly. To think Hattie had accused her of trying to buy Ella! She sent that money to put food in those children's stomachs, and Hattie had reduced it to a bribe. She'd taken the money though, hadn't she?

Hattie had never been easy to love. She was too quiet, it was impossible to know what she was thinking. And she was angry all of the time and so disdainful when her high expectations weren't met. When they were girls, Pearl tagged along behind Hattie wherever she went. Hattie held some part of herself back no matter how devoted Pearl was, no matter how much Pearl loved her. She still loved her, though Hattie made her feel like a failure. Even now, poor as she was and crammed in that house with all of those children, by all accounts Hattie was as proud as she had been when they were girls in Georgia and their father was the only Negro business owner in town. Likely, even the dole hadn't broken her. Pearl reminded herself that it was Hattie who had failed, not Pearl. Hattie had married the wrong man and she had failed.

When Pearl told Benny that Hattie had finally come around, he'd been almost indifferent. Oh, he hauled the baby furniture down from the attic and paid the man who came to repaper the nursery, and he smiled and nodded when the people at church congratulated him, but he never mentioned Ella when he and Pearl were alone. Just before they left for Philadelphia, Pearl came into the house with an armload of new baby clothes. Benny frowned.

"After all this time and trial, I thought you'd be pleased to have a daughter," she said.

"A niece," Benny replied and turned back to his paper.

That man spent so much time with dead people that he hardly knew how to be with the living.

Pearl came upon a tree still laden with nuts. The branches were teeming with squirrels and Pearl wondered if Ella would be the sort of child that was afraid of animals. She tried to imagine what the baby looked like: ivory like Hattie or cinnamon like August, sandy-brown hair or wavy black? She'd be a pretty baby. All of Hattie's children, the ones Pearl had seen, were pretty. Chestnuts had fallen from the tree and lay in heaps on the ground. Pearl took off her slip and piled nuts into it. Well, all that gathering made her feel carefree as a girl. She got twigs stuck to her sweater and crumbly bits of dirt on her skirt, but she kept collecting chestnuts until they bulged through the silk of her slip.

Benny was calling Pearl as she walked through the wood toward the highway. She stepped through the trees and onto the graveled shoulder of the road, ruddy cheeked and giddy with her slip made into a satchel.

"Will you just look at all these chestnuts!" she said.

"Is that your slip?" Benny asked.

"I'm going to give them to Hattie so we can roast them together. Won't that be fine?"

He sighed. "I think it's going to take more than chestnuts."

"It might ease things a bit, roasting chestnuts like we did when we were girls."

"Get in," he said. "We have at least five hours left."

They stopped once more—ham sandwiches at a roadside stand eaten so quickly the engine didn't have time to cool before they started off again. Just past noon they crossed the Schuylkill River and drove into Philadelphia.

I OUGHT to pack up Ella's things, Hattie thought. She rubbed her cheek against the smooth spot on top of the baby's head where the hair hadn't grown in yet. She stood in the doorway and scanned the street for Pearl and Benny's Buick. Ella had gotten old enough to hold on to things with her fist— Hattie's nose or chin or a lock of her hair. And she had learned to give kisses, though she kept her mouth open in a round O, suction kisses, August called them.

He was delighted with her, as he was with all of the children. He treated them like bear cubs at the circus, and they loved him for it. He let the little ones come into the bathroom while he shaved, and they watched him as raptly as they would a picture show. He taught them to whistle songs he'd heard on the radio. August was a buffoon, and they adored him; Hattie kept them alive, and they barely smiled when she entered the room. Hattie didn't know how to be a different kind of mother. She squeezed Ella. Maybe with you I could do better, she whispered in her daughter's ear. Maybe this time . . . But it was too late, everything was decided.

Ella closed her fist around Hattie's earlobe and giggled. I ought to put her in her blue dress and pack her things, Hattie thought again. But the blue dress was for company or for outings, and they still had another hour together. Hattie decided to put the milk bottles out on the stoop. Maybe she'd sweep too, before Pearl arrived. Fallen leaves were thick on the steps, and Hattie's was the only porch not swept clean.

Ella cooed at the butterflies flitting around the bushes near the porch steps. It was her first autumn. Hattie wondered what she must think of it or if she'd even noticed that the summer had faded into the burnt yellow and orange of fall. At least, Ella wouldn't have to endure the northern winter. Hattie had never gotten used to it. She didn't suffer from nostalgia—the South was gone from her—but the northern winter left her raw and heartsick. It had taken two of her children. Ella squirmed against her.

"Oh, it's the butterflies you want," Hattie said. She got a mason jar and captured two of them inside. She refused to look at the clock again but she was as aware of the time passing as she was of her own heartbeat. The butterflies, white as two slips of paper, flitted in the jar. Ella was transfixed. In the summer Hattie's girls trapped fireflies. They ripped the glowing bits from the insects' abdomens and put them on their fingers like rings. "Princess emeralds!" they shouted and ran down the block with the green glow paling on their fingers. Ella banged the butterfly jar with her hands.

"Ain't that a purty sight? You poke some holes in that lid and put some grass in the bottom and they'll live till sundown," Willie said. She stood in the middle of the sidewalk leaning on a cane.

"It's a shame to kill them. I thought I'd set them free when she gets tired of them," Hattie replied.

"Everything got to meet its end somewhere. Over by that bush or in that there jar, I reckon it's the same to them."

Willie gestured to Ella. "Look like she got a good disposition. Cranky baby's a hard thing to take. But not as hard to take as a cranky man, I reckon." She chuckled. "And she full of rolls. That's good coming into winter. Fat baby'll do alright even if there ain't much besides butter beans and her mama's milk. Fat baby do just fine in a lean winter."

"Yes, ma'am," Hattie said. "I guess that's true. I suppose I've managed before."

"We all have. Well, I better get on. You ought to step in sometime soon. I'll give you something help you sleep better. You don't look like yourself." Willie moved off down the street.

It was true that many a baby, Hattie's own children, had done alright on butter beans and cabbage. The next spring Ella would be a little older and stronger, and Hattie could work somewhere. Maybe Mrs. Mark would come back from Florida, or Hattie could find a job cooking at one of the restaurants. August and Marion and Pearl wanted to rip her child from her, and that Pearl throwing around twenty-dollar bills like they were pennies. She's always wanted something from me, Hattie thought. I never knew what it was, but she's been trying to worm her way inside of me since we were girls—the way spiders get into butterfly cocoons and eat them from the inside out until they're nothing but husks.

I can't do this, Hattie thought. If I give my child away, I'll crumble. I wouldn't survive it. Maybe it's selfish to keep her from piano lessons and pinafores, but I'm not that strong. I'd disintegrate into nothing and blow away.

To Ella she said, "We'll take our chances."

THE HOUSE SMELLED faintly of mildew, like laundry left too long on the line on a rainy day. It made Hattie think of things she couldn't stand: hair in the drain, the bathroom grouting gone black with mold. She tidied the living room and put the butterfly jar on the low table near the sofa. Across the street her neighbor's late-blooming roses drooped on their stems. It occurred to Hattie that it was roses she needed to brighten the living room. She didn't care for them but Pearl liked sweet, cloying things.

Hattie decided to cross the street and cut a few. She'd just gotten her kitchen shears and was standing on the porch when Benny's Buick rolled to a stop in front of the house. "You all are early," she whispered. The sun glinted off of the Buick's chrome fenders, shined on the hood as though it had been blessed by God, and there she was standing in front of her rented house about to steal some roses from her neighbor. She didn't feel up to the battle she'd have to wage in order to keep Ella.

"You're early," she said, more loudly this time.

Marion was with them. Pearl powdered her nose in the passenger seat. Her hands shook. She looked out at Hattie standing on the steps with the baby in her arms. Her baby, her Ella. Hattie was older, that was sure, more lined and serious. She looked tired too, and her hair was coming loose from the bun at the nape of her neck, but she stood straight and tall and she still had that something in her bearing that made Pearl feel a little shabby, a little scuffed. She put the compact back into her purse.

Hattie looked down from the porch steps. Benny opened Pearl's door. He had always had good manners. Pearl was powdering her nose like a princess. She looked well, well-fed, manicured. When she got out of the car, she smoothed her skirt with both hands and walked toward the house. Yes, she looked well, though not quite sure of herself. Her eyes were fixed on Ella. She and Hattie looked at each other, then at the baby. Marion broke the silence.

"Hattie, my gracious, you are in a state. What are you doing out here with those scissors? You look like you've been at the cordial." She glanced anxiously from one sister to the other. "It's gotten so breezy! Isn't it breezy?"

Hattie took a deep breath and descended the stairs. "You all must be tired after all that driving, though it does seem you made good time. Did you make good time, Benny?"

"Alright time, I guess, Hattie." He took off his hat when she addressed him.

There was silence again. Marion said, "Don't you think we should go inside?" She edged past Pearl and Hattie and opened the front door. "Come on then," she said.

"You look well, Hattie." Pearl said. "And the baby . . . You painted the house since the last time I was here. But that was . . . well, that was so long ago. My goodness. Glory be. Well, this was always a nice respectable street."

Pearl could not recall ever wanting anything as badly as she wanted to take Ella into her arms. "A very quiet street." Her voice shook.

Hattie felt a rush of sympathy for her, all trussed

up and gloved and too much powder on her face.
If the circumstances had been different, she would
have reached out and squeezed Pearl's shoulder.
Ella nuzzled Hattie's neck like she did whenever
strangers came around.

"I almost forgot about my chestnuts! Benny, go
get the chestnuts."

He went back to the car. The women entered
the house.

The living room was all shadows. Pearl stood in
the foyer with her arms hanging limp at her sides;
she looked around as though she'd unexpectedly
found herself in a barn. Hattie offered to make
them some coffee and started toward the kitchen.

Pearl blurted, "Can I hold the baby while you
make the coffee?"

"I suppose everyone takes milk?" Hattie asked.
As she turned to walk down the hallway, she kissed
Ella's forehead and pulled at her earlobe because
that always made her daughter laugh.

She put the water on to boil. There was a little
coffee in a tin at the back of the cupboard, just
enough for two or three cups. I'll tell them I don't
take coffee in the afternoon, she thought. She balanced Ella on her hip with one arm and with the
other hand took an old serving tray from the hutch
and the good cups and the creamer and sugar bowl.
Ella kept reaching for the dishes, and Hattie nearly
dropped the saucers. She whined as though she

might cry, so Hattie wet the tip of her pinky, stuck it in the sugar bowl, and put it in Ella's mouth. She leaned against the counter and whispered in Ella's ear while the baby sucked the sugar away. Hattie felt as though she were sliding off of the side of the earth.

Marion came in. "You need some help? At least let me take the baby while you do that."

"No!" Hattie said. "No, I'm alright."

"You all are going to have to get on with things, you know."

"Coffee's ready. You can carry the tray," Hattie said.

Benny had put the things from the car in the middle of the living room floor: a basket of apples and one of string beans, a couple of covered boxes, and a big bag brimming over with what looked like clothes. Next to these, Pearl's slipful of chestnuts. It looked as though he'd unloaded a ship. Hattie shifted Ella from one hip to the other.

"I am grateful for all of these things, and I do certainly appreciate the trouble you went to, but"— Hattie took a deep breath—"you should keep your things. Ella is staying with me. You can't have her for a bucket of string beans."

"Hattie! I brought these things because you're my sister, like I do whenever I come visiting. I brought some things for Marion too. Didn't I?"

Pearl looked at Marion.

"I don't know how you could say such a thing," Pearl said.

"I'll help you take them back out to the car," Hattie said to Benny.

He shook his head and looked up at her from beneath his eyelashes.

"I think you ought to keep them, if you would. I'd like you to have them even if . . . ," he said.

"What is the matter with you, Benny!" Pearl cried. "Hattie, I thought you might need these things!"

"You don't know what I need, and I'll thank you not to speculate on it," Hattie said.

"I have never known anyone so full of foolish pride. Anybody can see you need our help. Just look at the state of this house!"

"Pearl!" Marion said.

"I'm sorry, Hattie. I truly am. Excuse me. I'm a little agitated," Pearl said. "I think we're all just a little excited. Let's drink our coffee. Why don't you sit down so we can have our coffee?"

"I'll stand, thank you," Hattie said, rubbing the small of Ella's back.

"I didn't mean what I said. We ought to talk this out. We had an agreement, Hattie. It's all decided. You said yourself that I should come."

"Now I'm saying otherwise."

"But Hattie . . . you have to be practical. There's clothes and food to consider, and all of you squeezed into this little house. I know it must be hard, but it's the best thing. For Ella."

"You don't know anything about it. You've never had a child, so you can't say how hard it might be. Can you, Pearl?"

Pearl began to weep. Hattie stood in front of her, rocking Ella. She was sorry to see Pearl cry. She was sorry for her loneliness. Benny looked at his wife like she was a stranger to him, like she was somebody who'd wandered in off the street. But, Hattie thought, her problems aren't mine to fix. She wanted them to leave. She wanted some quiet, an hour of silence before the other children came home from school.

"There's not much point in going on with this," Hattie said.

A whistled tune drifted in from the other side of the door. The knob turned. August stepped in.

"Y'all already here?" he said. He saw Pearl crying and Benny staring at his shoes and Marion sitting there looking like somebody's old aunt. And Hattie, Hattie like a thundercloud in the middle of the room.

"I guess things ain't going so well. I didn't reckon they would," he said.

"Please, August, say something to her," Pearl said. "She says she won't give up Ella, but we had an agreement. You know we did."

"Nothing I can say. She thinks I'm lower than a cockroach."

"For goodness' sake, August. Please! Can't you just—"

"You know what? Don't nobody ever act like this child is one bit mine. Y'all act like she hatched from an egg. Don't nobody never think maybe it hurts me to see her go."

"We agreed!" Pearl said. "We all agreed!"

"This our child, Pearl. You got no right to act like you better than us. A blind man can see that's what you think, and that don't endear you to nobody. You all come from the same parents. Things took a different turn for Hattie, but you strutting around like a cock in the yard ain't right."

Hattie looked over at August, surprised to find an ally in him, hesitant to believe he really was one.

"I halfway hoped y'all'd already be gone when I came home 'cause I didn't want to see another one of my children taken away."

"She's not going to be taken away," Hattie said. "I changed my mind."

August nodded. "I was of half a mind to call Pearl myself and tell her not to come. I couldn't stand the thought of losing a child again. I thought it would put me in the floor, but then I realized it ain't the same thing as before."

"Where are you going with this, August?" Hattie asked.

"I need to say this to you, Hattie, even though you won't want to hear it. You watched our two babies go, you nursed them, and sang to them and rocked them, and it didn't do no good in the end."

August's voice cracked.

"I won't stand here and tell you what you should do, but I want you to know that this ain't that. Ella ain't dying. We had that pain, Hattie, and we'll have this too, but you got to understand it ain't the same thing."

Hattie looked at August a long while. No one spoke. Finally, she nodded and he nodded back.

Pearl stood and took a step toward Benny, but he was sitting with his head in his hands and did not look at her. Benny won't love Ella, Pearl realized. She had fooled herself into thinking that he would. "Oh!" she said aloud and sank down onto the couch.

Hattie cupped Ella's head in her hand; her hair tickled her palm. She touched her fingers to the baby's plump calves and dimpled knees and small translucent toenails. After a time, August took Ella in his arms and sang to her so quietly she fell asleep. Hattie watched him nuzzle her and remembered his smile when she told him she was pregnant. She remembered her panic and her rage. She had nearly gone to Willie for something to get rid of the pregnancy. And certainly Hattie was glad she hadn't done that—here was her baby girl in the world. Hattie was grateful for Ella's life, however briefly she'd had a place in it. But then there was this unbearable fact: Hattie was losing another of her children. And she couldn't help but ask herself, God help her, if it wouldn't have been easier if Ella hadn't ever existed, and Hattie had never had these six months as her mother. How was she supposed to bear a life like this? She looked around the room as if she might find the answer in August's face or Marion's or Pearl's, but her eyes settled on Ella. In that moment it was no consolation to think she was doing the right thing for her child. Best not to think at all, best to move, because if she didn't, she would fall down and she wouldn't get up again. Hattie stood and climbed the stairs. She came down a few minutes later with Ella's Moses basket and a brown bag.

"Here's some of her things," she said to Pearl. "There's a doll baby in there that I made for her. I'm sure you have something fancier, but she likes this one and it smells like me, so you can give it to her on the ride back if she fusses."

Pearl looked at her sister as though she wanted to say something but didn't know what it ought to be.

Hattie took Ella from August's arms. The baby snuffled and whimpered, so Hattie shifted her onto her shoulder and rubbed her back.

"She fidgets in her sleep," she said to Pearl. "You

have to pick her up and rub her back like this or she'll wake up howling."

She's only my child for a few more minutes, Hattie thought. She wished Ella would wake up so she could see her eyes one last time.

"You ought to go now before she wakes up," Hattie said.

She handed her daughter to Pearl. I'm in the floor, she thought.

Marion and Benny, Hattie and August, and Pearl, holding Ella, walked out to the street. Benny opened the car door and settled Pearl and Ella in the passenger seat. He pulled off slowly. Pearl raised her hand in a wave and held it suspended until the car rounded the corner and was gone.

"The children will be home from school soon," Hattie said.

"I guess they will be," August replied.

They went into the house and began carrying the baskets of food into the kitchen. The butterflies were still alive in the Mason jar. August turned to her and said, "We gon' make it through, Hattie."

She snatched the jar from the table and hurled it at the wall behind August. The two of them watched the butterflies, stunned and struggling in the broken glass.

Alice and Billups

1968

6:30 a.m.

ALICE STOOD IN her bathrobe at the top of the staircase. The sun had not yet risen. Outside, she heard the muffled thump of car doors in the driveway, Royce getting into the town car that took him to his office, his driver shutting the door behind him, then the fading engine rev as the car pulled into the street and was gone. The grandfather clock tolled the half hour, and the wooden stairs creaked with cold. Eudine would not come for another two hours. This morning of all mornings it seemed to Alice unjust that she should have to descend alone into the house to turn on the furnace and put the kettle to boil. Eudine ought to have been there already, neatly uniformed, pouring the coffee and doing the toast while Alice gave her instructions for the party that evening. The guests would not arrive until nine—a lifetime away—but there were the caterers to keep after, the good china to be gotten out of the credenza, the liquor to be delivered.

Alice went down. In the foyer she bent to straighten the corner of the throw rug Royce had kicked up as he left the house. He never failed to kick up the rug, as he never bothered about turning on the lights or the heat. But of course, she was lucky to have him, there were so few colored doctors, and from such a prominent family! She walked through the chill rooms of the first floor. Well, what did Royce know of **love's austere and lonely offices**? A couple of years before, he'd insisted they attend a reading of Robert Hayden's poetry, and Royce nodded with great feeling when Hayden recited that line. But later, when Alice mentioned the poem, Royce didn't remember it at all and he had looked at her with pity as if to say: silly, unsophisticated Alice, starry eyed over a trifle. The point, she realized too late, was to go to the reading with the other colored elites of the city, not to remember the poems. She still made so many errors in conduct, even after five years of marriage.

Alice switched on the heat and sat in the kitchen waiting for the whoosh of the pilot and the gurgle in the radiators. Barely past seven! She did not like to admit she was lonely, though she listened for the click of Eudine's key in the front door. If only her brother Billups were there with her. Alice missed him most in the early morning. How many times had he arrived at six, bleary eyed after a night of terrible dreams? They would sit drinking tea until he had calmed, then he would kiss her on the cheek and thank her and go off to whatever little part-time job he had. In the last few months his visits had dwindled to once every two weeks. He hadn't even called her back about the party. Even Mother had phoned to say she'd come. Mother who never phoned, who did not like parties, who did not, Alice sometimes thought, like Alice.

Hattie's house was only thirty minutes away, but Alice never went there now. When she did see her parents and siblings, they had to come to her, dine at Alice's table and be served by her help. They were all coming for the party. They'd eye her lovely things, sit on her settees and sofas, and chat with her as though she had never been one of them. Bell would walk out of the powder room and make a joke about how she could sell the hand towels to pay the month's rent. Of course, the trouble was their jealousy. Though it was also true that, when assembled, the family put her in mind of a group of roaming, solitary creatures rounded up and caged together like captured leopards. It would help that Floyd's concert occasioned the party. He had been away for fifteen years, since Alice was a girl of ten.

She only knew what he looked like from his pictures in the paper. Mother cut out articles about him and sent the clips to everyone in the family. Who would have suspected Hattie of sentiment? Oh, how the prospect of their arrival terrified her. Alice stood so abruptly she nearly upset her chair. Five minutes later she was out on the street, her panic burning away in the frigid air.

7:30 a.m.

Alice had been walking for thirty minutes when Saint Mark's Lutheran Church came into view. She needed a few minutes' warmth. The cold morning, so calming when Alice left the house, had turned brutal. The church loomed over the block, three stories with a steep flight of granite steps that led to red double doors. Royce's family had been members for seventy years. A pew at the front was inscribed with the family name, the same pew in which Alice sat every Sunday with the brim of her mother-in-law's hat poking into the side of her face.

When Alice and Billups were teenagers they used to go in secret to Catholic churches. They'd skip school and skulk around parks smoking cigarettes, then catch the trolley to Our Mother of Consolation or Old Saint Mary's or Holy Trinity. They took turns unburdening themselves to the priest in the confessional. Alice told the story in a flat little voice, reciting the facts as though she were reading a grocery list. She told it so often she was immune to its effects on her listener, and if the priest gasped or paused in shock, she was almost surprised. On the way out she and Billups lit candles for the preservation of their souls. More often, they did the reverse: they whispered a name, always the same name, and blew out a candle to extinguish his soul. Well, now Alice and Billups were grown up and they both knew there wasn't any way to rid the world of malignant souls.

The icy landing at the top of St. Mark's steps had already been salted. An older man came out of the church holding a white bucket. Alice did not recognize him for a few seconds, bundled in a coat and scarf as he was. But then she noticed the slope of his shoulders and the way he held his neck at a forward angle, as though he were peering at something in the distance. Alice gasped. She couldn't see his face, but it was surely him—he wore that same fedora, had that same rodent skittishness.

"Thomas!" Alice tried to call out, but her mouth only opened and closed like a fish mouth. Each time she encountered him she had the same vision: she beat him with her fists and scratched him bloody with her fingernails, kneed him in the groin until he fell onto the sidewalk. But she was too afraid to even point at him, much less attack. He descended steadily toward her, throwing fistfuls of salt on the stairs. She told herself she would hold her ground this time, at least that, and when he reached her, he would have to look into her face and acknowledge her. He drew closer, his heels clicking on the stairs.

Alice had never met another man who wore such noisy shoes. How the sound had echoed in his empty house when she was a child. He had so little furniture: the stand-up chalkboard in the kitchen and the square table where he went over Alice's and Billups's lessons, the loveseat in the little parlor where Alice waited with her school workbook pressed open on her knees. The latch would click softly as he closed the parlor door behind him and again as he locked her inside. He'd pause on the other side of the door and jiggle the handle to make sure Alice could not get out. She was alone in the little room. The house filled with the sounds of his shoes tapping against the tiles in the foyer. Then the clack of his heels against the wooden floors in the small dining room. Then nothing as he walked on the rectangle of carpet in the hallway that led to the kitchen.

Alice looked up at him on the steps. He was not far from her now. Wait, she thought. Hold on. He's almost here—he's nearly scratching distance. But as he grew closer, the air around them seemed to contract and push her toward him until it was as though they were side by side, and she could smell his chalk and shoe leather scent. She turned and fled.

8:30 a.m.

"Billy! Billy are you there?" Alice called. She rang his bell a fourth time. "Billy!" There were only three units in the apartment house. Alice pressed all of the buzzers. A woman she had never seen before opened a second-floor window and stuck her head out.

"Miss! Stop that carrying on! He must not be here. Lord Jesus!"

Alice pulled her coat more tightly around her. "Billy!" she called again. Her toes ached with cold. The soles of her tennis shoes were thin as crackers. But she was determined to warn Billups that Thomas was not far from the neighborhood. Alice scanned the street to see if he'd followed her from the church. "Billy!" she shouted.

The neighbor woman opened her window again, "I told you he's not here!"

"Couldn't you please knock on his door? Apartment three?"

"Miss, I'm trying to get some sleep! I haven't seen him since yesterday."

"Was he alright?" Billy was so fragile, with his insomnia and his headaches.

"I have half a mind to call the police if you don't get out of here."

"But I'm his sister!"

The woman shut her window. Alice descended the steps and stood in the middle of the sidewalk. She glanced one last time at Billups's window. The curtain moved. Or was it the play of the tree branches' reflection in the glass panes?

"Billy?" she called, more quietly this time. Alice's eyes welled with tears. She looked down the empty street and felt a sudden foreboding. It was as though the iron sky and the aching cold and the minutes hurtling past—here it was already 8:30, already February, already her twenty-fifth year!—bore her some ill will. Alice shivered and turned toward home. Surely it was the strangeness of the morning that made her feel so unprotected.

9:30 a.m.

A white van pulled out of the driveway as Alice crossed the lawn to her front door.

"Who was that?" Alice called as she walked into the house. "Eudine?"

Eudine padded into the foyer like a great cat, all long strides and silence. She was neat as a pin, her hair twisted into a chignon at the base of her neck, her apron sun-blind white, and her face, not just her skin, but her expression, as smooth as melted caramel. Alice pulled her coat more tightly around her, as if she could hide her dungarees and canvas shoes dirtied with melting slush. She pushed a stray lock of hair back under her wool cap.

"Who was that in the van?" Alice asked again.

"Caterer."

"The what? The caterer? They're not scheduled until the afternoon."

"I couldn't say," Eudine replied.

She could say, of course. Eudine knew everything about the running of the house. She was the most efficient person Alice had ever known—up at five every morning and always fifteen minutes early to work.

"Well, they made a mistake, didn't they?" Alice said. "I don't know why you didn't send them away."

Eudine did not reply. She was indecipherable, so ageless and immaculate. Her eyes were the same caramel shade as her skin. Her face was a placid lake, such depths. A woman with a face like that could be a confessor, could be told anything, no matter how awful, and remain steady as granite. When she hired her, Alice had hoped Eudine might become her confidant, like in those films in which the lady of the house sits at her vanity telling her secrets to a maid who unclasps her necklaces and lays them in the jewelry box. Or was it only white women who made confidants of their servants? Or only white women with whom colored maids could be forced into confidence? Maybe Alice was only an imitation of a rich white woman in a big house. She was not entirely certain what she was imitating. That is to say, the object of her efforts was nearly always unclear.

"I'll just call them."

Alice kept her papers for the party on a desk in the sitting room. Weeks of lists: linens needed, menus, the phone numbers for the florists and the agency that sent extra help, and the catering manager whom Alice had dismissed. The woman had lorded about as if she were the lady of the house. Why, she had stopped consulting Alice at a certain point! In the interest of expedience, she'd said. As if Alice couldn't plan her own brother's party.

"You know, Eudine, I'll bet that awful woman is mixed up in this somehow," Alice said, knocking scraps of paper and tea-stained invoices onto the floor as she rifled through the heap on her desk. "She was just determined to sabotage me."

"It don't think it was her," Eudine said.

"Pardon?" Alice didn't look up from her papers. It was so difficult to keep track of all of the details.

"I believe, I think maybe Dr. Phillips had some people he wanted . . . I mean, some things he ordered separate."

"Royce? No, that can't be. He said he wouldn't . . . I handled all the details myself." Alice blinked rapidly. She felt a tightening in her throat.

"Is the other caterer still coming later?" Alice meant to ask the question boldly, but when she opened her mouth to speak, all that came out was a small, little-girl voice.

Eudine gazed at her. "I don't believe so," she replied softly.

"I'll just . . . I'll just go upstairs and call to straighten this out," Alice said again.

Humiliation burned her cheeks. She wondered when Royce had canceled her caterer, and in what other ways he'd embarrassed her, and when he'd conspired with Eudine. Alice could feel her smirking. She climbed the stairs slowly, head high and back straight. At the top, Alice paused, picked up a vase with both hands, and threw it to the floor. What delight, what release in its shattering.

11:00 a.m.

Gloom crept through the house like an ice age. The morning was all but gone, and Alice had managed only to change out of her dungarees and back into her bathrobe. Time so often passed that way—Alice foundering until the day had dwindled to a sliver and she was forced into frenzied action: the household requirements, dressing for dinner in time for Royce's return from the hospital, shopping for the groceries and sundries Billups couldn't manage to get for himself. Alice sighed. It was clear the day would not brighten. She wanted to go back to bed, to spend all of her days in bed until spring came. But then what? Spring would arrive with its loud colors, and people would go about happily because the season had changed, and Alice would have to go about happily as well. In summer she and Royce would spend July at the house on the Vineyard, the large airy rooms, the champagne-colored curtains lifting and billowing in the breeze, the ice cubes tinkling like wind chimes against the crystal glasses, and the conversation tinkling in that same delicate, frivolous way. The air would smell like taffy and drying seaweed, and they would wear white, and there would be still more happiness. So much happiness. It was almost as exhausting as this relentless February.

12:30 p.m.

The doorbell gonged. Alice hurried to the top of the stairs and peered down as Eudine opened the door. Billy! He hadn't come to see her in weeks. He did look well, taller somehow. Alice caught a glimpse of herself in the hall mirror as she ran downstairs:

hair still in pin curls, face still unwashed. She didn't like for Billups to see her unkempt, but what a joy, what a wonder that he had come.

"Billy!" She raced downstairs to greet him. "Eudine! Tea!" she called.

Alice took her brother's arm and led him into the living room. "I've been thinking about you every minute. I went by your apartment this morning and you weren't there. The party's tonight. Did you forget?" She paused and stepped back to appraise him. "Are you alright?"

"I'm fine, Alice," he said.

"Why are you standing around with your coat on?"

"You didn't give me a chance . . ."

"Well, you look so fit. I can't imagine what you've been doing these last weeks! Is this coat new? It's very nice. Where did you get it?"

"Alice, I need—"

"Navy. Well, I prefer black or gray for a man's coat. I always buy you black or gray but . . . Did Royce give it to you? He has so many things. You ought to look through some of his old suits. You'll need to let them out, but—"

"Alice! Alice, please. I want to talk to you."

"Talk to me? My goodness but you sound so serious. What on earth about? It's not even lunchtime. Too early to be so grave, Billy!"

"It's 12:30, Alice."

"Is it? So late as that? The day is getting away from me! And so much left to do." She looked around the room. Eudine had set out the bottles that didn't require chilling, and she'd put out the good ashtrays and stacked pewter coasters on the side tables. Alice leapt up from the sofa with a little gasp. "I've got to get in the bath. You'll wait, Billy?"

"Tea," Eudine announced, entering the living room with the tea things on a silver tray.

"Well, I . . ." Alice said, looking from Eudine to the stairs and back. "I suppose I have time for just one cup."

"I need to talk to you," Billups said again.

"Oh, Billy! I didn't tell you." Alice waited for Eudine to leave the room. She sat next to Billups and said quietly, "I had a terrible morning. I saw him, on the steps outside of my church. He was wearing that same fedora."

Billups tensed.

"I'd know him anywhere," Alice whispered. "I didn't say anything. I should have said something."

"It wasn't him," Billups said.

"It **was** him," Alice replied.

"Please, Alice. Can we talk about something else?"

Alice's Thomas sightings upset her brother. Most she did not tell him about. In the last year she'd seen Thomas near her favorite shoe shop and outside of Bonwit Teller downtown. He hadn't aged, but then some people are preserved in the appearance of youth for years and years.

"Those clicking heels, Billy. I went running straight to your apartment, to warn you he was near." Alice could almost smell the angel food cake Thomas had made them eat every week when she and Billups went to his house. Alice locked alone in the parlor, Billups in the kitchen with Thomas.

"I thought I was going to vomit," she said.

"I don't want to talk about this."

Alice leaned forward in her chair. "What would you do if you saw him now?"

Billups didn't answer.

"What would you do?" Alice said.

"Nothing," Billups said.

"What if he tried to talk to you, then what?" she insisted.

"Nothing!"

Billups's hands shook. He had such large, strong hands. In winter they were cracked and ashy and hard looking. If Billups saw Thomas now, surely he would kill him with those hands; he would beat him until he was a tomato someone had stepped on. It was terrible to see a tremor in his thick fingers.

As Billups lowered his teacup to the tray on the coffee table, it slid from the saucer and cracked on the wood floor.

"Oh, my poor Billy!" Alice said. Billups balled his hands into fists in his lap. He looked as though he were going to cry. The puddle of spilled tea spread toward the Persian rug.

"Eudine!" Alice called. "Eudine!"

She appeared with a bucket and rag and got on her knees to sop up the mess. She looked up at Billups. Alice saw something in her eyes. Judgment? Pity? "I'll thank you to keep to your task, Eudine," she said.

"Alice!" Billy cried.

Alice put her arms around her brother. He stiffened in her embrace.

"He's cursed by God. I believe that," she said. "He was limping. He probably had an accident or—"

"I don't want to talk about it anymore!" Billups shouted.

Mother and Daddy, their sisters and brothers, none of them took care of Billups. She didn't expect them to understand what he needed, she and Billy had never told anyone about Thomas. It was Alice who comforted her brother through his night terrors, Alice who'd found him an apartment in the good part of town and helped him pay the rent, Alice who kept him in nice clothes, the best clothes. She knew Billups needed looking after even when he insisted he didn't. She was all he had. It took all of her strength not to call after him when he slammed the front door on his way out.

1:30 p.m.

After two attempts, Eudine had stopped calling up the stairs to consult Alice about arrangements for the party. Just as well, Eudine managed it all expertly, and anyway Alice couldn't face her just then. Instead, she inspected the rooms of the second floor, though most of them were unused and didn't need cleaning. What could Billups have wanted to talk to her about, she wondered, passing from spare bath to guest bedroom. Alice did not like that he had something to tell her that she didn't already know. She used to know everything about him. They had always been united. Royce said Billups's only real problem was that he indulged his dark moods. He advised increased daily activity and physical exercise. Ridiculous. Royce was so intent on uplifting the race—Billy was just another of his improvement projects.

Royce volunteered his services in the slums and donated to the SCLC and Edward Brooke's campaign. Of course, he also had his shirts sent from London. When he discovered Alice used a colored tailor near Wayne Street, he'd told his mother, who'd bustled her off to a shop downtown where the white seamstress was contemptuous even as she kneeled at Alice's feet to pin her hem. Royce's people were bitter and triumphant and invulnerable, they were as cold as the farthest star. How Alice yearned to be like them! And how she hated them—five years she'd been trying to please them and still they treated her like a dog that couldn't quite be trained.

Royce wanted to have a child. He'd converted one of the spare bedrooms to a nursery just after they married. He wouldn't allow anyone in there now. Alice opened the door with the key he kept in the bottom of his sock drawer. The walls were papered with yellow ducks in rain hats, fine for a boy or a girl, he'd said. No child came. Royce sulked and he blamed. In desperation, he took Alice to specialists in New York and Boston. Alice's childlessness was the only thing about which he'd ever displayed genuine emotion—but in this he would not have his way. Alice made sure of it. This was not an act of aggression, Alice told herself when she opened the new packet of pills each month. She was only buying time until things between them were better. And she was still a young woman. There were plenty of years, so many years. As she walked out of the nursery, Alice tucked the key in the pocket of her robe. She left the door wide open.

The sewing room was at the end of the hallway. Alice quickly lost interest after it was outfitted, but she kept the machine because it reminded her of the little corner in the living room on Wayne Street where Hattie had set up a makeshift sewing area. What Mother wouldn't have done for a sewing room back then. Hattie hated Wayne Street. She used to say they were crammed in like rats in a hole. She couldn't stand its shabbiness. Every couple of years she painted the living room a fanciful color: antique rose or Casanova blue or sea breeze green.

A few months ago, Hattie had taken Alice to see a house she hoped to buy. There had been so many hoped-for houses over the years. The place wasn't much bigger than Wayne Street, but it didn't need to be; most of the children were grown up and gone. Hattie led Alice through the rooms. "Finally!" she kept saying. "Finally!" She was to sign the papers at the bank in two days' time. It was absurd to rely on August to put up his share, but Hattie was bitterly disappointed when the sale fell through. And she wouldn't accept Alice's help. Foolish pride, not money, stood between Hattie and the only thing she'd ever admitted to wanting.

All of their lives the Shepherd children had heard Hattie declare the family diminished because they didn't own their home. Renting made them poor and common. They were defenseless, Hattie said, and subject to the whims of the landlord. "All these years," Alice once overheard her say to August, "and we've accomplished nothing. Don't you want to have something to give our children?"

When Alice was a child, Hattie would periodically calculate the sum she'd paid in rent in the course of her years on Wayne Street. Days afterward, she'd roar through the house gesturing at the cracks in the bathtub or the nicked and dingy baseboards. These rages were dangerous. She switched Franklin because he left a window open during a rainstorm and the bedroom floor warped. He was only eight at the time. Hattie dragged him into the hallway and hit him until he urinated on himself from the fear and the pain. Alice applied Mercurochrome to the welts for a week.

It must gall Mother to come here, Alice thought. All of these bedrooms and parlors and not a child in sight. All of these rooms filled with my fine things. Alice returned to her bedroom and sat on the edge of the bed, her hands limp in her lap. The party would begin at nine; next week or next month there would be another gathering, and eventually another and on and on and on—so many conversations to be had in all of these rooms, so much chatting and hosting and pretending to be done. Alice couldn't imagine she'd ever be adequate to the years ahead of her. She felt the house around her as if it were a great maw that had swallowed her whole.

3:00 p.m.

Alice stepped from the tub, skin tingling from the heat of her bath. She spritzed on her favorite gardenia perfume and selected her jewelry: the diamond and platinum choker, her tennis brace- let, pearls for her ears. She stood naked in front of the mirror—the jewels buoyed her, they made her courageous. I am a wealthy woman, she thought. I don't have to be afraid of anyone anymore. Alice put on her slip and bathrobe and went downstairs to tell Eudine she needed her party dress.

The ironing room door stood open. Alice crossed the kitchen and went in. The back window was steamed over, but she could just make out a bril- liant red bird perched on a bare branch of the back- yard's oak. When Alice turned her head and saw Billups and Eudine all wrapped around each other, she nearly said, "Isn't that something? A cardinal in February!" Because both bird and embrace were impossible, Alice thought she'd imagined them and she squeezed her eyes shut. She looked again and the bird was gone. But there was Eudine smooth- ing her hair and Billups springing away from her and clearing his throat. Alice stepped backward into the kitchen. "Excuse me," she stammered. As though it were she who had done something she shouldn't.

Billups came into the kitchen. "I've been . . . I

was trying to tell you . . .." He faltered. He looked at Eudine, who'd followed him out of the ironing room and stood a few feet away. She nodded at Billups in encouragement; when he returned his gaze to Alice, there was something light and lifting in his eyes.

"We're going together," he said.

Alice couldn't stand the authority in his voice. The declaration of this thing he'd done behind her back, this decision he'd made without consulting her. Eudine held her chin high; her eyes were fixed on Billups as though Alice were not there.

"Snake," Alice whispered. "Jezebel."

Eudine tugged at the bib of her apron, though it was already straight, and said, "I think I better go."

"You ought to be ashamed!" Alice shouted. She started down the hall after Eudine. Billups blocked her path.

"Calm down, Alice. You're just getting yourself worked up."

He rested his hand on his sister's shoulder. She tensed.

"I know this is a shock, but I tried this morning . . . I've been making some, some changes. I'm . . ."

Billups looked around the room as though something could save him from this discussion, as if something might scoop him up and fly him away from Alice.

"I'm moving next week. I found a place I can afford on my"—Billups hesitated—"on my salary."

Alice stood in front her brother, shaking like a terrier, but she didn't say a word.

"Alice? Alice?" he said. "Maybe I should go. This isn't the best time, with the party and everything."

"This is what I'm talking about, Billy," she said at last. Her voice was low and strained. "You can't make right decisions. A tryst with the maid? And moving? To what neighborhood? You can't afford anywhere nice."

"I got a job. I'm the new filing clerk at Girard Hospital, $5,600 annual salary. I'm done with part-time and switching from one thing to the next."

Look at him. All puffed up with pride.

"That's a woman's job," Alice said.

"It's a good job," Billups replied weakly, eyes downcast.

Poor Billy! He wasn't up to all of these changes. He wouldn't be able to manage it.

"You're not thinking, Billy," Alice said. "We've been through this. You know part-time is best. You don't need to work at all if you don't want to. There's plenty of money."

"**You** decided part-time was best," Billups said. "**You** decided I had to have that expensive apartment. I can stand on my own!"

"By working as a flunky at the hospital."

Billups shook his head. "I knew you'd do this.

I've been working for two months and I didn't tell you because I knew you'd act this way. Look, look at this." Billups pulled some folded pieces of paper from his pocket—Alice's weekly checks, uncashed. "I've been fine without them," he said.

"You think you don't need me? Because of a silly little job? And Eudine? Really, Billups. She cleans my toilets."

"Who are you to decide who's good enough for who? Royce's family thinks you should be cleaning their toilets."

"All I wanted was for you to be happy! I've done everything so that you could be happy."

"I never asked you for anything. I'm sorry you feel so guilty but I can't do anything about that."

"Guilty! I have been trying to help you!"

"You wanted to buy your way out. And what good has it done you? Look at yourself, Alice. You turned into some kind of black Miss Anne sitting up in this big house zonked on those pills Royce gives you—wandering around here like a zombie and staring out of windows. Let it go, Alice. It's making you crazy."

"Look how you blame me. You blamed me when we were children and now you're blaming me for being upset about it!"

"It wasn't you Thomas took in that kitchen every week!"

The two stared at each other in shock. Billups

had never said it aloud. He inhaled deeply to steady himself.

"I don't blame you, Alice. I used to think you should have told somebody, because you were older and you were supposed to be looking out for me. But I haven't thought that for a long time. We were just kids. But you have to stop talking about it. Stop apologizing, stop trying to drag me back there. You know what I want, Alice? I want to be normal. I'm twenty-three years old. I want to get married. I want to go to my job every day. I want to pay my bills and make my way and be a man."

"I married Royce so I could take care of you," Alice said.

"You married Royce because you wanted to be better than everybody."

"You don't think much of me, do you?" Alice asked. "How could you say I don't care for you?"

"I didn't say that."

Not my Billy too, Alice thought. The only person on this earth who needs me, who doesn't condescend or undermine. Not him too. They stood in silence. After a time Billy shifted his weight from one foot to the other and straightened his jacket as though he were going to leave.

"Billy?" Alice asked quietly. "Does Eudine know about Thomas? Maybe she should. Maybe I should tell her." Alice called into the living room, "Eudine!"

Even as Alice felt the sting of her brother's palm against her cheek, she could see he couldn't quite believe he'd done such a thing. She fell under the force of the slap. She must have cried out because Eudine ran into the kitchen and helped her into a chair. Alice's lip throbbed, and her thigh was cold where her bathrobe flapped open. One of her pearl earrings had fallen onto the floor. Billups bent to pick it up, but Eudine waved him away.

"She's just a little thing, Billups," she said. "You shouldn't have put your hands on her."

"I know," he answered, near tears. "I know."

"Go for a walk and get yourself together," Eudine said.

She was talking to Billups, but it was Alice who stood. She walked past the black-suited caterers in the dining room. She waved away a woman carrying an armful of lisianthus and calla lilies and another with a tray of serving silver. No one called after her, for which Alice was grateful.

5:30 p.m.

The day had cycled from darkness to darkness, and there was Alice at the top of the stairs as she had been that morning. The guests were to arrive in three and a half hours. Royce's return was imminent. Alice had been trying for some time to rouse herself and finish dressing before Royce got home, at least that, to spare herself his reprimand and its consequences. She rubbed the side of her face where Billups had slapped her; the corner of her mouth was slightly swollen. The family would gossip about it. She hugged her knees against the chill that settled over the upstairs at nightfall.

"Mrs. Phillips?"

Alice didn't reply.

"Mrs. Phillips," Eudine called again. "I got to get the last of my things from the kitchen, then I'll be going. Do you think . . . can I come up instead of yelling up the stairs?"

"You most certainly cannot!" Alice ran down the stairs, but when she found herself face-to-face with Eudine in the foyer, she was suddenly unsure what to say, what tone to strike.

"Well, I guess that's all then," Alice said. She wanted to ask about Billups, where he'd gone and if he'd come to the party later, but she couldn't bring herself to acknowledge that Eudine might know something about her brother that Alice did not.

"I'd appreciate it if we could settle up now," Eudine said.

"Settle up?"

"My pay."

"Oh, yes. Yes." Alice didn't have the wherewithal to tally Eudine's hours or find her checkbook or any of the rest of it, so she said, "I'll mail the payment. I need to review your hours."

"It's nothing to review. I worked three days this week. Three days' pay, I'm owed."

"Dr. Phillips should write the check, since it's the last one."

"I don't understand . . ." Eudine sighed. "Alright. It would be a help if you could send it sooner than later." She turned toward the kitchen.

The caterers banged and clattered in the dining room—a troop of paid strangers readying the house for Alice's family, another troop of strangers. Eudine would soon be gone. She would not return the next morning or the next and nor would Billups. Oh, this empty house!

"You can't just walk out of here!" Alice called. "You know there are things that ought to be said!"

"What do you want me to say?" Eudine asked, turning to Alice.

"That you're sorry! Aren't you decent enough to be sorry?"

"I'm sorry you had to find out about us the way you did. And I'm sorry for what Billups did this afternoon."

"That's none of your business!" Alice said. "Don't say a word against him! You shouldn't have his name in your mouth!"

Eudine shook her head. Alice felt her disapproval like a second slap. In a rage, she rushed to her desk in the parlor and pulled out an envelope.

"Take it and go," she said, reaching into the

envelope for a thin stack of twenties. "I never want to think of you again! After all of my kindness!"

Alice shook the money in Eudine's face, and when she did not step forward to take it, Alice flung it at her. She would have spat had she thought to. The bills, thrown with such scorn, fluttered in the space between the two women and landed near Alice's feet. Even in her disdain, she was ineffectual. A uniformed young man pushing a cocktail trolley paused briefly at the parlor doorway and gaped at the spectacle—the twenties on the floor and the lady of the house a shrieking harridan in a bathrobe. Alice began to sob with such force that she was bent double and had to rest her hands on her thighs to steady herself.

Eudine took a handkerchief from her bag and held it out toward Alice. The gesture, despite its pragmatism, its lack of emotion, seemed the greatest of kindnesses to Alice. She was a starving thing that had been offered a morsel of food, however meager. She kneeled on the carpet. Eudine disappeared briefly and returned with a glass of water. She stood next to the weeping woman, eyes tactfully averted, until Alice calmed.

"I better be going now," she said, handing her the glass. "It takes me a while to get home."

Alice wiped her eyes on the sleeves of her bathrobe. "Are you going to keep carrying on with my brother?" she asked quietly.

"That's not the right way to call it."

"He has a lot of problems, you know. He's a good boy, but he can't take care of himself. He might think he can but he can't. What will you do, live together in North Philadelphia? He isn't accustomed to that kind of . . ."

"I don't live in North Philadelphia."

"Well, wherever, but . . ."

"No buts. I don't live in North Philadelphia. And wouldn't be nothing wrong if I did. It's just a place like any other place, don't mean you can put me in a box."

"I never put you in a box."

"You done nothing but put me in a box and now you're mad 'cause I won't stay in it."

"I wanted to help you!"

"Help me? By talking down to me all the time? You're plain bedbug crazy, you know that? Either you put me down or you moon after me, like I'm supposed to love you up like a baby."

Alice felt on the verge of some knowledge, as if all of this time there was something she needed to know, and if she knew it, she might be free. She rubbed her cheek. She wished she could take Eudine's hand; her palms would be warm and dry, a bit calloused—healing hands. The opposite of Royce's indifferent, clinical touch or Billups's huge trembling paws.

"I've been by myself, you see. And I never had

anyone to tell things to. So much has happened to me. You have no idea. I get confused sometimes about what . . . about how to be. I've tried to be so many things and I haven't managed any of them. You seem like . . . I thought you knew how to manage."

"I don't know nothing more than you do," Eudine said.

"You know Billy," Alice leaned forward. "Do you think . . . do you think Billy will abandon me?" she whispered.

It was not the right question. As soon as the words were out of her mouth, Alice realized she had asked the wrong question and didn't know what the right one was. Eudine looked away. Alice had embarrassed herself. I have embarrassed myself, she thought. But what am I if I don't have Billy to take care of? What kind of person? What kind of life would I have if we weren't both so ruined? And more, what if my ruin is not the same as Billy's? All of this time Alice had been thinking Thomas was their shared affliction, but it could be, it could be that something had changed, and it was just her, just Alice, ruined all by herself. Here was her precipice, here was her verge. Alice backed away from it as if it were a cliff's edge.

She stood and wiped her eyes, tucked a strand of hair behind her ear.

"You can't imagine what a job it is to take care of my brother. It'll take you all up," Alice said.

"He can take care of himself. You got to let him be."

"I have tried."

"That's not true."

"You won't be able to do it. I'm the only one who can."

"That's a shame you think that," Eudine said. "For your own sake."

The front door swung open. Billups stood on the threshold. He was pale with cold.

"Billy!" Alice cried.

They would make up; they had to. Alice stepped toward her brother. Eudine stepped forward too. Billups angled his body toward his girlfriend and smiled. He smiled I'm sorry and I didn't mean to disappoint you and thank God you're still here. Their embrace slashed into Alice like the first flare of a migraine—that sudden and that breathtaking.

The living room's chandelier shine and the light caught and gleaming in the cut crystal glasses and silver candelabras were reflected in the bay window. There was Alice, small and dull in the foreground. Outside, it had begun to snow. The flakes, white and fat as dandelion fluff, shone in the light from the street lamp. A man, head down, approached the house. The collar of his dark coat was pulled up around his neck. When he passed beneath the streetlight, Alice saw he wore a fedora.

"Billy! Do you see him there?" she said, pointing to the figure advancing in the snow.

"Call the police! He's right here!" Alice looked at Eudine and her brother. "Why are you just standing there? Don't you see him?"

She crossed the room to the phone on the desk and began to dial. Billups and Eudine exchanged glances.

"Billy, we have to do something!" Alice said.

Billups gently took the receiver from his sister's hand and led her back to the bay window. He put his arm around her shoulders to stop her shivering.

"It's Royce, Alice," he said. "See?"

"Royce?"

"Yes, Alice. It's alright. It's just Royce."

Alice looked through the window. It was true. The approaching figure was her husband. Though he looked at her with concern, though he raised his hand in greeting with such kindness, Alice knew that after the party Royce would convince her to excuse herself to Floyd and her guests. He would tap two white pills into her palm and tell her she needed her rest. The evening would go on without her while she lay upstairs in the bedroom, the blankets pressing on top of her like a body, the skin of her lips cracking in the hot dry air. She would wake deep in the night feeling light and heavy at once, as though her head were a balloon filled with water. She had failed today: she wasn't dressed and she hadn't managed her household, she'd fired Eudine. Billups too was going. He'd leave the house and walk along the slippery flagstones until, as if a curtain had closed behind him, his figure was lost to the falling snow. A little while after even his footprints would disappear. Alice knew these things were coming, and she rested her head on her brother's chest. She wished the man outside really were Thomas, so she and Billups could again have the same enemy and the same fear.

Franklin

1969

A sampan appears. Low to the black
water and grenade distance from my post
on the shore, it sails out of the mist that
descended at nightfall.

Yesterday morning I was given my
assignment: I am one of a ten-man squad
to be deployed to an island at the edge of
a large bay. I'll keep watch on the beach
while the others plant mines. We sail
out at 04:00. In the briefing I was told
to look out for indigenous vessels, junks
and sampans. Later that day Pinky and
Mills and I were walking to the chow
hall when the lieutenant yelled over his
shoulder, "Seaman Shepherd! Don't fuck
this up." Mills and Pinky laughed. Pinky

said, "You can't watch for sampans on the bay at night." I asked why, and all he said was, "You'll see."

Three men ride in the sampan, two at either end and one in the middle; the conical peaks of their paddy hats are pressed close to their heads. They paddle out of an inlet at the far end of the beach. Their arms move in graceful downward arcs. The oars dip; the water ripples. The oars come up; the water ripples again, and the canoe pushes forward. The one sitting in the middle trails his hand along the surface of the bay. Between his legs sits a large sack of something heavy and soft, creased in the middle and slumping over on itself. The sampan is black and wooden, less than two feet high with ends that turn up like a banana's. The men sit straight as toothpicks, squinting against the beam from my flashlight. The boat does not list.

I fire two warning shots in the air. "Identify yourselves!"

The men in the boat throw up their hands and in their haste one of their oars falls into the water.

Fishermen in sampans are not to be trusted. In our briefing the lieutenant said it should not always be assumed that they are fishermen. They paddle along in that quiet way they have, then reach under their bundles of fishing net and pull out grenades or MAC-10s. Some even have napalm; brass did not tell me that. Mills and Pinky did, and I believe them.

"Stand up! Stand up with your hands in the air."

I hear the wet suck of boot falls on the sand behind me. Mills yells, "Drop it! Fucking drop it!" even though none of the men in the boat is carrying anything.

First one stands and then another. The boat trembles and lurches. Two more shots are fired. "I said stand up, motherfucker!"

This, I realize, is my own voice—hoarse and frenzied, shouting at them though I know that they have to rise slowly and one at a time or the sampan will overturn.

"That one in the middle won't fucking stand up!" I glance at Mills to my left. "He won't fucking stand up!"

I took my eyes off the target. Never take your eyes off the target. The one in the middle finally stands, and the boat nearly tips over. He squats to steady himself. I almost fire. I almost do. One man turns out to be a woman. She is steadier on her feet than the other two. She turns her head slowly and looks at us like we are a bunch of wilding monkeys.

"What's in the sack?" I call. They don't respond.

"They don't speak English," Mills says.

"They understand. They're faking. Dump the sack!" I motion toward the bundle with the muzzle of my rifle.

I fire a fifth warning shot, this one into the water near the sampan. The man in the middle reaches down and heaves the sack over the side. It sinks silently into the bay.

"Get out of here," I say. I keep the woman in my sites. She looks sneakier than the others. She's the one that will fling the grenade if there's one to be flung. Mills motions for them to keep going. He moves his rifle laterally in two swift motions.

"Move along! Fucking move!"

"Shit, Shep. They leaving!" Mills says. I don't tell him about the burning at the base of my spine. I used to think the pain was just fear but now I know it's a premonition. The sack on the sampan set my back on fire.

"Get the fuck out of here!" I shout once more, though one of the fishermen has begun to paddle with the remaining oar, and the sampan is creeping forward.

Mills walks away, shaking his head. I am alone again, pacing my small territory, a narrow strip of sand at the edge of the island. I imagine the fisherman's bag was filled with specially kitted-out grenades that will wash onto the shore and explode in the sand.

I squint into the darkness. A fist of thick gray cloud drifts back and forth across a high half moon. The bay and beach are moon bright and then dim and moon bright and then dim again. Now, with the moon hidden behind the clouds, I see only the outlines of things: tall blocks of rock rising out of the water, our junk moored a half mile down the beach, the silhouettes of my squad members on their knees in the sand. In the shallows, turtles knock their shells into one another and hiss. I cock my head to the side and listen for human sounds, more paddles in the water, more sampans gliding over the sea.

In a few hours we'll have completed our mission and then we'll load up the junk and sail away from here. Behind me my

squad is busy digging holes in the beach.
I lived near a butcher when I first got
married. He was always working when I
walked by. He hummed while he worked,
which made me think he was a happy
man. Listening to the shovels pushing
wetly through the sand, I remembered the
sound of his knife cutting through flesh.

I am afraid the mist over the water
will creep onto shore and settle over the
sand so that I can't see snakes coming
toward me. My neck aches with the strain
of scanning the sand for them. I squeeze
the trigger of my rifle, softly, slowly until
I feel the pressure building under my
fingertip, until I am a fraction of a second
away from the satisfying pop of the
trigger's release. I light another cigarette.
I have written a letter to my wife—my
ex-wife, I suppose I should call her—our
first communication in almost a year. I
think she's really finished with me this
time. I'll never be finished with her.

Sissy. She's back in Philadelphia. If
she is at her sister's house, she might be
laughing with her mouth wide open, her
fingers gesturing as she talks. Or more
likely, she is a little blue and staring out
of the window with her hands folded in

her lap. I know all of her moods and the way they play across her features, but I am still awed at the configuration of lips and eyes and cheeks that make up that face that I love. Out of all of the others I could have loved. My Sissy.

When we crossed the threshold into our apartment on the day we got married, a maple leaf blew into the living room. It had turned a deep crimson that darkened to burgundy around the edges. Sissy said that fall was all blood and gold, and I held the leaf and said, "Well, here we got the blood." We went back outside to look for the gold. I found a yellow leaf on the sidewalk across the street, not a speck of brown on it. I can't imagine doing that with anyone else—something as silly as looking for fallen leaves in the street, but with her it wasn't silly at all. I gave her that gold leaf, and she put it on top of the red one and wrapped both in a handkerchief that she pressed into a flat neat square with the iron. We didn't have any ribbon, so she cut a scrap from the lining of the dress she got married in and she tied up that handkerchief and put it in a pull-out drawer under the bed. That was only two years ago.

The clouds roll back, and the moonlight throws the area into high relief. There

are hundreds of small islands in this bay.
In some places they are so close to one
another that if I floated between them
on my back, my toes would touch one
and the crown of my head would touch
its neighbor. The smallest are just hunks
of dirt no bigger than city block squares
of cement, but they have crazy colored
flowers growing all over them. I don't
even know if you'd call them flowers,
they're waxy and spiky and bright as neon
signs. Mills told me this bay is one of the
Seven Wonders, but I've never heard of it.
I patrol the biggest island; there's a whole
jungle growing in the middle of it. I wish
I could have seen all of this in some other
way, without a rifle and the junk full of
bombs.

I don't know where Mills gets all of
this beer. We've been drinking since
reveille. There's a glimmer of something
bright in the sky—can't be a star because
it blinks too much, or a flare because it
didn't sail upward and then fade, or a
plane because it's stationary. I've never
seen so many unidentifiable lights in the
sky as I have since I've been here. Pinky
said the sky over the bay is haunted. "Sky
can't be haunted," I said. "You'll see," he

answered. Then he laughed, and I knew he was making fun of me.

A few feet out from the shoreline something splashes. I get my rifle up quick. Something's coming for me right out of the water. I'll shoot it to tatters; I'll make it Swiss cheese. It breaks through the surface. A fish, a goddamn flying fish. It glides for a hundred feet or so and dives. I lower my rifle. Something black and convex floats right next to the place where it disappeared under the water. It doesn't move, so it must be one of the islands. The small ones are no bigger than a coffee table. Must be one of those, must be.

I smell like stale cigarette smoke and rancid meat. I taste the smell in my mouth. My tongue and teeth are mossy. I can't imagine what my breath must be like. I ate a can of tuna earlier and some crackers; my other meals were beer and coffee. I can't remember the last time I went an entire day without feeling like vomiting. My beard has grown in irregular patches. Beneath the hairs, red bumps flare in clusters.

I'd like to think Sissy wouldn't recognize me, but that's a lie. She's seen me this ugly. When I get back to the ship,

I'll start a new regimen: I'll limit my beers to the evening, after chow. I'll stay out of fights and the brig. I think I can do that, get myself together. I've done it before, though sometimes I think I am just a bleary drunk, and the periods when I am clean and shaved and useful, I am only hiding from myself.

I got a letter from Sissy last week. She wrote: You have a baby girl, born September 13th. I wasn't going to tell you, but she looks just like you, down to the flecks of hazel in her eyes. I don't know what you're going to do now that I've told you. I don't know if I want you to do anything. I was going to keep the secret but I know that the things you try to hide come out when you least expect them to. I don't want my baby to have a liar for a mother. She is five months old. Her name is Lucille.

I met Sissy on Chicken Bone Beach. White folks started calling it that because they said we dropped chicken bones everywhere; it's the only colored beach in Atlantic City. We started calling it that too. Ain't that a shame? There were a few bones scattered in the sand. Mother went with us once and she spent the afternoon shaking her head and clucking her tongue. "Negroes don't know how to keep anything nice," she said. The beach wasn't really as bad as she made it out to be, and it wasn't so much that we were dirty as it was that the county didn't clean it up like they did the white beaches. Seagulls swooped down to peck at the chicken bones. They cracked them with their beaks, ate out the marrow, and left the hollow bones to bleach in the sun. You had to be careful, I remember, or you'd get little bone splinters in your feet. That summer Uncle Lewis bought a brand-new Buick but he'd only take four of us at a time. He said it was unseemly to drive around with a car full of Negroes piled up on top of each other.

I saw Sissy standing in line to buy a pop from the man who walked up and down the beach dragging his portable icebox along the sand. She had a brown mole on her cheek, and the first thing I thought was how pretty she was despite that blemish. I was barely out of high school but I'd had my share of girls, I liked them thick in the thigh with Dorothy Dandridge faces. Sissy had that mole, but there was something in the way she held her pop bottle, as delicately as if it were a china cup. I didn't talk to her that day, but I spent the week scheming about how I could get her. I knew enough to realize that I'd have to say just the right things and mind my manners, maybe make some promises. I'd let her know I had a good job as an electrician's assistant down at the Navy Yard. I'd borrow Uncle Lewis's Buick and drive her downtown to a concert at the Latin Casino. I'd pull her chair out for her, buy her a cocktail, and look her in the eye with this Romeo stare I'd been perfecting. She'd let me kiss her when I dropped her off, and then it would be only a matter of weeks. I knew just how to play it. I would start the next week.

The following Saturday came, and she wasn't there. I drank my pop and laughed with my friends but I never stopped looking for her out of the corner of my eye, and the more I didn't see her, the more the beach looked squalid. The sun felt too bright; the bathing-suit-clad bodies around me were oily and speckled with birthmarks and bumps and hair. I passed the afternoon walking from one end of the colored beach to the other. It wasn't very long, but it was far enough for the soles of my feet to scorch on the sand and the skin on my nose and shoulders to burn. The gulls annoyed me. I was so out of sorts that I didn't go out that night. I spent the following week trying to convince myself that what I felt was just disappointment at not having the chance to mess around in the backseat with a nice girl. When she didn't come the next Saturday, I felt a buzzing in my temples.

That week I asked around and found out her name and where she lived. It wasn't easy; she didn't come from our part of town. I took a bus down to

South Philadelphia. I hadn't been there before. I had lived in the same city my whole life and I had never been there. I remember I was surprised at the quiet and the neat row houses. I had imagined trash in the gutters and shifty niggers on the street corners. Sissy answered the door, and I took off my hat when I saw her. She stood looking at me from the other side of the screen, and I held my hat in my hands and said, "I'm Franklin Shepherd. I'm sorry to disturb you but I saw you at the beach in Atlantic City and I wondered . . . I wondered if we couldn't go out walking one evening." I never talked like that, but standing there in front of her, my head emptied and all I could call up were old-fashioned, country things. She smiled and nodded and told me to come back on Friday evening, so I did. I was nineteen then, and Sissy was twenty-two. We married six months later.

I missed the sunset this evening. Night fell while we were surveying the area on the junk. I was drunk and playing cards with Mills and Pinky. One minute it was day and the next, darkness had fallen. I make a point of seeing the sunset. Even if I am on duty, I go on deck to watch the sky darken into twilight. It helps me remember that this strange place is still the earth, and I am still on it.

In the briefing they told us there are
enemy hideouts all over this island. If I
were to walk deep into the trees near the
beach, I would find a village. The people
that live there would hear me hacking
and stumbling through the jungle and
by the time I arrived, they would have
disappeared into the bush, babies and all.
Protocol says we should burn villages we
find in enemy territory. But we don't have
to do that; we're laying mines instead.
The enemy will paddle their sampans to
the beach or moor their junks or walk out
of the jungle. They will step onto the sand
with their load of supplies, and the mines
will blow them apart. Their eardrums
will shatter; their legs will blow off of
their torsos.

"Shit!" someone says behind me. I turn
and see some of the guys backing away
from a hole in the sand. "Fuck, fuck,
fuck," someone says. They triggered a
mine, but it's a dud. I don't want to die
a rotting drunk patrolling a beach so far
from home it may as well be the moon.
I have a daughter in Philadelphia who
doesn't know she needs me. Lucille is
made up of all of these things that are
like mine—maybe she has my mouth

and chin, or maybe she'll be good with numbers like me—and she doesn't even know that I am somewhere in this same world with her. She's still a baby, but when I think about her, I see an older girl, four or five, in a pale green dress. She calls me Daddy, or maybe Pop, and all the work I have to do to prove myself worthy of her is already behind us.

That dark thing a couple of hundred feet out is bobbing. I don't think it was moving before. I could ask one of the guys to take a look, but they already think I'm crazy, which is why I'm patrolling instead of laying mines. I shine my flashlight on it, but the beam doesn't make it that far. Is it closer to the shore than it was a few minutes ago? It's a little darker than the other islands, maybe. Everything out there is just a silhouette, but it's blacker, I think, than the rest. I walk out into the water until I'm up to my knees. I wish I could remember if I'd seen it during the daylight, if there was an island right there. I heard the enemy have little black submarines with periscopes no wider than a stovepipe. Command put us out here like sitting ducks. That dark thing is bobbing, I'm sure of it now.

Earlier today, after our recon, Mills and Pinky and I stripped off our clothes and ran into the sea. I expected to feel a firm sandy bottom like at the beaches at home. Instead, I slipped on the slimy muck beneath the surface. The water looks so clean, so transparent and warm. I had been looking forward to a swim all afternoon, but the seawater was syrup on my body. The others whooped and dove. I waded out of the water near tears. I wanted the Atlantic. I wanted Chicken Bone Beach—the water always a little too cold, the waves knocking the wind out of you, the granules of sand scratching against your calves when you swim in the shallows.

It is 03:00 hours. A washed-up jellyfish glows on the sand. This whole place feels as though the sea spit it up. I've been carrying my response to Sissy's letter in my pocket. I take out the letter and squat in the sand near the lights my squad set up. I smooth the paper open on the butt of my rifle and write: I would like to hold Lucille and to feel her beating heart and see the soul of her looking out through her eyes. My handwriting is scratchy and uneven; the letter doesn't look like it was written by a man worthy of fatherhood. What I have written is flowery and insufficient. What I want to say is let's try to be a family. I am here and still alive. Give me another chance to become somebody decent. Sissy doesn't want to hear all of that again, so instead, I tell her I'll be furloughed in one month. She likes things to be clear, and my furlough is the only fact I can offer her. The paper is damp from being in my pocket, and I have to press hard with my nub of pencil. I put the letter back into my pocket.

I don't mention my life here. There isn't much I could say that Sissy would understand—the warm beer and the waiting and all of the chores we do to fill the time, checking the same lines and cables we just checked the day before or polishing the railings even though they're not dirty. I used to think the discipline was noble, but now I wonder if the brass understands that people are getting killed. It's ridiculous, disrespectful even, to keep mopping the same patch of deck when men are dying. Mills says it's better when you go on missions. Better than what, is my question. I've been on plenty of missions and I have begun to feel that

I am not quite as human as I was when I came here. I don't know if I can get it back. I try to hold on to that image of Lucille in her pretty green dress, but I have another vision too, in which, a few years from now, I stand across the street from Lucille's school. Every day I watch her climb the steps holding Sissy's hand. She hasn't ever met me, and I know that's for the best. Nobody ever thinks he's going to become one of those failed men, those bums that normal people won't make eye contact with, ashy old men with cirrhosis and matted hair and a room in a flophouse. And nobody ever thinks—I didn't before I got Sissy's letter—that those old men probably have wives and children who have had to forget them.

My squad has almost finished seeding the beach. When it's done, we'll get on the junk, finish the job, sail out of here.

When Sissy and I lived on Bevere Street, I used to go to a local bar called Fat's. It was a nasty little place that stank of spilled beer and Lucky Strikes. Sometimes the southern guys came in to play the spoons—cracked-knuckled, rheumy-eyed old men with raspy voices. All of the songs were work-gang chants or blues about how a bow-legged woman left them in Alabama. But those old guys would sing, and I felt my heart unzip. I mean it; something in my chest unfastened. I have never felt anything as profoundly as I felt those songs, not love or regret or wonder, not even, until I came to this war, fear. I would have been a musician like Floyd if I had known that part of myself sooner. It's too late now. I'm always saying that; I wonder what I think I still have time for.

I used to stay out late playing cards at Fat's three or four nights a week. I had a good poker face. The more I drank, the better. When I won a decent amount of money, I would give some to Sissy or buy something for the house. One time I bought us an armchair, paid outright from a furniture store on Greene Street. I had them deliver it to the house while Sissy was visiting her sister. When she came home, she found me sitting in that brand-new chair and grinning. She looked at me and at the chair and said, "I appreciate the thought but not the means." She never would sit in that chair. Later, after it was gone, she said it stank of liquor that had leaked through my pores; she said the smell of it broke her heart.

It got so there weren't enough games at Fat's, and I had to travel all over the city. I played men with wads of twenties in their pockets who would break a bottle and cut you if they didn't like the fact you'd taken their money. I never got stuck up. Most of those guys liked me alright because I clowned them and could drink them under the table. My hands would be numb with whiskey, but I could always drink one more, and nobody ever carried me out of a bar. Those games lasted until five or six in the morning, until there was nothing left to bet.

One time a guy bet his sister. What the fuck kind of world is this, I thought, but I won that game and took my prize. I didn't go home to Sissy for days after that. I stayed out playing until the wee hours and then staggered into the prize's bed. I can't remember her name. I don't believe she ever knew mine. She was too drunk to do anything but fall asleep. In the mornings I went back out to drink. There are a lot of bars, more than I would have imagined, open at eight o'clock in the morning. I went to a few and felt like I was stepping into all of the sadness in the world. After a couple of days I ran out of money, so I borrowed some. I ran out of that too, and I went back to work at the Navy Yard. When I showed up, they said I didn't have a job anymore. I stayed away from home for two more days because I was too ashamed to face Sissy.

On the sixth day, I crawled home like a roach. Sissy was gone. I was too drunk to do anything about it, so I slept for a long time. I kept waking up to varying stages of daylight: dawn, then midafternoon, then dusk, then midafternoon again. The liquor cleared out of my system, and I sat straight up in bed shaking and thinking of Sissy. My liver hurt, that's not supposed to happen but it did. I had a liver ache, and the only thing keeping my heart pumping was Sissy and the thought that I could get her back. I cleaned myself up and put on a nice suit. I looked like the guys I played cards with. I saw in my own face the slack-jawed, dull-skinned puffiness that old drunks have. There's a rabid look that goes with that doughiness; if somebody drops a nickel, those guys will run out in the street to pick it up, like a dog chasing scraps.

I splashed on a quarter bottle of cologne and went searching for Sissy at her mother's house and her sister's apartment. They looked at me like a piece of filth and wouldn't tell me where she was. I tracked her down at her friend's place and went over there the next morning. It was cold, but she was sitting out on the stoop in her coat. She saw me before I saw her. She cursed me and all my ways. She cursed my mother for bringing me into this world, and my sisters for doting on me, and every bar in the city for serving me a drink.

"Doesn't anything matter to you?" she asked.

I got down on my knees. It wasn't an act to win her back; I would have laid on the ground in front of her if there had been room on the stoop. I told her I loved her and that I'd do better and all of the other things men say when they don't deserve forgiveness. I meant every word, but she shouldn't have taken me back. You can't let somebody like me off so easy. I don't know what's wrong with me. It's not like I don't know I'm doing wrong or like I'm powerless to stop myself. I just do what I'm going to do, despite what it'll cost me. After, I'm truly sorry. I regret almost everything I've ever done, but I don't suppose that makes any difference.

Sissy's father was a gambler and a drunk. She wasn't innocent of my faults. I got a job unloading trucks at a department store and I took her my earnings. I told her to put it aside for the house, for when she came home. I didn't touch a drop or play a single hand. It took two months for her to agree to try again.

The day Sissy came home I bought a broom and mop so I could scour the house with new, clean things. I didn't want her to have to cook, so I went around to Wayne Street for a batch of fried chicken and some collards. Mother knew Sissy liked gizzards, so she fried some of those too—though she hardly spoke to me. She had saved four thousand toward a house she wanted to buy, four thousand dollars from taking in laundry and working part-time in the high school kitchen. I was to contribute another thousand. I had to badger her into accepting it. She said it was shaming to take money from her children, but she really wanted that house so she finally agreed. Well, she and I both knew what had happened to that money. When I got to Wayne Street, I was too embarrassed to bring it up to her; though evidently I wasn't too embarrassed to take her chicken.

I laid the table for Sissy and me. She walked into the apartment tentatively, like you would step onto a sheet of ice if you weren't sure it would hold your weight. She looked at the food and said, "I guess you've been around to your mother's." She went into the bedroom and sniffed the sheets. In the living room, she moved an end table and straightened out the doily on the back of the sofa. The food got cold while she walked through the rooms rearranging things.

"I like to keep the cooking oil in this cabinet next to the stove," she said.

And, shaking an empty box, "How'd you make out with no sugar? You must have been getting your coffee at the diner."

Then, "I don't want any liquor in the house."

She unpacked her suitcase and hung her clothes in the closet. What a relief it was to see her dresses hanging next to my suits. She put a little bar of blue soap in the dish next to the tub and ran her fingers over a dark line of mildew in the tile grouting.

"I can get that out with some lye."

After she pulled on her slippers, she said, "I guess we ought to eat your mother's supper."

We ate in near silence, like a rich couple in a movie. I reached for her hand, and she flinched, so I waited a few minutes, then tried again. A crease in her brow looked as though it had deepened, and I noticed that she had put on rouge and lipstick. I didn't like that. I wanted us to be husband and wife again with no pretenses between us, nothing for show. She hadn't worn makeup since we were dating, and it made me feel like a man she didn't know and who didn't know her. I wanted her to walk around in her slip like she used to, with her hair in pin curls tied up with a silk scarf.

"I never took you for a fool," I said. "I never mistook your kindness for weakness."

She sighed. "Well, I don't suppose you meant to. I don't suppose my father meant to do that to my mother either. But he did."

"I'm not him."

"You're not far off."

"I'm not him," I said again.

For the first time that evening, Sissy looked me in the eye. "I put aside my better judgment for you. I did when you came to my house and asked me to go out walking on our first date, and I'm doing it now. I'm terrified, but I'm doing it anyway. I want you to understand that."

She came over to my side of the table to clear my plate. The lilac powder and hot-comb smell of her knocked me out. The nylon whisper of her stockinged thighs brushing together made my hands twitch.

"Baby," I said.

She put those plates down and led me into the bedroom. When I woke up at 6:30 to get ready for work, she was still asleep, but the room was warm, and I realized she had gotten up sometime before dawn to turn the heat on for me.

"What the fuck?" That's Mills talking. We're shouting at each other. The blood is pounding in my temples and my palms are slick. "What the fuck?" he yells again.

"There's something out there, man," I say, pointing to the dark thing just off shore.

"That's a goddamned rock, Shep! And you ain't even aimed all your shots at the water. You just discharged half a round into a beach full of live mines. What the fuck?"

"You don't see that? I've been watching it for hours." I raise my rifle again, staggering a little with the effort.

Mills is mad now.

"Put that down! Put it down!"

I lay the rifle on the sand, and Mills is up in my face poking his finger into my chest and shouting. I shove him away; the force of it makes me fall backward onto the sand. He's on me, all swinging fists and flying spittle. He's half drunk himself and only manages to land one on my shoulder before Pinky comes and breaks it up. He pulls me to my feet, says maybe I should take a break, maybe all three of us should take a break. The other guys in the squad have stopped digging. It's dark but I swear one of them is looking at me and shaking his head.

"I don't need a break. I'm protecting you motherfuckers. There's some kind of sub out there. What the hell else was I supposed to do?"

"You figured you could shoot the sub?" Pinky says.

"Right there, two hundred feet out, to the left."

"That ain't nothing. It's a rock."

"Look close," I say.

"Look like a rock I'm looking at close," Pinky says.

Mills is standing a few feet away from

us, but I can tell he still wants to take a swing at me. "I see it. It's a fucking rock," he says.

"You got to calm down." Pinky leads me over to a stand of mangroves, and we sit on the sand. It takes me a few minutes to realize that he's taken my rifle and propped it against the roots of the trees. I think I might throw up.

"It was a sub," I say, though now I'm not so sure. Pinky lights a joint and hands it to me.

"Alright, man. Okay. If it was a sub, don't you think they'd come out by now? We been here all night." Pinky's laughing. "You was going to sink a sub with a rifle, huh?"

We sit and pass the joint for a few minutes. My nerves settle. I don't know if it's the joint or Pinky. It's true, if they were going to get us, they would have by now. He calls over to Mills, "This nigger really thinks he saw a sub."

Mills doesn't answer.

"Come on, man. We ain't blown up. Come on and help me laugh at this fool."

Mills walks over and sits. It's like that with us. One minute you're angry enough

to draw blood, the next you're sharing
a joint. I want another beer but I don't
think they'll give me one.

Pinky has a tattoo on his arm that
reads Black Patti. He says she was the one
that got away. I need a good laugh, so I
say, "Tell us about Patti." Pinky has a
thousand Black Patti stories.

"No man, not now." Pinky says.

"Come on. Mills here wants to hear it,"
I say. Mills cracks a smile.

"Yeah," he says. "Let's hear a little
Black Patti."

"What'd she do?" I ask.

"What'd she give you?" Mills adds.

Pinky's grinning now. He says, "That
bitch gave me the mess around.

"I used to go around her house, made
a date first and everything. Then I would
show up, and her mama would answer
the door and tell me Patti wasn't there.
So I say, 'Respectfully, ma'am, where'd
she go?' And that big woman would rear
up and say, 'I believe Patricia had another
engagement.' So fa la la, that damned
lady. She had her nose so high in the air
she could smell the birds farting. She
thought she was Leontyne Price. And

she'd slam the door in my face. Then I go to a party and damned if Black Patti wasn't there with some other cat."

Mills pulls a beer out of his back pocket. We pass it between the three of us.

"Now y'all know Patti was knock-kneed. She was not a nice-looking woman. But she could wind. I'm telling you she could put it on you. She had me all messed up."

"She was shaped like a chicken, right?" Mills says. "With little bitty chicken legs."

"And her mama ain't know nothing about how she was," Pinky says. "I remember this one time she had me come over in the afternoon. Her mama was sleep in an armchair with the *Ladies' Home Journal* in her lap. And how about she was snoring with her head hanging down? Reading about how to make a lemon meringue pie and she's making noises like a truck. So me and Black Patti go to her room and we get it going. I don't know how long we was at it. But I had a good start. Patti liked to pretend she was shy, you know. So you had to sweet talk her. You had to say, 'You sure are a pretty girl,' and call her sugar and spice and all that stuff. She did have a pretty smile, I'll say that about her. And she smelled like heaven, like silk and rich ladies. She had a little dresser covered with perfume her mama had bought so Patti could get the Negro doctor lived around the corner. So anyway, we going good when Leontyne starts hollering in her fa la la voice. 'Patricia, Patricia, Dr. Nelson has come calling. Isn't that a delightful surprise!' "

"Aww shit," Mills says.

"Don't you know Patti pushed me off her! I tried to hold on to her 'cause we was in the middle of something, you know. So she's there with her bra undone and starts whaling on me. She smacking me all in my head and neck like I was a wayward child. Then she's kind of hissing at me under her breath, 'Dr. Nelson is here. Get up, you idiot. We have to finish this later.' She pushed me right down to the floor, and I'm laying there stunned. She had strength like she been working in the fields. I saw stars. There's Patti staring at herself in the mirror and spraying herself with damn near every perfume on that vanity. I'm on the floor tangled up in my pants. Then she looks at me and says, 'Oh, you gon' get out of here.' She starts smacking me again. That bitch smacked me all the way to the bathroom and out the window. I'm falling out the window and last thing I hear is Patti's mama, 'Patricia, let's don't keep Dr. Nelson waiting.' I'm half naked so I get behind a bush and damned if Patti don't come outside with a lemonade on a silver tray. I'm behind a bush with grass up my ass, and Patti's having a beverage on the porch."

Mills is slapping his thigh, laughing. "And how long this went on?"

"A year. A whole year climbing out windows and getting stood up. I had a broken heart."

Mills guffaws.

"I did, man. I think Patti worked some roots on me. I was walking around town all jacked up. I went to the hardware store and cried all over the wrenches." Pinky's laughing at himself now.

"Some women get in your soul," I say.

Mills and Pinky look at me. "It ain't all that deep, man. Damn," Mills says. "What happened after a year?" he asks, but just then our commander walks over.

"Y'all want a fan and some drinks with

umbrellas? Get the fuck up so we can finish and get out of here." He spots the beer Pinky tries to hide behind his back. "And throw that away," he orders. He probably has one in his own pocket.

I pick up my rifle and walk, carefully, back to my post. It's true, that black thing isn't big enough to be a sub. Could be a mine though. Could be whatever that fisherman heaved over the side of the sampan. Could be a diver's back, if he were dressed in black and his head and legs were submerged. But why would he float like that? That doesn't make sense. Pinky and Mills said it was a rock, so it's a rock. The pot has stopped working. I'm so tired I can't feel my legs, but the fear is vibrating in me like an engine. I walk to the edge of the sea and throw up in the water. Maybe it'll wash out to that floating diver. Heh. That'd be a nasty surprise for him.

Sissy bought some new houseplants and borrowed a rug from her mother's house. The apartment looked nice, more like a home than it had before. I guess that was because we'd earned it, because we'd survived something.

We had been back together for a month when a

couple of repo guys knocked on the door. I didn't have enough money to settle what I owed, and all my begging and pleading didn't stop them from taking that armchair I'd bought and the sofa and table and bed with the pull-out drawer.

At least I can say I didn't run away that time. When Sissy got home, I stood in the empty living room and told her what happened. I remember I had my hands in my pockets because I wanted to be a man about it. I didn't want to fidget or cover my face with my palms. Those guys had emptied the pull-out drawer under the bed, just turned it upside down and let the contents spill out onto the floor. Sissy's things were in a pile in the middle of the room: a camisole and a slip, her music box with the lid that broke when it hit the floor. There was a shoe print on the folded handkerchief with our blood and gold inside. I don't know why I didn't think to pick that stuff up. To this day I wish that I had. I wish she hadn't had to see her private things scattered on the floor like that.

Sissy looked at me the way her mother must have looked at her father a hundred times, with disgust and resignation and disappointment. She stared at her precious things for a long time, then picked them up and packed them into her suitcase. "I'll be back for the rest of it," she said.

I started crying then.

"I'm sorry," I said. "I'm sorry. I was going to pay them when I got . . . it's from before."

Sissy rushed at me, her hands balled into fists. She hit me in the gut. I mean, she punched me hard enough to wind me. Do you know that I was relieved? Sissy was on me with both fists, and I was so relieved because something true was happening between us. She was going to leave me for good, because I was the ruin of her. I have looked at my father many times and wondered how he could stand knowing he was my mother's ruin. He was too weak to leave her. Mother should have thrown him out and saved them both, like Sissy was saving the two of us.

My squad puts the last mines in the ground. They level off the little mounds of sand where the mines are buried. If the enemy is coming, they'll come now. We'll be out of here in twenty minutes. I realize that I have spent the last twenty-four hours thinking I was going to die. They have only twenty minutes left to kill me. I trot up and down the beach with my rifle sights on the dark thing out there. Twenty minutes ticks down to fifteen. My legs are shaking and my chest is tight, but I keep moving. I want to see my daughter. I want

to explain to Sissy that I couldn't possibly be the same fool after what I've been through tonight. In my hours on this beach I have been so close to death that I am almost my own ghost.

We've finished packing our gear. I try to get another beer, but Mills refuses me. Behind his back, one of the other guys tosses me one. Mills sees him and says, "You want him shooting at invisible choppers this time?" The guy shrugs. "Could have been worse," he says. We walk toward the junk, and all I can hear is the frog song swelling and the hiss of my beer opening.

Our junk is black and old and stinks of rot and fish like everything else in this bay. I take my place on the starboard side in the rear, and we push away from the shore. The black hump in the water is just visible through my rifle sights. I beat you, I say. We clear the shallows, and two of us open a hatch at the back of the ship. A retractable plank is lowered, and two of the hands roll the sea mines down the gangway. They slip with a little splash into the black water. They will detonate when something interrupts their magnetic field. I was told that fish are not big enough to do this nor a man swimming alone. We head toward the open water.

Mills is standing next to me. I whisper, "Cheat death and shame the devil."

"You one crazy nigger," he says.

"I'm not dead though," I say.

"Nah, not today, anyhow."

I don't want to look at that island for one more minute. I stand at the prow and look out toward the sea beyond the bay. I'll have to rewrite my letter. I practice folding it into different shapes; if I make it pretty, Sissy might not throw it away. Maybe she'll let Lucille hold it, a paper toy her daddy made her. I fold it into a boat, just flat, you know, with a triangle for a sail, but I don't think little girls like boats, so I change it into a swan.

Sissy borrowed the money to get the bed back; she let them keep that armchair. A few months later I joined the service, and after I left, she took up with a man who wouldn't gamble away the furniture. Alice told me about it in a postscript to one of her letters. Just a postscript to tell me my wife was living with somebody else. Imagine that. Sissy's mother must have been half dead with the shame of it. When my leave came up, I went to Philadelphia.

I went around to Sissy's apartment in the middle of the afternoon. She and this man had a little place on a block in West Philadelphia where neither of them knew anybody. I wore my dress blues. The brass buttons shone in the sun. I felt like the son of a king come to claim his bride. I didn't deserve to feel that way, but the fantasy helped me keep my head up. As I climbed the steps to the apartment, I realized that it was remarkable that Sissy hadn't found another man before now. I'll tell her, I thought, that I had come to offer her a divorce. We could go down to the courthouse that same afternoon. I'd free her so she could have an honorable life with this man she'd found. But then she opened the door and she was every inch my Sissy, with the mole on her cheek and her iron gaze.

"I came to get you," I said.

She stood on the threshold looking at me and blinking quickly. I thought she might cry, but she wouldn't give me the satisfaction.

"We're still married," I said. "What kind of way is this to live?"

"I'm living like a woman, Franklin," she answered. "My mother and my sisters won't speak to me, but it's worth it to live like a woman. I don't know when you suddenly got so concerned about my sacrifices."

And there we were in a movie with me as the penitent husband and Sissy as the wronged wife. I said my lines and she said hers. I don't know why I didn't take my hat and go.

"I came because I love you," I said.

"I believe you think that's true," Sissy said.

She never moved from the doorway. Her hands hung at her sides, and she made a fist, then released it again like she did when she was nervous. Little circles of gold, the sunlight reflecting off of my brass buttons, played across her face. I looked over her shoulder into the living room. It looked alright; it was cozy. Everything in the room was light and lifting, white curtains, a cream sofa, a pale rug on the floor.

"I'm a better man after being in the service." I knew better than to say that to her, but I couldn't think of anything else. "I arranged for a truck to help you move your things. I can call right now. It'd be here in ten minutes."

"A truck!" Sissy laughed in spite of herself.

She knew I didn't have a truck. I don't know what I would have done if she'd called my bluff.

"A truck!" she said again and shook her head.

She let me into the apartment. I sat on her white couch. She sat opposite me in a straight-back chair with wooden armrests. I should have bought her a chair like that, instead of the armchair I got. It suited her better, she was not a slouching woman.

"I haven't had a drink for weeks," I said.

"I can't go with you this time, Franklin."

"So you just going to live like this with this man!"

"He has real feeling for me. I won't call it love, but he's steady and kind. I feel like a lady on a rest cure. You know the kind in books, that sits in a chaise lounge all day and looks at flowers? That's just what I do. I go to work and come home and tend the house and don't think about anything. You wore me out, Franklin."

I had come begging to Sissy before, and she beat the hell out of me and left. I hadn't changed since then, but I was still so arrogant I thought I could go over there and win her back. I thought of all the things I could do: I could rage and drag her out of there with my hands, throw myself on the floor and beg for her mercy. I could tell her again that I was a changed man. But I had done all of that before. I had played all of my cards, and Sissy wouldn't be lied to or cajoled. I caught my reflection in the living room window. I looked like a pile of fool's gold, you had to squint from all the shine coming off of me—buttons, shoes, epaulets. I asked myself why I wanted her back so badly. I couldn't answer the question, but I couldn't leave that apartment either.

I got up from my place on the couch and stood crying in the middle of the room.

"I love you," I said.

"We have to be finished, Franklin."

She got up and took my hand. I didn't understand how she could hold my hand like that and
tell me no. She stroked my palm with her fingers. I
leaned into her because I needed some strength to
walk out of that door, and she was the only one I
could get it from. We hugged for a long time, and
then I kissed her neck and her shoulder. I kissed
her eyelids and the hollow between her collarbones,
and we sank down onto the white couch together.

After, while she was buttoning her blouse, she
said she'd walk me out to the corner, and you
know we walked out to that corner holding hands
like we did when we were dating, before I messed
everything up.

"You take care of yourself," she said and turned
quickly toward the house before I could reply.

That was over a year ago. I had not heard from
Sissy since then, until I got her letter about Lucille.

**We steer the junk toward the gulf. It's
slow moving, but we are making distance.
The stars and fog fade in the pre-dawn
and the sky brightens. Behind us the
island is a ridged black silhouette, ever
receding. A sampan glides along the
surface of the water near the shore of
the island. Probably a fishing boat, they
come out at this hour. The occupants, a
boy and an old man, look into the water**

and then at us. The boy is pointing at our junk, at me. I swear he's pointing right at me. The old man pushes the kid's arm down.

The sampan is lifted on a low wave, gently, like a ballet dancer lifting his partner, and pushed closer to the island. There is a boom. The boat is lifted higher on an upward moving column of water. The explosion echoes and echoes. It bounces from one island to the next. It knocks in my brain and chest. I am holding my breath but do not notice until it is quiet again, and I take a deep inhale that makes me cough and sputter. Mills lets out a low whistle, says softly, "Shit."

I get another beer and drink half in one gulp. I look into the water for floating body parts. I want to see the boy's head. I ought to be forced to acknowledge what I have done. Most of my missions are at night. I shoot into the darkness and sail away before I have to count bodies. It was the same with Sissy. I was a violence in her life and left before I had to face the damage I'd done; with Lucille there would be more recklessness, more hurt, more promises I don't keep, more destroying the people I love.

I make a wager: if I see any evidence
of the boy whose life we took, I will
never drink again. I set my beer on
the deck and wait. I scan the water. A
light-colored unrecognizable something
floats toward me. I lean so far over the
starboard side I nearly topple into the
water. Behind me Pinky calls, "Suicide
ain't the answer!" I hear a round of
guffaws. I lean and squint. The floating
object appears to be a finger, then a leaf,
then a discarded bandage. The current
shifts, and the thing is carried away
from me. I pick up my beer, finish it off.
When we get back to the ship, I'll go to
sleep, and when I wake up, I'll have the
shakes and I won't have the willpower to
sit on my bunk sweating and throwing
up until the liquor's out of my system.
I'll take a swig of the whiskey stashed in
my footlocker, and the days will go on
as they've been. And it's not like I don't
know I bet my family on an exploded
boy's body parts. I know that. I know
what it means about the kind of man I
have become. Or always was? I can't tell
anymore. It is almost a relief to know
that the people I love are free of me, that
I don't have to lie to myself, that I don't

have to pretend Lucille would be better off for knowing me.

I reach into my pocket and throw my letter for Sissy into the bay. There was a picture in the envelope, which lands in the water next to the folded paper swan. In the photo I am standing at the dock with my ship behind me. I'm in my dress blues with my white hat pulled low over one eye. On the back of the photo it says, For you and little Lucille. Love, Franklin. Saigon, 1969.

Bell

1975

AFTER WALTER LEFT, Bell decided to lie down and not get up again. For a month she lay in bed looking out the window to the street below. The glass was sooty. Had she known this window would be her last and only portal to the outside world, she would have cleaned it while she still had the strength and the will. Music thumped in the apartment next door. The bass seeped into her bones and skull with a thud-thud like a nail into soft wood. Bell lifted herself onto her elbows. She was feverish; the sheets hurt her skin. She renounced the pain, as she had renounced her life a month before. It had been surprisingly easy to decide to die. She simply stopped doing the things required of her: taking her medicine or getting out of bed in the morning or going to work or hoping

Walter would return. There wasn't any food left in the apartment. Bell was hungry. She felt as though her insides were nothing but air—if she got up from her bed, she would bounce lightly along the floor like a balloon.

If Bell kept still, her cough wasn't as bothersome. It wasn't too bad in the daylight hours, but at night it was persistent. Like most of the men I've known, she thought. Ha! Some nights, between the cough and getting in and out of bed for water, she hardly slept at all. The bouts bent her double and left her gasping for air. When Bell was a child, she'd gotten whooping cough and pretended the wheezing was caused by moths fluttering in her chest. My moths are restless today, she'd say, or my moths are sleeping. Now her moths were always restless, and her chest ached as though their wings were knife blades beating against the walls of her lungs. She was thin and growing thinner. Right after Walter left and Bell still had some desire, she'd reached under the covers to pleasure herself and felt her hipbones jutting out like the hard angles of a table. She had always wanted to be thin like her sisters. Careful what you wish for. Ha! Now her stomach was almost concave. Bell rubbed her hand over it and coughed.

When she could sleep, Bell dreamed of her moths. In the dreams she was a length of broken tree bough, no wider around than a sapling. Her arms and legs were bare branches growing out from her tree body. She was burnished brown like the cane Walter carried. At the top of the long stalk of her, her head was elongated and graceful like the statues they sold at the African bazaar in West Philadelphia. The cough never hurt in her dreams; it was a vibration in her chest that moved up through her lungs. When it reached her throat, she threw her head back and opened her mouth. Her moths flew out—legions of them, all moon-light silver.

If she stayed in bed long enough, she might fos-silize into a wooden carving of herself, Bell thought. Eventually someone would come into the apart-ment and instead of finding her flesh and bones, they would find a whittled pole polished to a high shine. It would probably be the city marshals and wouldn't they be surprised to find they had evicted a stick! A notice had been slipped under the door: Bell had thirty days to vacate for nonpayment of rent. She wondered when Walter had stopped pay-ing the rent and what he'd done with the money she'd given him for that purpose.

A couple of months before, he'd given her a dress, a loud, ugly fuchsia thing that made her look like a whore. It didn't have any tags, he'd probably taken it from some other woman's closet. Maybe he'd brought it to her to assuage his guilt, if he had any. Likely he gave her the dress because he wanted her to look cheap. Bell was happy to please him in that way. It was the correct size, though by the time he gave it to her she was already losing weight and it was too loose.

Walter said, "You losing your sugar."

"I ain't losing nothing, baby," Bell replied. "I got my sugar right here."

She thrust her hips toward him. With Walter she could be as dirty as she wanted to. He had no interest in where she came from or who she had been before they met. Bell told him that she was from a neighborhood like the one where they lived now, with trash in the gutters and cool, predatory young men hanging around in front of the chicken take-out place. She pretended that she spoke like him and acted like him and was like him, though that wasn't true, though she was Bell Shepherd from Germantown and had graduated from high school and had one year of college. But these things were so distant they seemed like the details of someone else's life. She knew now that she had always been a woman of base instincts. She had cycled through men of varying fortunes and possibilities until she arrived at Walter, with whom she could indulge every whim and to whom she was accountable for nothing.

He didn't talk about his past much. He didn't talk much at all, and if he did, it was generally about something that had happened within the last few hours. He had tried at various intervals to make his living as a number's runner, a pimp, and a drug peddler, but he wasn't successful because he couldn't keep the past, even the recent past, in his mind. So he had become a petty thief and a hired hand for the neighborhood loan shark. He never had much trouble with the law. He was damned, but he was lucky, and smart for a man who couldn't remember what had happened the day before yesterday. Bell appreciated that about him. She had been with her share of schemers and men who were forever building castles in the sky. All of those dreams made out of clouds; when it rained—and it always did—they were left with nothing but the soggy shirts on their backs. That kind of disappointment was exhausting. Walter was mean as a rat, but he didn't tax her spirit in that way. He was the perfect man for Bell because her spirit was already worn out.

In the two years they were together, Walter had never tried to make Bell believe anything. He didn't even try to make her laugh. Of course, he had the sense of humor of an armored car. He told her a story once, while they were in his car waiting for one of the loan shark's defaulted customers.

"This a waste of my time. The man ain't got the money to pay," Walter said.

"So what will you do when he comes out?" Bell asked.

"Don't worry about it." Walter replied. They sat in silence for a few minutes.

"That discharge money they give you when you come out the service ain't enough to buy a round of drinks. Ain't enough for a pair of shoes. Ain't enough for nothing."

"That's a shame," Bell replied. "A damn shame."

She leaned back on the headrest and closed her eyes. Walter drummed the steering wheel with the pads of his fingers.

"Baby, you have to do that?" Bell asked. "I was going to take a nap."

He didn't answer for some time.

"I washed windows on them platforms." He nudged Bell with his elbow. "You listening?"

Bell, who had fallen asleep, bolted upright in her seat. "What? Yeah, baby, mmm hmm."

"I said I washed windows."

"I heard you say it."

"My cousin had a window-washing business he started, and he came up to my mom's house and asked me to do it 'cause I ain't afraid of shit."

"Mmm hmm," Bell said, struggling to keep her eyes open.

"They hoisted me up there. That thing moves all around. And they got a lot of dead bugs on the windows. You wouldn't think they'd be up so high. You ever been in a boat?"

Bell shook her head.

"This was like being in a boat," Walter said.

"Uh-huh."

"I was washing those windows just fine. They had me tied to a rope that hangs over the top of the building. I did tip the bucket and all the water spilled. I heard some lady yelling on the street. Heh, heh. But it don't do to look down or you might get dizzy."

"Sure," Bell said.

"I was like a surfer up there. Like a mountain goat, sure of my steps, you know."

"I thought you said you spilled the bucket."

"You gon' listen or not?" Walter lit a cigarette.

"Alright, baby. You were up there like a goat."

"I cleaned forty buildings the first week. Second week more buildings. Maybe sixty that week. Good money too, for all that dare deviling."

"How much?"

"That ain't the point!" Walter replied.

"Oh," Bell said.

"Maybe a hundred a building."

"Really? That seems like a lot."

Walter gave her a dirty look.

"Usually it's just me up there, I never saw nobody. But one day there's white cats."

"Where?" Bell asked.

Walter sighed, exasperated.

"In the office! Ain't you paying attention?"

"I am, baby, but you said . . ."

"Suits up in there. Talking. I'm trying to be professional, and friendly. I give them a nice smile and a little wave."

Walter's smiles were a little like a snarl you might see on an animal about to attack.

"These crackers pull the shade! Right in my fucking face. I say to myself that ain't nice, or professional, or friendly. Right?"

"I guess not," Bell said.

"What you guessing for? What if I smiled at you right now, and instead of smiling back, you start the car and drive off? It was just like that."

"I see your point," Bell said.

"Anybody sees my point. A monkey sees my point."

"Okay."

"Shit!"

"Okay."

"I kicked the shit out that window. I mean I put my boot in it. I almost fell off the rig. Next thing I know they hoisting me back up to the roof. I get up there, and they're asking all kind of questions. I go down to the street 'cause my cousin's there, and the police. And he's talking about I had a fit 'cause of the war. I said, 'Nigger, I lay you out right here.' And he says to the police, 'See, I told you, he can't control himself.' "

"So what happened?" Bell asked.

"I ain't washed no more windows."

"That's all?"

"What else you want to happen? Shit."

Bell chuckled. That Walter. She had a sudden craving for the soup her mother made when Bell was a little girl. If she were at Wayne Street now, Hattie would put hot mustard poultices on her chest and feed her syrup made with cooked onions and honey. No matter that Bell had tuberculosis and that nasty stuff wouldn't do a bit of good; Hattie would give it to her anyway. How many times had she and her siblings choked down that mixture? It had cured more often than it hadn't. Hattie had kept them all alive with sheer will and collard greens and some old southern remedies. Mean as the dickens, though. Well, she's an old woman now, Bell thought. She hadn't seen Hattie in nearly a decade. And she didn't have a single picture of her and would die without seeing her face again. Alice and Ruthie said Hattie had mellowed, she laughed now and again and smiled a lot and bounced her grandchildren on her knee. You're going to have to go and see her sometime, they said. But it was Hattie who hadn't called her in all of these years, Hattie who wouldn't forgive. Of course, Bell didn't deserve her forgiveness, that was true.

After Bell took up with Walter and moved to Dauphin Street, her sisters stopped coming around; Walter was a criminal, and Dauphin Street was the ghetto. Bell wondered if they knew which building she lived in or what the cross street was. She had been excommunicated from the family. It was the Shepherd way—if one of them was disgraced, she was cut out like a bit of rot on a vegetable. The family might not even hear of her death before she was put in a pine box and buried in the potter's field. Was there still a potter's field? Maybe the coroner would just burn her up and throw her away. They could dump her body in the river for all Bell cared. Maybe she should leave a note for whoever found her: **Just throw me in the Schuylkill and let the fish eat me.** She liked the idea that the men who fished the river would eat bits of her with their suppers.

Bell's craving for soup grew stronger. If she could get out of bed, she could go to the Chinese takeout around the corner for wonton soup. She hadn't felt desire for anything in weeks. The sensation was thrilling. She swung her legs over the side of the bed, planted her feet on the floor, and put her hands on the mattress on either side of her hips. One good heave and she'd be standing. The church in the middle of the block ran a soup kitchen on Saturdays. As if people only needed to eat on Saturdays! Anyway, it wasn't Saturday. She would have seen the line of hungry souls stretching from the church's front door down to the corner. That was a catcalling bunch—mostly the men, and some of the women too. Ha! She recognized a few of them as the men she used to serve at the Belmore Lounge, raggedy drunks trying to hustle her for cheap liquor. She rarely made tips at that place, though now and again some fool flashed his cash—imagine flashing money around in a dump like the Belmore—hoping to get in her pants.

The Belmore was the worst place Bell had ever worked, and the dirtiest. She used to relieve herself in the alley behind the bar; it was cleaner than the bathroom, and there was less risk of somebody drunkenly walking in on her. The customers were harmless for the most part, though Bell's coworker Evelyn kept a knife in a sheath around her calf, like a villain in a Western. She was quick to reach for it. She'd bend at the waist like she was going to tie her shoe and the next second that knife was glinting in her hand like a silver tooth. The boss said, "You can't go threatening the regulars."

"How else will they know to mind their manners?" Evelyn replied.

"I don't want no police in here," he said.

"Won't be, if folks act right."

The first time Walter came to the bar Bell introduced him to Evelyn, and they spent the evening eyeing each other like feral cats. He played pool with one of the customers and lost twenty-five dollars. After the game he asked the man to go into the alley with him to smoke a joint. He came back alone fifteen minutes later, tucking money into his pockets, his knuckles bruised. Evelyn turned to Bell after he left and said, "You need to learn to use my knife if you gon' take up with niggers like that."

One evening Bell was out behind the Belmore having a coughing fit when Evelyn stepped out for a breath of air. "That don't sound like nothing for Robitussin," she said.

Bell still had some cough syrup. It didn't help the cough but it made her sleep. The bottle had rolled under the bed. My God, what wasn't under there: remnants of peanut butter sandwiches, dust bunnies the size of her fist, dead roaches. They would find her body on dirty sheets with all of that nastiness under the bed. She ought to die on crisp white sheets with some soup in her belly. Just a push with her hands and she'd be standing, nothing could be easier. She took a deep breath and a coughing fit came over her. Her eyes teared. She forgot that she couldn't take deep breaths anymore. Those restless moths would get her. She looked out of the window and tried to ease her breathing. She thought she saw Evelyn's car at the intersection at the corner. Evelyn to the rescue, like a Saint Bernard. Ha! As though Bell were trapped on a mountain and waiting for rescue. She wasn't trapped; she'd made a choice. Bell waved at that car on the street below.

———

ON AN AFTERNOON in early summer, months before Walter left, Evelyn took Bell to see a friend of hers who could give her something for the cough. She steered her car down 19th, then onto Morse. Bell looked out of the window at the men standing in knots at curbside. They watched Evelyn's car glide by, sharp eyed as a pack of lions chasing a gazelle. One young man walked in front of the car. When Evelyn hit the brakes, he put his hands on the hood and bent low to peer inside. Bell gasped. He saw that it was two women and sauntered off toward the curb.

Evelyn said her friend lived at the end of the block. They approached what looked like a cul-de-sac. Bell glanced at Evelyn and realized that she had never seen her in the full light of day. The Belmore was sunk in a perpetual twilight; opaque window glass kept it dim even in the daylight hours. Evelyn had something of the Belmore's waxy gray film—too much cigarette smoke and not enough sunlight—but she had high cheekbones and her hair was picked out into a short Afro that shimmered in the sunlight. She wore a man's wide-collar shirt, fitted bell-bottom pants, and lace-up shoes that were double knotted. Bell liked that Evelyn knotted herself up so she wouldn't trip and lose her balance. She couldn't imagine her as anything less than sure-footed. And the way she drove, easy and confident, one hand on the steering wheel and the other arm slung along the top of the seat. Bell leaned back so her head just touched Evelyn's forearm, and Evelyn shifted so her fingers grazed the top of Bell's shoulder.

At the end of the block the crowd disappeared. There wasn't a single loiterer in front of the last house, as though an invisible barrier held the people back. The steps and sidewalk were swept clean, and flowerpots sat on either side of the door. They climbed the steps, and Evelyn tapped lightly with the door knocker. An old woman answered.

"This is the friend I told you about," Evelyn said.

"Good afternoon, ma'am," Bell said.

She knew she sounded too proper. Evelyn glanced at her. At the bar Bell lowered her voice half an octave and coarsened her diction. She told herself that her affectation made her coworkers and customers feel more comfortable around her, but she really did it so she wouldn't feel like a tourist among them and because she thought herself better than they were, and she assumed they agreed. Her feigned accent made her feel generous—like a queen stepping down from the throne to kiss a poor woman's cheek. Now she was embarrassed, Evelyn had caught her in her lie.

The old woman's house was cool and dim and smelled of piecrust and soil. Evelyn and Bell followed her down a corridor to the kitchen at the back of the house.

"Oh ma'am, isn't it nice back here!" Bell said, looking at the butter-yellow walls and lace curtains and the light coming in as though the sun were lemonade pouring from a pitcher. Three places were set at the table, and there was a pie next to a jug of iced tea.

"Folks think it must be a cave in here on account of I keep the front room so cool," she said and let out a low laugh that bubbled up from her belly. She rummaged for something in a drawer.

She must be a hundred years old, Bell thought. She was deep brown and had white hair cut close to the scalp.

She squinted at Bell.

"What's this gal's name again?" she asked Evelyn. "What's your name, gal?"

"Bell, ma'am."

"Bell."

"Yes, ma'am."

"Who's your people?"

"My last name is Shepherd."

"I knew it! I don't never mistake a resemblance. You Hattie's child, from round Wayne Street," she said.

She looked at Bell again, appraising her clothes and shoes and hair. She looked into her eyes so long it made Bell uncomfortable.

"What you doing with yourself, gal?"

"I don't know what you mean, ma'am," Bell replied.

"Firstly my name is Willie. I cain't stand nobody calling me ma'am. Second, you know what I mean. You work with Evelyn at that ol' crazy bar?"

"Yes, ma'am. Willie."

"When's the last time you saw your mama?"

"I don't . . ."

"I lay odds it's been a minute."

Willie had exposed her. Bell was grateful that Evelyn was gracious enough to keep her eyes on her pie plate. What would Walter do in a situation like this? Overturn the table, probably, and shout obscenities at the old woman. Bell rose from her seat.

"Thank you, ma'am, for your hospitality but I think I'd better be on my way," she said.

"Oh, sit down, gal!"

Bell felt a pulling in her chest. She coughed long and hard. Evelyn stood and put her hand on Bell's back.

"You better sit down, gal," Willie repeated.

The coughing fit weakened Bell; she didn't have the energy to leave. Willie's kitchen made Bell miss her mother, though the kitchen at Wayne Street was drab white and Hattie ran it like an army mess. It had never been a place to sit in the sun and sip lemonade. That wasn't her mother's fault, but Bell was angry about it just the same—she had always found in Hattie a place to put the blame. Willie pushed a glass of tea across the table.

"How long you had that cough?"

"Oh, it comes and goes," Bell answered.

"Sound like it's mostly coming," Willie said. "The Belmore ain't no place for somebody got TB."

"I don't have TB! People don't even get that anymore. It's just a cough."

"You been to the doctor?"

"No."

"Where you live?"

"Dauphin Street."

"Long way from home."

"It's only half an hour on the twenty-three trolley."

"You know what I'm talking about."

"I'm alright where I am."

"Don't look like it, but ain't nothing nobody can do about that but you," Willie said. She sighed. "I was there at half your kin's birthing. I guess you don't remember. It's a long time since I lived on Wayne Street. I remember the last boy your mama had, bigheaded thing. Seem like he wanted to bring half your mama's insides with him when he came out, for a souvenir." She chuckled. "Hattie was alright in the end. Your mama was strong as a plow horse. I don't usually find the high yellows to be so."

Willie leaned forward and peered at Bell.

"You ain't strong like she is. You got a soul that cain't be still. Your mama did too at one time, but she wrestled it down. Yours look like it's running you."

Bell pressed a napkin to the sweat beading on her forehead and upper lip.

"You come on with me," Willie said.

Bell followed her through a door at the back of the kitchen and down a short corridor with a creaky wooden floor. The smell of the outdoors intensified, not the city's outdoor scent of tired trees and hot asphalt, but a clean roots and rain smell. Willie opened another door, and Bell stepped over the threshold onto something dense and springy. High windows on three of the four walls faced the backs of other row houses across an alley. The room was bright and hot, the floor layered with pine needles. Earthenware pots, some no wider around than a fist and others so big Bell could have climbed inside, sat on the floor. In the middle of the room a picnic table was covered with multicolored bottles and droppers and thin glass stirrers, stone mortars and pestles, vials of liquids of various shades of brown, drying plants hanging upside down from a small wire rack, and jars brimming with powders. Willie dragged a folding chair from the corner and opened it next to a wooden bench. Bell didn't move.

"I expect you done enough standing around with your mouth open," Willie said.

Long green tendrils drooped over the sides of planters suspended on hooks from the ceiling so it seemed that the room was hung with tattered green curtains. Bell half expected a flock of hummingbirds to rise from one of the pots and hover over her head.

"Half of what's wrong with people today is that they ain't got no place to go that makes them peaceful. I don't reckon you got no place like that."

"No ma'am, I don't," Bell answered.

"I know I couldn't live without the smell of pine needles."

Bell nodded and sat in the folding chair. Willie asked her again how long she'd had the cough and whether it was worse at night and if she had the sweats and how she'd been sleeping. She asked her if her dreams had changed since she got sick and what they had been like before that. Did Bell dream about blood, Willie asked, or crossing dry riverbeds? While she listened to Bell's answers, Willie's hands moved among the vials and bottles. She placed a few in front of her and asked a question. Depending on Bell's answers, she poured something into a mixing bowl or whisked the bottle away and replaced it with another.

"What's that?" Bell said, pointing at a green husk in a jar.

"Praying mantis. Don't worry, you don't get none of that."

"What's it for?"

"Lots of things. Could be to get a man you want but don't want to keep for long. Could be for getting rid of one that won't go away. Mostly it's for show. Folks like to see something strange when they come in here."

Willie crushed the contents of the mixing bowl into a powder. She poured in a clear liquid and made a syrup.

"What's that?" Bell asked.

"Water."

Willie funneled the mixture into a brown glass bottle.

"Make sure you have something on your stomach when you take this. No cow's milk or cheese and nothing cold 'sides a little fruit. Just hot things, spicy if you can."

She handed Bell the bottle. "Nastiest stuff you ever gon' drink. Two tablespoons in a cup of hot water. Hold your nose and drink down three cups every day. And if you got a man or somebody 'round you all the time, you gon' have to tell him you got TB."

"I don't have—"

Willie got up from the table and walked out of the room before Bell could finish her sentence. She followed the old woman, blinking to readjust her eyes in the dim hallway.

"Y'all done?" Evelyn asked when they walked into the kitchen.

"Much as can be, I reckon," Willie answered. She turned to Bell. "Pride brought down a lot of folks. One of these days you gon' have to turn around and look at whatever it is you running from."

Evelyn pushed some money into Willie's hand, but the old woman refused it. Then they were out the door and in the car maneuvering through the crowd. After Evelyn dropped her off, Bell sat on the steps of her building for a long time before throwing away the bottle Willie gave her. Upstairs in the apartment Walter was rolling joints and listening to the stereo at a volume that made Bell's teeth rattle. She went to the bedroom and lay on the bed with Stevie Wonder's tenor in her ears. She fell asleep and woke up to darkness and quiet. Bell never returned to work at the Belmore.

PURPLE AND ORANGE STRIPES appeared on the horizon above the buildings on the other side of Dauphin Street. Bell's hunger had passed, and her arms were stiff from tensing and relaxing her muscles in the afternoon's efforts to rise from her bed. She wouldn't get her soup; she was too weak to stand. Another night was coming, and she would cough and dream of her moths and maybe she would wake up the next morning and maybe she wouldn't. She was too tired to go to the bathroom to fill the water jug she kept by the bed.

Walter, you coward, Bell thought. You liar. What a scene you made, kicking the wall and yelling about how you weren't going to take care of me like some white woman in the suburbs. "This ain't **Leave It to** fucking **Beaver**," you said. "If you ain't going to get another job, I'll be damned if I'm going to pay the bills while you lay around all day." Oh, it was a fantastic show. He'd overturned a chair and shoved her onto the floor and raised his fist as though he were going to bring it down on her jaw. And all because he couldn't admit that he was scared he'd catch her TB or scared that he'd already caught it. Isn't that something—tomorrow-be-damned Walter had an instinct for self-preservation after all.

Bell had fantasized that she and Walter would die together romantically and decadently and in squalor. She had believed in his emptiness and his meanness and his utter disregard for himself and everyone else. But turns out Walter wasn't fearless at all. And if wild, reckless Walter wasn't fearless, then nobody was. Maybe no one could be passive in the face of death, not even Bell. It's true that she had taken to her bed and refused to get up again, but that was the opposite of apathy—it was suicide. All of this time she had been wanting to die and wanting someone to die with her, and she'd thought Walter was perfect because most of what was human in him had already been killed by the time she met him. You fraud, she thought. He'd stormed out after his big blow up and come back the next day with a friend to help him move his things. They took everything but the bed. Bell didn't know if that was an act of compassion or if he just didn't need it where he was going.

She looked around the bedroom. The walls were smudged; the paint was chipping. The carpet was matted and stained. She was seized with the sudden urge to walk to the kitchen—one last walk, one last time to feel her muscles moving and the floor beneath her feet. Maybe something's living in that refrigerator that'll give me a little company. Ha! Before her strength had given out, she paid a neighbor boy to go to the store and bring her a loaf of bread and a jar of peanut butter. A heel of bread still moldered in a cupboard. When Bell was a child, Hattie couldn't afford peanut butter. Sick as she was, Bell had felt a kind of decadence sitting in bed nibbling on a peanut butter sandwich. She wished she could conjure up that neighbor boy now and send him to the store for a can of chicken soup.

What a mess she'd made of things. She let herself want the soup and now a host of other wants marched in by the hundreds. They'd trample her to death, all these things she wanted. What's that Marvin Gaye says you can't avoid? **Taxes, death, and trouble.** Well, I'm dying and I've had my share of trouble, but I haven't paid taxes in five years. Take that Marvin! Ha! Bell leaned back on the bed. She didn't know if it was the tuberculosis causing her to gasp for air or if it was the rush of all her disappointments and her mistakes and her loneliness. Bell lifted her hand to her chest. Her heart beat too quickly. She was floating out on a tide of agony, and soon she would be carried so far she'd never come back.

Walter's eyes used to slide all over the room when Bell had a coughing fit, he'd look anywhere but at her. That bastard. She would give anything for a last glimpse of him, and of her mother. Imagine the two of them in a room together. Hattie would look at Walter like a roach and pretend he wasn't there.

That soup Hattie made must have been a vegetable broth; there wasn't money for meat when Bell was a child. It was salty, with little bits of potato. Bell thought of the soup from the Chinese takeout, the warm liquid going down her throat and the firm give of the wonton under her teeth. She remembered a bakery that sold the sticky buns she used to buy years ago. She couldn't quite recall the taste, but she remembered walking down Henry Avenue with Cassie, holding the warm bun in her hand and pushing down the wax paper so it wouldn't get in her mouth when she took a bite. Cassie would make them walk all the way home afterward so they could burn off the calories. Bell's sisters used to take her to dances. She was never the prettiest one in the room, but she'd always met boys just the same. Two had wanted to marry her—good decent men who had families now and lived in nice houses on Tulpehocken Street. Bell had been disdainful of them; she'd thought them small and ordinary. She'd taken such pleasure in saying no to their proposals and breaking their hearts. Women who married men like that did nothing but shop for groceries and nearly die of boredom. But here I am dying anyway.

BELL REMEMBERED sitting with her friend Rita on a school bus when they were girls of sixteen or seventeen. They were returning from a field trip, and the bus stopped at a red light in a neighborhood some distance from Germantown. Where had they gone on that trip? Bell had been trying to remember for years. She and Rita were deep in conversation, sitting close and leaning into each other in the way girls do. The bus jerked to a halt, and they looked up and out of the window.

"Oh!" Bell said. "There's my mother!"

Hattie was in her early forties then, Bell's age now. Her skin was the color of the inside of an almond, and she had chestnut hair curling down her back. She looked like a woman of twenty-five. When Bell saw her, she wanted to shout, "Isn't she beautiful! Isn't she something!"

In her surprise she didn't notice that Hattie wasn't alone.

"Is that your father?" Rita asked.

Hattie walked arm in arm with a tall slim man. They shared the same long stride, the same rhythm in moving down the block, as though they had been made to stroll down the avenue together. The man looked at Hattie and said something. They were intimate and snug and comfortable with each other. Hattie threw back her head and laughed. Bell nearly cried. She'd never seen her mother laugh that way. She'd never seen any joy in her at all. Hattie had been stern and angry all of Bell's life, and it occurred to her that her mother must have been very unhappy most of the time. She wanted to know her mother as she was in that moment, so beautiful and happy that the bright afternoon paled in comparison. This man brought out a light in Hattie that Bell hadn't any hope of seeing.

"No," Bell said to Rita. "That's not my father."

———

BELL PICKED at some lint on her bed sheet. She coughed. How stoic and constant Mother was, how seething and unfathomable. Bell's sisters used to say that she had Hattie's temperament—secretive and quick-tempered. She had never been afraid of anyone the way she was afraid of her mother, she had never been so angry with anyone and never wanted anyone to love her as much as she wanted Hattie's love. But Hattie was always so remote, like a receding shore as a ship moves farther out to sea.

Bell insisted upon her disappointment with Hattie. She reviewed every moment of her childhood and found it full of Hattie's hands bringing down the belt on her children's thighs, full of Hattie's rages and silences. Maybe she was trying to protect her children or teach them discipline and respect, but Bell could hardly remember a tender word or a kiss. Bell missed her. Wasn't it funny that when she left her mother and the rigors of her house, she had disintegrated bit by bit? She had been free-falling until she landed in this bed on Dauphin Street.

Bell was thirsty. It'll pass, she thought. My thirst will pass and these waves of desire will pass, and I will become tired. I'll be too tired to make a fist, too tired to think, and then I'll go to sleep and that will be that. I'll lie here and silver moths will fly out of my mouth and then . . . If the church is to be believed, I've done enough dirt to send me to hell three times over. I should be scared, Bell thought. But all she felt was regret.

Bell's eyes burned and she grimaced as she would if she were crying, but her body could not make tears. She was a husk, an old dried-up leaf curled in on itself.

Lawrence, as he looked when Bell saw him walking down the street with Hattie all of those years ago, came to her mind. He wore a gray suit and white shirt unbuttoned at the collar, no tie and no hat. He was graceful and strong as an athlete. Lawrence wasn't more handsome than August, but he was a different sort of man. There was something regal and striking about him. He had stayed in her memory like a movie star. She could see him still as he was then, with a burgundy handkerchief in his breast pocket and the wind pressing his jacket against him.

BELL HAD RECOGNIZED Lawrence instantly despite the nearly twenty years that had passed since she saw him with her mother. She was still healthy then, she could not have imagined that Walter and tuberculosis were coming in less than a decade. She was buying a hat. The shop girl was putting her purchase in a hatbox when the bell on the door jingled, and Lawrence came in alone wearing a suit much like the one that Bell remembered. His hair had grayed and there were hollows in his cheeks, but he was still fit and handsome.

"That's a nice one," she said when he paused in front of a wide-brimmed red hat.

"Do you think so? I don't know anything about ladies' hats," he replied.

"It's very stylish." She paused. "Depending, of course, on the age of the lady it's intended for."

"About your age. Too young, if you ask me, to be wearing grown folks' hats."

"I'm sure she's a woman of good taste. Not many people wear hats these days."

"I'm glad that you consider yourself a woman of good taste," he said, chuckling and nodding toward the hatbox in Bell's hand.

Lawrence leaned toward Bell while they talked. He told her the hat was for his daughter. Bell saw how a man so confident and elegant had charmed her mother. This man could have swept any woman off her feet. He knew it; he was sixty if he was a day and he was still turning it on like a faucet.

"I'm Lawrence Bernard," he said.

"I'm Caroline," Bell replied. "Jackson."

They left the store together.

During the third week of their acquaintance, Bell invited Lawrence to a jazz concert. They drank brandy Alexanders. An old man's drink, she thought. While they danced to the band, she told him she would like to see his house. After the con-cert they sat on his narrow front porch drinking lemonade spiked with rum. The April night was cool. He wrapped his arm around her. He kissed her shoulders and took her to his bed. She was prim in her lovemaking with him. Though her eyes were squeezed shut, the experience was not entirely unpleasant, until Bell thought of Hattie. She shook her head violently to rid her mind of her mother's image. Lawrence mistook the gesture for sexual ecstasy. He fell asleep soon after. She lifted the sheet and studied him; his body was still firm. He was vain—his toenails were clipped and filed smooth, the heels of his feet were buffed. He did not look like an old man in the way she thought he would. His stomach was going soft but was still flat. She was suddenly embarrassed and guilty. She rolled to the opposite side of the bed. Here was her mother's lover lying naked next to her. She was thrilled and revolted and decided to stay the night with him.

Bell woke Lawrence next morning and pretended to take her leave. She'd wrapped herself with the coverlet as though she were shy about her naked-ness. He wanted her again, as she knew he would. He was emboldened by the previous evening. They'd forgotten to draw the shade, and the sun-light made the room as bright as a beach at noon. She offered herself to him on all fours. Gone was the previous night's reserve. He was almost aggressive with her; the noises he made were guttural and primal. She enjoyed herself with him because she had reduced him to a grunting, rutting man, just like any other man. Bell felt a fleeting triumph. She had her revenge on her mother, though, of course, she would never tell Hattie. She was doing a terrible thing, but in the doing she was equal to Hattie; equal in pain inflicted and punishment exacted. More than that, she had become her mother in some way—not the angry, exhausted Hattie but the laughing beautiful woman Bell saw from the school bus window.

Bell resolved not to let Lawrence turn the affair into a romance, though he continued to ask her to go to dinner with him or to attend this concert or that one. If I did not have the upper hand, she thought, I might be smitten. She refused to go on dates with him. Instead, they met on Lawrence's porch at twilight and ate sandwiches followed by too many glasses of spiked lemonade. Now and again they took his car to the Chinese place a few blocks away and ordered takeout. He talked about the Panthers and how he thought them too violent. "That Huey Newton is going to die, you mark my words," he said. He told her he might go to Mississippi or Alabama to campaign for Robert Kennedy. The churches were doing good work with voter registration, he said. My brother Six has a church down there, Bell almost told him. That fool's been married for fifteen years and has children by more women than you could count on your hand, but that doesn't stop him from going on about how the Lord would uplift the race if we pray and do right. There's the Church for you! But of course Caroline didn't have any brothers, so Bell kept silent.

"I guess I'm too old for all that woolly hair and fist raising. It broke my heart to see regular colored folks, with their regular clothes and regular hair, sitting at those counters. I've never seen anything so brave."

When he asked her questions about Boston, Bell answered in sweeping generalities that gave the impression of truth. She'd grown up in Roxbury and had an uncle who liked the Red Sox, and, yes, the winters were colder. He would look at her and say, "It's the strangest thing. You look so familiar sometimes." Then he would wink at her and laugh and say, "I must have seen you in my dreams."

It wasn't hard to keep Lawrence from prying; he didn't really want to know much about her, and he was, in his graceful and good-natured way, as withholding about his life as she was about hers. And anyway, they both knew their conversations were only a prelude. Bell would have liked to eat their Chinese food upstairs, to lean against the pillows naked and sweaty and slurp the noodles out of the carton. But Lawrence insisted on setting the small table on the porch. What will we do in winter, Bell wondered. Would they eat in the living room or in the kitchen? By then the affair would surely be over. By then Caroline would be called back to Boston on a family emergency, never to return to Philadelphia. In a few months, maybe less, Bell knew she'd tire of Lawrence. The skin on his neck was beginning to sag, and his erections failed occasionally. She wanted to be disgusted by these things, but she was not. She had stopped seeing other men, but that was, she told herself, merely because she didn't have time. She could not deny that he had become Lawrence Bernard whom she'd met in a hat store a few months before and was less and less the man she'd seen with her mother so many years ago. But that was normal, surely, and didn't signify that her feelings toward him had deepened.

In the fourth month of their relationship, the weather changed abruptly. Bell woke one morning to the crisp, clean air of fall. That evening after work she found herself jumping into a pile of leaves that had been raked to the edge of a lawn. And still in her heels and office clothes. Ha! She walked home smiling and called Lawrence.

"Maybe it's from when I was a little girl and used to get so excited about the new school year, but I am so happy in the fall. I feel like everything is starting again," she told him.

"You want to start again with me too?" he asked.

"Oh, stop it," she said.

"You stop it. I'm sick of you hiding me in the house and using me for your pleasure." He laughed. "Just because I'm old doesn't mean I don't ever want to take my girl out."

"Your what? Your g——?"

"That's what I said."

"Well, I'm not hiding anybody," Bell replied.

"Then meet me at Wanamaker's tomorrow at six o'clock," he replied. "There'll be a surprise."

At 6:00 the next day, Bell rushed down the center aisle of Wanamaker's to the bronze statue of the eagle, where she and Lawrence had arranged to meet. There he is! she thought when she saw him. She quickened her pace. He'd brought her flowers—the bouquet flared crimson against the slate gray of his suit. A small brown shopping bag hung loosely from his fingers. The store was crowded. Shoppers milled around him carrying boxes and bags or tugging children behind them. How striking he was standing among them, how handsome.

"Lawrence!" Bell called. It was only then that she noticed he was in conversation with someone obscured behind the eagle.

She called again as she drew closer, "Lawrence!"

He turned. "Here's my girl!" Lawrence said, extending his hand toward Bell in greeting. The fabric of her skirt fluttered against her legs. She was glad she'd bought a new dress for their date; he was the sort of man who was pleased by new dresses.

The woman Lawrence had been talking to stepped into the aisle, expectant and smiling. His hand was on her elbow.

"This is my dear friend Hattie," he said.

My God, Bell thought, looking at her mother, we're so alike. She knew she ought to say something, or feel something, but her attention fixed on the flat, leonine slope of the bridge of Hattie's nose—the same slope as Bell's own nose. And our eyes have the same slight downward turn at the outer corners. Mother and daughter stood facing each other, each with her hand on her upper chest just below the clavicle. Bell was suddenly enraged with Lawrence. Pathetic old man! So easily duped by sex and youth and flattery. If he had looked at me at all, she thought, if he had bothered to really look at me, he would have seen Mother in my face. The resemblance would have leapt out to him, as it leapt out to Bell in that moment. But then she remembered that she too had been blind to their likeness. She had denied it as a kind of revenge against Hattie. As if to say, I don't want you either. I don't even see you.

"Bell!" Hattie said.

Lawrence looked from Bell's face to Hattie's and then at Bell again. His hand flew to his mouth, such a feminine gesture.

Hattie backed away from them. She bumped into a man behind her and lost her balance. Lawrence rushed forward, throwing the bouquet and the little brown bag to the ground, and caught Hattie as she fell. With Lawrence's hand on her arm, she righted herself clumsily. She looked old just then; it seemed to Bell that the flesh of her face was slack and wobbled a little around the chin. Despite the horror of the moment, the sweetness in the way Lawrence reached for Hattie made Bell think of an old man reaching for his old wife whom he had loved for years and years, whom he had picked up when she faltered for years and years. Hattie had a shopping bag that fell to the floor when she tripped. Lawrence picked it up and held it out toward her. She took it and pressed the brown bag to her chest. She was crying.

"I'd better get to my shopping," Hattie said and lowered the bag. She tried to take hold of the handles, but her hands shook.

"I'll finish my shopping," she repeated, but she didn't move.

Lawrence was talking. He had been talking all along, Bell realized, but she had not heard him because her mother was standing in front of her fumbling with an old shopping bag and weeping.

"She said her name was Caroline," Lawrence said. "She told me she was from Boston. I didn't know, Hattie. I swear I didn't."

Hattie shook her head. Her feet still didn't move. A clerk approached them and asked if everything was alright. She was smartly dressed and suspicious. Hattie turned to her.

"I'm just . . ." She took a deep breath. "I'm just looking for the linen department."

The clerk began to give directions, but Hattie walked away from her toward the exit.

Bell was left alone with Lawrence. There was nothing she could say. She reached toward him. He let her put her hand on his arm for an instant. He picked up the roses and the little bag, handed them to her, then dashed after Hattie. Bell did not hear from either of them again.

BELL'S MOTHS BEAT their knife wings in her chest. The pain was astonishing. Her limbs went slack and her eyes closed, and she was suddenly thrust into a sludgy half-conscious darkness from which she was sure she would not return. She dreamed that someone was knocking on the door. She was in a house like the one Lawrence lived in, and her body was as robust as it had been when she was with him. Bell walked through the rooms effortlessly, taking in great lungfuls of air, feeling the oxygen in her blood, the molecules of it quick as minnows in her blood. She opened the front door. It was hailing. The hail crashed against the railings of the porch and on the eaves. Someone called her name. She couldn't find the source of the voice in the storm.

"Bell!"

She wished the voices away.

"Bell! Bell!"

She woke. The hallucination persisted.

"Bell!"

She was too weak to answer the door. She couldn't keep her eyes open for more than a few seconds. "Please stop," she whispered. "Please stop."

"It's Willie. You in there, gal?"

Willie. Juju Willie with the jungle in her back room—now I know I'm dreaming, Bell thought.

Something crashed in the living room. She heard wood splintering and then a voice.

"Ain't no lights in here?" and "What's that stink?"

Then there were footsteps and someone shaking her shoulders.

"Bell! Dear Lord Jesus. Bell?"

She opened her eyes long enough to see Hattie's face hovering above her and Willie a step behind.

"She's alive," Hattie said.

Sometime later there was a commotion of light and hands, sirens and street noises. A mask was placed over her face. A needle pricked her arm. She slept.

BELL WOKE TO various discomforts: an itching on her cheek where the plastic edge of the oxygen mask irritated her skin, a dry mouth, an ache in her hand from the IV. If she wiggled her fingers, she could see the needle move beneath her skin. How fragile we are, she thought. An apparatus next to her bed flashed green and red and beeped steadily. All of this just to keep one body functioning.

The hospital room didn't have a window to the outside. Half of one wall was a rectangle of glass facing a busy corridor. Hattie was asleep in a chair pulled close to the window. Her head was tilted so it rested on the back of the chair. Someone had tucked a blanket around her; only her face was visible. Look, Bell thought, as she had when she was a girl on the school bus, there's my mother. Bell could have cried in gratitude. Hattie's glasses had slipped down her nose. Her neck will hurt when she wakes up. She ought to have a pillow.

Bell didn't know if it was day or night, a clock above the nurse's desk read simply 11:00. Nurses hurried down the hallway outside of her room, but that gave no indication of the time. And Hattie was sleeping, but that was no indication either. Bell's moths were still. She could feel the weight of them crushing her chest, the knife-winged legions clinging to her lungs like sleeping bats in a cave.

A nurse wearing a surgical mask approached the door to Bell's room. Hattie woke and gestured toward Bell. The nurse shook her head and came in alone. Hattie stood at the window with her hand on the glass. Bell raised her arm in greeting, and her mother nodded at her. Another nurse came along and put her arm around Hattie's shoulder and gave her a Styrofoam cup of something hot. What a shock it was to see Hattie as the object of such affection.

The nurse told Bell she had been in the hospital for three days. She was in quarantine and would be there until the tuberculosis was no longer contagious—at least three weeks, maybe more. She would be given medication to kill the bacteria that caused the disease and other medication to break up the congestion in her chest. She would cough a lot but not like before. Until her lung function improved, she shouldn't try to talk. They would give her a chalkboard and a notepad. She was very lucky; she had nearly died. The nurse injected something into the IV, and sleep closed over Bell like water over a drowning person.

Walter came to see her. He was terrifying; his eyes were red and he paced in front of Bell's room like a caged leopard. Had he always been so frightening? He looked like he might strangle a nurse. When she waved, he came into her room.

"Walter!" she said. "You can't come in here! You'll catch TB."

"You already gave it to me. Look at my eyes. See how red they are? And my teeth."

He opened his mouth. His teeth were gone. A little black ball, not bigger than a marble, rested on his tongue. "What's that?" she asked. He told her it was her sickness, that he had sucked it out of her with such force that it knocked out all of his teeth. Then he swallowed the black ball and left the room. "Walter!" she called after him.

A nurse shook her awake. "Miss Shepherd! Calm down now. Calm down." Hattie watched through the window with both hands pressed to the glass.

Bell spat into a silver bowl the nurses gave her. As the days passed, she spat more and more. First the phlegm was frothy and red as strawberry soda. Her throat hurt from the coughing, but her chest wasn't as heavy, and her breathing was less labored. On her little chalkboard she asked the nurses about the time, or other practical matters, like what day she'd have her next round of X-rays. She couldn't think what else to write. She had intended to die and here she was living. Now her life stretched endlessly, bleakly, before her. She ought to rip the IV from her hand.

One afternoon the nurse came in with pills in small paper cups on a tray. Bell wrote: **No.** She shook her head as the nurse lifted the oxygen mask and held the pills toward her. "Miss Shepherd," the nurse said. "No funny business." She shook her head again. From the corner of her eye she saw Hattie rise from her chair in front of the glass window. When Bell was a little girl, and sick, Hattie had taken her by the chin and forced medicine down her throat. At the time Bell had not recognized this as love. Now, as her mother advanced toward the door to the room, her arm outstretched as if to turn the knob and enter, she wore the same stern expression. Bell saw the tenderness in it—Hattie's tenderness, which was always hard. She swallowed the nurse's pills.

Hattie came every day. Their interaction consisted of waving to each other. On the sixth day Bell wrote, **what is the weather** on her little chalkboard and held it up for Hattie to see. Immediately she felt ridiculous. She had probably written it too small for her mother to read, and Bell wouldn't be able to hear her answer anyway. Hattie would think her silly and trivial. There were so many other things she wanted to say, but she only had a chalkboard and she lacked courage. Tears came to her eyes. Hattie fished a piece of paper and a pen from her handbag. She scribbled something on the paper and pressed it to the window: a drawing of a big dark cloud from which a cascade of slanted dashes fell. "Raining," Hattie mouthed.

From then on their visits began with Hattie's drawings of the weather. She brought a ball of yarn and sat crocheting in the chair by the glass. Hattie was inscrutable as ever, but it was true what Bell's sisters had said—she was calmer, the old rage had receded. There was an ease between them that they'd never had. They had been uncomfortable with each other long before Bell's relationship with Lawrence. When Bell came to Wayne Street for holidays or the odd Sunday dinner, she and Hattie avoided each other's eyes and were stiff and formal if they found themselves alone in a room. Maybe, Bell thought, Hattie hated her because she knew Bell had seen her with Lawrence when she was a teenager. But that isn't true, Bell thought. I'm the one who hated her because she was so joyful with Lawrence, and all I ever saw at home was a miserable woman who heaped punishment on her children—for running on the stairs, for a hint of insubordination, for wanting things she did not think it would be possible for them to have.

Adulthood brought Bell a kind of freedom but no relief. She felt defective in some vital way, incapable of doing the right thing. She was constantly afraid that some force would strike her down for her failings. She wanted to ask her sisters and brothers if they felt the same way. But they'd made their peace with Hattie years ago, maybe because they already knew that the force that would strike them wouldn't be their mother, but something of their own making. At some point in their lives Bell's sisters stopped blaming Hattie for their messes. Maybe Mother didn't know that she was supposed to love us, Bell thought. But she's old now and life does not require her to be so ferocious.

The morning the quarantine was lifted, an orderly moved Hattie's chair into Bell's room and positioned it next to the bed. Nurses took Bell to have her lungs X-rayed. When Bell returned to her room, Hattie was sitting in the chair crocheting.

"This just touches my heart to see you two in the same room!" the nurse said. "You know your mother has been here day and night. Day and night."

Bell and Hattie smiled. The old stiffness returned. It had been easy to be comfortable with each other when there was a glass wall between them. She will not ever forgive me, Bell thought. The nurse left the room.

"The nurse told me you can go outside for a little while tomorrow," Hattie said. She paused and picked at a stitch in her crocheting. "The weather's nice. Sunny."

Bell nodded.

"There's a little park behind the hospital. You don't even have to cross the street to get to it. I guess I can wheel you over there."

Bell reached for her chalkboard, then remembered the doctors had said she could talk. She took a deep breath and said, "Aaaah." She made the sound tentatively, in the way one might put one's weight on a leg that had just been removed from a cast.

"Aaaah," Bell said again. "I sound like a frog." Her voice was gravelly and cracking.

"I don't suppose you should try to say much," Hattie said.

"I guess not," Bell replied.

Hattie's crochet hook flashed through the loops of yarn. Bell wished for a window to the outside—a bit of sky or a cloud, anything to draw her away from that room. She concentrated on her breath. There was a slight rattle when she inhaled and a faint urge to cough when she exhaled.

"How did you know to come and get me?" Bell asked after some time.

"Willie."

"And how did she know?"

"A girl you used to work with. A fellow you know told her you weren't doing so well."

"Walter."

Bell wondered if he'd gotten sick himself, if he was somewhere coughing and wasting in some woman's bed. Walter, that bastard. She wished him well. She clenched her fists to keep from crying at the thought of him.

"A dark-skinned young man came around one

day when you first got here. Didn't say a word to me just stood by the window looking like the devil and then went away."

"Walter."

"He didn't look quite right in the head."

Bell shrugged.

"Willie said you had been sick for some time. She said you came to see her months ago."

Hattie rested her crocheting in her lap.

"You told us to go away when we came to get you. You kept saying, 'Please stop. Leave me where I am.' I thought it was the fever talking, but I came to understand that you were—"

She picked up her hook.

"I guess you know you can't go back to that apartment. I don't suppose anybody told you Daddy and I are buying a little house in Jersey? There's room for you there."

"You finally did it, huh?"

"Only took fifty years," Hattie said bitterly. "It's just a little place, two bedrooms, but your father's happy to have you."

"Are you happy to have me?" Bell asked. She had not intended to say it.

"They said the thick humid air's no good for you. I guess we'll get an air conditioner. I never did like them. They give me a headache."

Bell coughed. Hattie poured ice water into a cup and handed it to her.

"They said you have to drink a lot of water."

A nurse poked her head into the room. "Everything okay?" she asked brightly. The two women nodded. "Meds in one hour!" she said and ducked out. Hattie watched her disappear down the hallway.

"I can't stand to think you were going to let yourself die like you don't have anybody," Hattie said. "You were all set to take yourself right out of this world, and we wouldn't have known. Maybe a few months later the police would have come knocking on my door to tell me. Or maybe they never would have come at all. You would have just disappeared from the earth as if you never were," Hattie said.

She yanked a length of yarn free from the ball in her lap.

"I don't know what brought you so low. I should have known. I didn't see you much, but when I did, you looked like something was tearing at you. I never did know what to do about my children's spirits. I didn't know how to help anybody in that way."

"I just didn't want anything anymore," Bell said.

Hattie looked at her and shook her head. "Everybody's been there. Everybody I've ever met. But you can't just . . . I didn't when I was way down there. "

Bell said softly, "I took you there."

"You mean Lawrence?" Hattie sighed. "No. That

hurt me more than I have words to say, but I've been in darker places. My children died. There's no place darker than that, except maybe another child trying to kill herself."

"It wasn't suicide," Bell said.

"Oh, no?"

Bell had rehearsed the moment when she would have to explain herself to her mother, but now that it had arrived, all she could think to do was apologize.

"I'm sorry," she said.

"Some things you can't apologize for, you just have to try to get around them," Hattie replied. "For your own sake too, so you can have a little peace."

"You're not angry?"

"Of course I'm angry!" She looked at Bell as though she'd have liked to shake her by the shoulders. "I probably always will be. But I've been mad all my life, and I finally figured out that I couldn't keep carrying that with me. It's too heavy and I'm too tired. Time will take care of it, like it does everything else."

"You know that Willie has a whole forest growing in her back room?" Bell asked.

"She did when she lived across the street. I imagine she still does."

"She made me some medicine out of those plants she has. I . . . I threw it away."

"I knew a juju woman in Georgia. She could make a blind man see. Everybody thought she was crazy."

They sat in silence. Bell noticed the heart monitor was gone. She tried to remember when they'd taken it out of the room. Lawrence had probably cursed her to Hattie that night outside of Wanamaker's. He'd caught up to her and told her how Bell had lied and manipulated him. Bell shut her eyes against the memory. She hoped she'd never see him again. He had called Hattie his friend, but Bell supposed he still loved her. She wanted to know how their affair had ended. She imagined there had been bitterness between them and years of separation, after which they had met again, recently and by chance. It was too painful to think Lawrence had been her mother's only friend over the decades of Hattie's loneliness, and Bell had destroyed that too. She wanted to tell her mother she didn't think anyone decent had ever loved her, aside from Lawrence, and that after the first month, her relationship with him didn't have anything to do with Hattie. Bell continued seeing him because he was a good man and because he cared for her. Bell and her mother had in common that joy at stumbling upon love after years of disappointment.

"I saw you and Lawrence on the street when I was a girl. I never forgot him. I took up with him out of spite and I'm sorry even if apologizing can't make it any better," Bell said. She blinked away a tear that had formed at the corner of her eye. "I wanted some of the happiness I saw in you when you were with him. I wanted to see if he could make me feel that kind of joy."

"My God, but you are hard to love," Hattie said.

"You never laughed like that with us, the way you did with him."

"You leave my memories alone! They're mine. Me and Lawrence all those years ago, that's mine and you can't have it."

"You won't ever forgive me, will you?" Bell asked.

"I have spent the last eight years trying. I've succeeded as much as I ever will," Hattie said. She rewound the ball of yarn. "The new house has a nice front yard—I'm going to put flowerbeds in. It'll just be a little garden, but I can spread out. I never felt like I could spread out."

"Ha! I feel like all I ever did was spread all over the place."

"Like a house on fire. You never did learn that sometimes all you have is your own dignity and self-control."

Ruthie had said once that Bell and Hattie were just alike. It wasn't true. Hattie was stronger than Bell could ever be. She didn't know how to tend to her children's souls, but she fought to keep them alive and to keep herself alive. That was more than

Bell could say. All of them—Hattie and Willie and Evelyn and even ruined, crazy Walter—were little lights; sparks flying upward in dark places, trying to stay alight though they were compelled toward ash. They were nearly extinguished one moment, then orange and luminous the next. Who was Bell to have tried to unmake herself in the face of their strength? Maybe it was her cowardice as much as her betrayal that Hattie could not forgive.

Hattie stuck the crochet needle through her ball of yarn. "I'll bring you some soup tomorrow," she said.

"Alright," Bell replied.

Hattie gathered her things: she put her crocheting and her sweater into a cloth bag. Bell remembered seeing her mother put clothes into a cloth satchel a long time ago, maybe a year after she first saw Hattie and Lawrence from the school bus window. Bell's stomach tightened, she didn't want that memory.

Bell was a teenager. She'd been reading in the living room when she heard Hattie and August shouting at the back of the house. There was a crash and the sound of plaster breaking. August charged out of the kitchen in his bathrobe, and as the door swung shut behind him, Bell caught a glimpse of her mother. Hattie leaned against the counter, head down. She squeezed the baby too tightly, desperately, as if Ruthie were all she had in the world. August was up the stairs in an instant, then down again a few minutes later. He slammed the front door on his way out of the house, and with that, Hattie flew from the kitchen with such fury that Bell ducked behind the couch. Hattie sent all of the children outside. She was crying. "Go on! All of you, go to the park!" she shouted. She waved her arms and shooed them out of the house. She went upstairs and came down holding Ruthie and carrying a bag. A shirt fell out of the satchel, and Hattie put the baby down on the couch and shoved it back in. She picked up Ruthie—the one she'd chosen above all the others—opened the front door, and stepped outside with such finality that Bell had scrambled from her hiding place.

"Ma? Ma, where you going?" Bell said.

The satchel fell from Hattie's hand as she whirled to face Bell. "I told you all to go to the park!"

"Are you going to come and get us later?"

Hattie slapped Bell with such force that the girl staggered.

"Don't you ask me anything! Don't you ever ask me anything about my business!" Hattie shouted and hurried down the porch steps.

"Ma!" Bell called as she hurried away. "Ma! Come back!"

Hattie paused in the middle of the sidewalk. Bell was sure she would turn around, but after a few seconds she kept walking, away from Wayne Street, away from Bell.

"Ma," she said again, in a whisper. "Ma. Please."

HATTIE MOVED toward the doorway of the hospital room with her back to Bell.

"Mother!" Bell called.

Hattie turned.

"You're coming back tomorrow right?"

"Yes, girl! I just said I was going to bring you some soup," Hattie said.

"Okay then."

"Alright."

She wanted to call out again, "Mother! Come back!" but Hattie had already left the room.

Cassie

1980

I WOULD LIKE TO wash my hair, but when I go into the bathroom, I think of the way the water will slide off of my body, fouled with particles of dead skin and bits of feces, and I have to return to my bedroom. I can't stand the sight of water pooling around a drain. Even now in the dry, warm backseat of Daddy's station wagon, I think about it and squirm in my shoes; my toes curl over the delicate creases where the fleshy pads meet the balls of my feet. My Sala, my sweet girl, is the only clean thing that I know.

This morning Mother suggested I take a shower before we go to my doctor's appointment. She led me into the bathroom and turned on the water, reached out to test the temperature as though she were drawing a baby's bath. I washed briefly, avoiding my hair and the private parts of my body. As the water fell over me, I wanted to throw myself against the shower doors. I stepped out feeling fetid, as though I had waded through a swamp. When I finished, Mother said, "Get dressed." For the fourth time that morning, she said, "Your appointment's today."

I sat on the bed and watched her lay out the clothes she had chosen for me: the skirt and sweater, my panties and girdle. When I was a child, she never did that sort of thing. There was never enough time to set out clothes for nine children. I wonder if she would have if there hadn't been so many of us. It requires a kind of tenderness, I think, laying out a little person's clothes. Mother was never tender. She still isn't. She put those clothes on the bed for me as though they were the ingredients for a roast chicken, as though I were to be trussed. Mother has always done what's necessary. I suppose she thinks she's doing that now by taking me off somewhere—though it's wrong, though she's wrong. I prayed for her. I wonder if she knows what she is doing to me, if it is conscious and pleasurable to her or if she just does it, like a hijacked spirit acting out someone else's commands. I sympathize with her. I know how difficult it is to resist certain urges. My urges are abhorrent. They have voices and whisper their suggestions so naturally, so calmly, that if I weren't careful, I might think they were my own thoughts: look at that man's crotch, they say; think about how he must look without his pants. Remember? Remember how it felt to be with men? I know, of course, that these are not my thoughts. I know that they come from whatever thing rules this whole business, whatever evil it might be. I can't tell about Mother and Daddy. I don't know if they understand the extent to which they have been corrupted. I would like to believe that they don't. I suspect otherwise, but I haven't told Sala because I don't want her to be afraid of her grandparents.

"This too," Mother said. She held my breast prosthesis out toward me. It trembled in the palm of her hand like half of an underboiled egg. Her hand, too, trembled. She blinked quickly. There was a movement in her throat as though she were swallowing something hard. Maybe she was. Mother always has butterscotch candies in her dress pockets. Right in that moment I saw something grand and terrible in her, a facial expression I recalled from years ago.

I remembered Mother in an apron in the kitchen of my childhood. I stood in the doorway. She tore the leaves from the stems of the collard greens and washed them in the double sink. Ham hocks simmered on the stove, the gas turned high and hissing beneath the pot. Now and again she stopped and stared out of the window, one dripping hand on her hip, and sighed. Sunlight shone on the side of her face. Her expression was soft and restless at the same time. Something wild was in that afternoon. It wafted through the kitchen like the music Daddy listened to after Mother sent us children to bed—juke music crept up the stairs and into our rooms. It curled itself around us and vibrated like a purring cat against our bodies. That music gave us inklings of things we weren't supposed to know: my parents hardly spoke at all, hated each other, it seemed to me, but Saturday nights, after they'd had a fight, they went upstairs and closed the bedroom door. I thought of that music too when a woman in a tight dress sashayed in front of our porch one evening, all hips and swagger. Daddy liked women like that. I saw him with one when I was a teenager. They were all wrapped around each other in a parked car while Mother was at home doing what needed to be done. I don't blame her for being so angry, though I couldn't help but wonder if she regretted us. When that woman peacocked in front of our stoop, everyone but Mother and I clucked her tongue. Aunt Marion said the switching woman was loose, but I thought she was free.

Mother washed the greens with a look on her face like she wanted to put on her own tight dress, walk out of the house, and never come back. Instead, she said, "Get the cordial out of the credenza."

She poured herself a glass and sat at the kitchen table sipping it. When it was gone, she turned the glass upside down and let the last drop fall onto her tongue. Mother was a beautiful young woman; the house was too plain, too small to contain her. I watched her; for the first time I understood that she had an inner life that didn't have anything to do with me or my brothers and sisters. She smiled and nodded her head as if to a remembered melody.

The Voice came last night. It's with me still: a gentle vibration against my rib cage, a ripple in the water, warm as Sala's breath against my ear when she was a baby. It says, "Go gently." It says, "Don't fight." I know my Bible. God told Jesus that the soldiers were coming; he heard their silver jangling in its pouch and he stayed, waiting. When The Voice comes, I can rest. Too often all I hear are The Banshees screeching at me like hyenas. Sometimes they are so loud I think other people must hear them, but I know they can't. They are my torment, my Furies, though I don't know what I have done to deserve them. For days they told me not to feed Sala her dinner. "The food is poisoned," they said. "The water is poisoned." I have been fasting so that Sala can eat; when they see that I don't eat, they won't poison the food. I don't mind. I have grown accustomed to hunger.

The Banshees screeched, "Everything is spying on you, everything has ears, everything reports."

Some of the herbs growing in Mother's yard would counteract the poison. I tried to get them but couldn't find the right ones. I go through all of this, all of this to keep Sala safe. I am so very tired and still The Banshees say, "You are failing. You are too small. You and that child are damned." It does seem as though my life is whipping away from me like a kite in a tornado. I pray for guidance and relief. When I am at my end, when I am going to collapse, The Voice comes and tells me to rest. Mother and Daddy are taking me somewhere today. I don't believe that it's a doctor's appointment despite what they say.

I try to find whatever loveliness there might be in a thing, even this afternoon as I stepped into the car and Daddy started the engine and Mother kept glancing at me furtively through the rearview mirror.

I try to find the beauty in things. Sometimes I am overcome with it. I have felt as though I were a single note of music, a high C trebling from a singer's throat, all shimmer and wing beat. It is really something to feel music, to feel as though one has become music. I don't feel that way very often anymore, but I remember that ecstasy.

Mother and Daddy tell me half-truths. I can't look at them, so I concentrate on the highway and the waning day. There is a particular kind of afternoon sun that exists only in autumn. A golden light drapes itself over the world of that hour. It falls through the afternoon sky, fine and faint as a swirl of cigarette smoke caught in the wind, nearly transparent. So sweet, that light, insisting softly, goldly against the windows.

I try to find the beauty in things. On dark days I sit in my armchair looking at clouds. I think about the vapor rising from the lakes and rivers and the dirty puddles on street corners and how the clouds take in the particles of water and rain down until they are exhausted into disappearing wisps. These clouds, they sacrifice themselves. It seems to me that everything is on its way to becoming something else, giving itself up in the service of another. In a little while this light will fade. The last few mosquitoes will come out, and the night creatures will eat them. I don't know where I will be then.

In the front seat Daddy fiddles with the dial on the radio and lets it rest momentarily on the Christian station. Mother says, "August, stop there. That's Reverend Bill's show. I can't stand you fiddling with the dial. All that static makes me want to jump out of my skin."

He says, "I want something pretty, Hattie."

He says, "I want to hear that pretty song Cassie taught me on the piano when she was a little girl. That's what I want. You remember that song, Cassie?"

He looks at me through the rearview mirror. I do

not respond. Yesterday Sala asked me the strangest question. She asked me if I loved my mother when I was her age. I can't remember who I was at ten, only that I tried to be a good girl because I didn't want to invite Mother's wrath. What I feel for Sala has eclipsed anything I thought was love before she was born; it has made me wonder if I ever loved anything before her. As for Mother, I think that I did love her. I think I still do. That's what I told Sala.

"You're not going to find that song, August. Just leave it. Lord, please just leave it," Mother says.

On the radio Reverend Bill takes calls from people who have questions about the Bible. A man calls from South Carolina. He asks an interesting question, one that I have had myself. I wait while Reverend Bill pauses to gather his thoughts before responding. I wait for what seems an eternity. I wait so long that I wonder if my father turned off the radio. When the reverend finally speaks, I have already forgotten the question, and his words are slow and distorted, like a record playing on the wrong speed. The more I concentrate, the more it seems that the words have nothing to do with one another. I focus on the minister's voice. I tune my ear to his pace so the words are whole: apostle and Paul and Damascus. I try to string them together like beads. They slide away from me. Mother and Daddy nod their heads to whatever the reverend is saying. I know that I should understand too. Please help me, Lord. These corners in my mind—I turn one and there is a tiger. Leaping.

The Voice is receding. The Banshees edge in. They take each bit of ceded ground and plant their loud and terrible flags; they begin their murmuring. I know how this goes. I am waiting for their awful crescendo. Something dark jumps at the edge of my vision. The Banshees, the three of them black and terrible. Or perhaps they are just large insects outside of the car window. It has become so difficult to distinguish one thing from another. The afternoon is deepening and these little monkeys jump on my shoulders. They bare their teeth and yelp. My heart is beating too quickly. I put my hand to my breast to steady it. "Where are you going? Where are you going?" they chant. In the front seat Mother sits rigid as a toothpick. There is a bit of her neck visible between the cloth of her collar and the place where her gray hair curls under. I look at that patch of skin. It calms me.

"Hear the silver jangling?" The Banshees ask. "Look at your awful mother. She never loved anybody. Tell her she never loved anybody."

I shake my head at them. I won't say it. In the front seat Mother tenses but does not turn around. Daddy reaches over and holds her hand.

"Good girl," The Banshees say.

"Now throw yourself from the car. Open the door and throw yourself out," they say.

There is a small brown mole in the dusky ivory of Mother's neck. "Out of the car, out of the car," The Banshees chant. I reach for the door handle. I grasp it, my hand flexes.

Daddy slows before the exit ramp. Ours is one in a line of cars moving toward it. Now is the time. I could jump out of the car and roll onto the shoulder of the highway. I'll get Sala from school, and we'll escape. We'll go to California or New Hampshire. I visited there once. It was the only time I've been on a plane. The day was gray. We flew up and up, and for a long while I couldn't see anything but thick fog. Suddenly we broke through the canopy of clouds and there was nothing—just the hum of the engine and the blue sky and the sun glinting off the plane's wings. I felt a weightlessness. I imagined I was flying without apparatus, without engine or metal casing, without even my own body, just the best part of myself—my soul?—borne along on the current of air. Wouldn't that be fine? Wouldn't that be grand?

I open the car door. I tumble. The side of my face burns; pieces of gravel cut into my palms. I taste metal; my mouth fills with liquid. I stand and run. I don't brush the bits of road from my coat. My shoes slow me down, so I kick them off and keep running. A wood edges the road. I am moving very quickly. My legs are ten feet long. With each step, I cover an enormous distance. The Banshees are pleased with me; they clack their teeth in celebration. I could go on forever. I take in great lungfuls of air. Atom by atom, the oxygen enters my blood and pumps in waves through my veins; it is tidal, this pumping blood. My heart beats mightily. If I ran any faster, my feet would pedal up into the air. I'd soar above the highway, and the cars would look like lines of speeding beetles, all chrome shine and hubcap glint. Behind me tires screech, horns honk. Someone is calling my name, Cassie, Cassie, Cassie. I don't need to look back; there's nothing there for me. The Banshees say, "Let them burn." I run into the coppering afternoon. I'll run all the way to Sala.

She'll be on the school bus now, going home. She doesn't know I'm not at the house. She'll run into our room and find it empty, the bed unmade. She'll wander the house looking for me then sit on the front steps and poke at the ground with a stick. The shadows will grow long, and a chill will come down. The street lamps will blink on, and her cheeks will grow cold and still she'll wait. She'll know that I am coming because I always come; my sweet girl, she'll be frightened but she'll wait. I've never let her down and I won't start now.

I stumble on a piece of blown-out tire. A truck pulls onto the shoulder of the highway and rolls slowly toward me, horn honking. A man leans out of the window as it passes, "You alright, honey?" I think I hear laughter. My chest burns. I turn toward the wood. A ditch runs the length of the border between highway and forest. It is filled with travelers' detritus: beer cans, potato chip bags, cigarette butts. I step down into it. A few feet away something hisses, something alive and wounded—a cat that someone abandoned. Its paw is twisted at an odd angle and its fur is matted and stretched across its rib cage. "Here, kitty," I say. "Here, kitty." It hisses as I approach. Poor thing. "Okay, kitty," I say. "Okay." Its good paw scratches at the air. It does not have the strength to lift its head when it hisses, but its eyes dart from side to side. "Pretty, pretty," I say. "Shh." I turn my pockets inside out looking for something to give it. I look down at the trash in the ditch. I don't want to touch that filth, but I comb through the garbage with my hands. "I'm coming, pretty," I say. "It's going to be alright." I don't want to scare it, so I take tiny steps toward its limp body. The mud in the ditch sucks at my feet. It is slimy and lumpy and cold. I kneel next to the poor wounded cat. It lifts its head from the dirt and sticks out the tip of its tongue and then, with the last of its strength, scratches my wrist. Blood beads up through the perforated skin. Poor thing. I crouch next to it. "Shhh shhh, pretty, pretty," I say. The Banshees urge me onward, "Go on," they say. "Get, you'd better get." But I don't think anything should die alone, so I stay on my knees next to the cat and wait for it to draw its last breath. I whisper to it until it lets me stroke its matted fur. It mews.

At the mouth of the ditch two pairs of boots appear. Two policemen look down. One says, "Ma'am, you come on out of there now. You gave your parents a scare. You come on out of there."

"Who sent you?" I ask.

The Banshees are in a rage. They are shrieking, "We told you. Now look, now look what you've done, you stupid woman. You miserable bitch."

I hear everything now: the kitten's shallow breathing, the men bending over the ditch, the cars whooshing by, the tree branches crackling in the woods, the tires against the road, the birds tweeting, the sandpaper sound of the air against my skin, the grass blowing, my labored breathing. All of it rushes at me, horribly articulated. I put out my hand to steady myself against the onslaught. The police officers are speaking again. It is impossible to hear them over the cacophony. I concentrate. I stare at their lips. One reaches for me, and I am lifted up and out of the ditch.

The roadside is a circus of police cars and flashing lights. Some of the motorists stop, and an officer waves them along. Daddy's car is parked with the passenger door open. Mother is talking to one of the policemen. I am led toward her. The Banshees say I should make a run for it, but I shake my head. "No," I say. "Nonononono." I thought I'd said it very quietly, in the voice I use to talk to them inside of my head, but I must have spoken aloud because Mother and the officer turn and stare. Daddy leans against the car with his head in his hands.

A policewoman takes my elbow and guides me to a squad car. She opens the door, and I perch on the edge of the seat while she squats in front of me. I am so tired. I am too tired to hear anything or understand anything. If only The Banshees would stop shouting, but they won't give me any peace now. Mother gestures toward me and then to her and Daddy's car. The officer shakes his head.

Paramedics arrive. They lead me to the ambulance, and I step up quietly. This morning The Voice told me to go gently. My parents sit in their car; blue and red lights flash on their windshield. The paramedic doesn't fasten the restraints on the stretcher, and she's given me a blanket, for which I am grateful. I try to look for the beauty in things. Mother in her apron all of those years ago, the amber twinkle of the cordial in her glass, and that song only she and I could hear.

Sala

1980

SALA WOKE AT sunset. Cold seeped through the window next to her bed. The sheets were too tight. Sala's grandmother had tucked them around her, pulled them so taut the girl's arms were pinned and she had to strain to straighten her feet. She didn't know how long she'd been sleeping. Outside, the trees and houses, wires and telephone poles were black silhouettes against the red-orange sunset. A few drooping leaves hung like sleeping bats from an oak's bare, black branches.

Sala's mother had been taken away the week before. Gone were Cassie's suitcase and bobby pins, her wide-toothed comb and maroon sweater, the tube of almond-colored concealer she dotted under her eyes.

In the backyard the light snapped off in Sala's

grandfather's toolshed. He walked onto the lawn and paused, his body turned toward Sala's window. "August!" Hattie called from the kitchen. "August, supper!" August's face was hidden in shadow. He leaned forward, as though trying to see into Sala's room. He was not so steady on his feet these days. Sala was afraid he would fall. The back door squeaked open, and a long rectangle of light fell across the grass. Hattie came out into the yard wearing her apron. August walked toward her with his hand outstretched. She took it and helped him climb the back steps. The door closed behind them, and the yard fell to darkness.

The wood behind the house was black and still. Good night, trees, Sala thought. She waited for her grandmother to come and turn on the bedroom light; she pulled at the sheets, squirming in her swaddling. She was afraid she might vomit. Sala had been sent home early from school that day. At mid-morning she'd felt a sudden vertigo. Her stomach churned, and the classroom brightened into a cube of light so white and disorienting that, though she willed it to, her body would not stay in the chair. She slid to the floor. A huge fuss followed. There was talk of an ambulance. Sala was carried to a cot in the nurse's office, where the adults talked about her as though she were not there. "I think there's something going on at home," they said. "She's been distracted in class," they said. The school nurse's face loomed above her. "We're calling your mother to come and get you." Twenty minutes later August arrived.

A pot lid banged. Hattie was in the kitchen, cooking and displeased. Sala struggled out of the sheets and sat up in bed, determined to appear well when her grandmother came to check on her. She would come in and see that Sala had recovered—she would realize people could will themselves healed and she'd bring Sala's mother back. Sala's eyes were gritty, as though there was dust under the lids. She picked up a pillow and hugged it to her chest, it smelled of her mother's hair-dressing oil. She drifted off and jerked awake again. Sometime later, two hands shifted her downward and tugged the covers up to her chin. A calloused palm passed over her cheek. "She asleep," August whispered to Hattie. He walked out of the room whistling a tune softly.

TWO DAYS BEFORE they took her away, Cassie dug up the front yard in the middle of the afternoon. Sala came home from school to find the lawn pocked with holes and scattered with clumps of browned grass and mounds of gray scraggly roots. There was dirt strewn on the slate pathway that led to the front door, dirt piled on top of the gravel in the driveway, dirt in Cassie's hair. Hattie's winter flowers, thick-leafed purple things that looked like open heads of cabbages, were hacked apart and wobbling, roots up, in the center of the ruined flower beds. Cassie kneeled next to the maple tree. She held a shovel by the blade with both hands and jabbed it into the ground.

"Mom?" Sala called. "Mom?"

Cassie raised her arms above her head and drove the shovel into the earth. Her leather gloves were ripped where the shovel's blade cut into them. The neighbors on either side of the house watched from their porches. Sala's grandmother stood in the doorway with both hands pressed against the screen, palms flat, as though she could push the scene away.

"Sala!" Cassie said, breathless. "Help me pull up this root."

Sala didn't move.

"Come on! Help me."

"What are you doing?" Sala asked.

Cassie set the shovel aside and used her hands to dig into the hole she'd made.

"Can't we go inside? Let's go inside," Sala said.

She bent over and tugged at the back of her mother's jacket with both hands. She began to cry.

"Mom, please let's go inside."

"Inside!" Cassie said. "Now?"

She glanced at Hattie standing in the doorway. She leaned into Sala and whispered, "We have to be careful with Grandmom and Grandpop. They're putting something in our food. But," she said, examining a clump of weeds, "there are plants out here that I can use to cure us."

"There's people watching," Sala said.

"Don't mind them. They're all in on it." Cassie looked at a neighbor woman standing on her porch. "I know what you're up to!" she shouted.

Hattie ran outside. "Cassie! Cassie, come on in now. That's enough."

Cassie sifted through the dirt with her hands.

"At least let me take Sala inside. You don't want her out here like this."

Sala tugged again at her mother's coat, but Cassie had gone back to her shoveling and swatted her hand away as though it were a fly. Hattie led Sala inside and the two of them stood side by side in the doorway watching Cassie move across the yard scooping clumps of dirt into bags. They shivered in the chill afternoon air coming in through the screen door. Sala wondered if she ought to stand so close to her grandmother, if Hattie wasn't transmitting something poisonous through her clothes. She wondered if there really was any poison, then she worried she'd betrayed her mother with her doubt. Cassie didn't have anyone but Sala, but Grandmom and Grandpop had each other and Sala's aunts and uncles. Sala tallied these bonds, measured the scale of defenselessness and need; she always concluded that her mother needed her more than anyone else. She sidestepped away from her grandmother. She decided she could stand next to her as long as there were a few inches between them. In this way she could satisfy everyone involved. In this way she would not lose anyone's love.

Cassie came inside at sunset. She hurried Sala into the bedroom they shared and locked the door behind them. She set a pack of razor blades and a pair of yellow rubber gloves on the bedside table. Cassie emptied the bags of pulled roots onto newspapers and sliced them with the blades. Sala watched from the bed.

"Don't cry!" Cassie said. "Remember that song about the Lord's army? That's us, the Lord's soldiers. He's taking care of us."

Sala did not feel taken care of. Cassie had not changed her clothes—her pants were grass stained and muddied, dirt streaked her face, her fingernails were black. She hardly glanced at Sala as she sliced the roots. She cut her finger, and the blood dripped onto the newspaper. Under her breath Cassie sang, **I'm in the Lord's army.**

"Sing it with me, Sala: **I may never march in the infantry, ride in the cavalry, shoot the artil-**

lery . . . Come on, Sala. Sing it with me. **I'm in the Lord's army. Yes, sir!**"

There wasn't anything to do but sing along. When she was like this, Cassie never tired; she could go on singing and slicing all night. There were times Sala would wake with the first light and find her mother sprawled across the bed, or lying on the floor, or sometimes, and this was much worse, awake and praying in the armchair near the window. Now, Sala sang, so that her mother would be comforted, and Sala would not feel so separate from her and so alone.

By the third round, Sala and Cassie were shouting. Maybe, Sala thought, there was medicine in the roots her mother had pulled from the yard. Mom knows lots of things. I'm only ten, what do I know about anything?

"Don't mind all of that noise," Cassie said. Sala's grandparents were knocking on the bedroom door. They wanted them to stop singing, to come out and talk. "Let Sala have her supper, at least," August said. Cassie ignored them. Sala didn't dare say she wanted to eat dinner with her grandparents. As the night wore on, the telephone in the kitchen rang with increased frequency. Long after the hour at which the house was usually silent, Sala heard her grandparent's voices and the shirr of their footsteps against the carpet.

Cassie covered the bedroom floor with grocery

store sales circulars piled with chopped roots. Sala sat in the middle of the bed with the quilt pulled around her shoulders. "Have you ever been in a boat?" she asked her mother. "This bed is a boat, and the papers are the ocean. See?" Sala said, bouncing on the bed to simulate the motion of waves. She drew her knees to her chest.

"Mom," she said. "Mom, I don't feel well."

What she meant was, what is happening? What she meant was, please stop this.

"Mom?" she called again.

"Sing some more," Cassie said without turning from the roots she was cutting up.

"I don't want to." Sala had tired of singing. She wanted her mother to wash her face and comb her hair. They could sit in the family room watching television and eating grilled cheese sandwiches if Cassie would only return to herself, but this other wild woman wouldn't let her go.

"I'm hungry," she said. "Mom? Did you hear? My stomach hurts. I'm hungry."

Cassie put down her razor blade. She crossed the room and sat at the foot of the bed. Sala kicked at her hand.

"Get away. I don't know you," Sala said.

Cassie crawled forward on the bed, trying to get a grip on some part of her daughter's body, but Sala flailed and bucked. Cassie grabbed both of Sala's feet and held on, head down, while the girl pummeled her shoulders. "Get off! You get off!" Sala shouted. She struck her mother with her knees and wheeled her arms. She slapped at Cassie's face and neck. Cassie lay on top of her, pinning Sala to the bed. Sala wriggled beneath her, winded from the weight of her mother's body. Cassie kissed Sala's forehead and her cheeks and her tears. "It's me, Sala. It's me, it's me," Cassie said. These were the first words she'd spoken that were free of the shrill-ness that came into her voice when Cassie had one of these episodes. Exhausted, Sala allowed her mother to pull her into her lap and rock her.

The next morning when Sala woke, Cassie had cleared the room. The chopped bits of roots were in brown bags on the windowsill. It was very early; the sky was tinged orange. During the night, Cassie had undressed Sala and put her pajamas on her. Cassie's hair was combed and the bits of grass were gone. She had put on red lipstick, which had smeared, giving her mouth a bloodied, just-punched look. Still, she had tried, and Sala, waking up to the sun and finding her mother groomed, could try to forget the night before. There were many things Sala tried to forget; sometimes she succeeded, for an hour or a day. More often, Cassie wearied and bewildered her. It had grown impossible to know what was real or true, and Sala was afraid all of the time. She learned to put aside things that were too confusing or too painful. And so she set aside the previous evening and hopped out of bed and asked her mother if she could wear her purple corduroy pants to school that day.

SALA WOKE in the deepest part of the night, when the furrowing, burrowing creatures are quiet in their dens and the night hunters have eaten their fill or given up the chase. Hattie was sitting in the armchair next to the bed. She'd turned on a night-light. A bit of the dark yard was visible through a gap between window shade and sill; Sala wanted to go out into the stars and the silence. She wanted some sort of enchantment.

"Let's go outside to see the owls," said Sala, half in a dream.

Her grandmother reached for the thermometer and shook it with two swift snaps of the wrist.

"Open up," she said.

"There's owls in the woods, right, Grandmom?" Sala asked.

Hattie sighed.

"All I know is you fainted at school and now you're talking nonsense in the middle of the night. Open up."

"Don't you ever want to go outside at night?"

"I've been outside at night. It's just like the day, only darker."

"Did you ever see an owl?"

"Sure."

"When?"

"Goodness, Sala, I don't remember."

"Was it pretty?"

"I'm not playing with you, child. Open your mouth."

"Where's my mother?" Sala said softly.

Hattie's hand dropped to her lap. She leaned back in her chair.

"She's alright. She's alright where she is."

"Are they nice to her there?"

Hattie didn't answer.

"Are they nice to her?" Sala repeated.

"I think they are. I called all around for the best . . . I hope so."

The two of them sat in the dark and the quiet together. When Sala began to cry, Hattie didn't hug her or take the girl's hand or rub her shoulder, but she didn't shush her either. After a while Hattie said, "They're kind of silver with the moon shining down on them. There were a lot of owls in Georgia when I was a girl. One time I saw one with a little rabbit in its mouth."

Here I am, seventy-one years old, and still no end to sick children, Hattie thought. Now this, and who would care for this little one if Cassie didn't get better? God help her.

When Hattie's children were young, they'd called her The General. They thought she didn't know, but she knew everything about each one of them. She could feel their vibrating souls. When he was a boy, Franklin joked that Hattie had superpowers because she always knew which children were upstairs, which were out on the porch, which had gone down the block to the corner store. She'd be in the kitchen and get an odd sensation on the back of her neck, like someone was tapping her there. She'd look up from whatever she was doing and call out to one of the girls, "Go tell your brother I said to stop fooling around up there in the attic." Sure enough, that's where he'd be, about to fall through the trapdoor onto the second-floor landing.

Sala had fallen asleep again. I'm sorry, Hattie thought, looking at her granddaughter. She'd seen Sala running after the car the afternoon they took Cassie to the hospital. But she hadn't said anything to August. He would have wanted to stop and explain things. And what could they have said? Hattie had looked through the rearview mirror at Sala waving and running; she glanced at Cassie, who was so taken up with whatever was in her head that she couldn't see anything outside of herself. Every bit of Cassie was twitching: eyes twitching and hands twitching and mind and the very soul of her twitching. How Hattie had wanted to sit in that backseat with her and hold her hand until she stopped shaking. When Hattie was a girl in

Georgia, they'd have taken Cassie to the preacher, and if that hadn't healed her, they'd have kept her fed and clothed and left her alone to be how she was. Hattie snorted. We couldn't go to the hospital bloody and dying, much less when somebody went wrong in the head. It was true that a part of Hattie blamed Cassie's condition on a failure of character, a creeping weakness that had gotten the better of her. But when she saw Sala running toward the car, she knew Cassie wouldn't have wanted her child to see her in her worst hour. That was Hattie's kindness. She had spared her daughter and grandchild that pain.

Hattie knew her children did not think her a kind woman—perhaps she wasn't, but there hadn't been time for sentiment when they were young. She had failed them in vital ways, but what good would it have done to spend the days hugging and kissing if there hadn't been anything to put in their bellies? They didn't understand that all the love she had was taken up with feeding them and clothing them and preparing them to meet the world. The world would not love them; the world would not be kind.

She had been angry with her children, and with August, who'd brought her nothing but disappointment. Fate had plucked Hattie out of Georgia to birth eleven children and establish them in the North, but she was only a child herself, utterly inadequate to the task she'd been given. No one could tell her why things had turned out as they had, not August or the pastor or God himself. Hattie believed in God's might, but she didn't believe in his interventions. At best, he was indifferent. God wasn't any of her business, and she wasn't any of his. In church on Sundays she looked around the sanctuary and wondered if anyone else felt the way she did, if anyone else was there because they believed in the ritual and the hymn singing and good preaching more than they believed in a responsive, sympathetic God.

Hattie was an old woman when August began attending church regularly. He had taken to telling her he loved her—and Hattie let him, because he said it had something to do with his newfound belief in Christ. Besides, what did they have after fifty-six years but each other's company, and wasn't it something how, as her body lost its vitality, so did her desire to leave him and begin again? August was seventy-four, sick and getting sicker—it was just so typical of him to run into the arms of God when his heart was too weak for him to run into the arms of some woman. He persuaded Hattie to go with him to the local church, and she discovered, to her surprise, that it was a place of solace and beauty. The church brought her great peace, and if she only pretended to believe, if she was a fraud, well, that was the price she had to pay for comfort and fellowship.

Hattie pushed a coil of hair back from her grand-daughter's forehead. No point in waking the child to take her temperature, and anyway, Hattie could see fever, and Sala didn't have one. She ought to go to bed, but she was too tired to get out of the chair; these sick children wore her out.

In the car on the way to the hospital, Cassie had said—how could she have said that?—that Hattie had never loved anything. It was just a whisper, barely audible. "You never loved anything," Cassie said. Hattie had done the best she could. She was done with regret and recrimination, there was no sense in it for an old woman. And there had been so many babies: crying babies and walking babies, babies to be fed and babies to be changed. Sick babies, burning with fever babies. Hattie's first babies. They fell ill on January 12 and were dead ten days later. Penicillin. That was all that was needed to save her children. They would be fifty-six now, grayed or graying, thick at the waist and laugh lined around the mouth. Maybe they'd have grandchildren. The lives they would have had are unoccupied; that is to say, the people they would have loved, the houses they might have owned, jobs they would have had, were all left untenanted. Not a day went by that Hattie did not feel their absence in the world, the empty space where her children's lives should have been.

Sala feigned sleep. She peeked at her grandmother from under her eyelashes. Hattie was looking up toward the ceiling, and Sala wondered what she was thinking. She didn't dare ask. Hattie was like a lake of smooth, silvered ice, under which nothing could be seen or known. When she was angry, the ice creaked and groaned; it threatened to crack and pull them all under, the way Cassie had been pulled under. Cassie would have said there wasn't anything wrong with her, that her own mother had turned on her in a betrayal so spectacular it defied belief. August would say Cassie had been sent away to be cured. Hattie, Sala thought, wouldn't say anything at all.

ON SUNDAY Sala was well enough to go to church with her grandparents. The members of the congregation were kinder than usual. They bent at the waist to greet her, took her hand in theirs. Brother Merrill, the pastor, knelt to speak to her. "We've been praying," he said. "Such a brave girl," his wife said. Hattie looked embarrassed.

The church was a squat brown building off the New Jersey Turnpike. It was a poor place, with a packed-dirt parking lot and a large white cross that had dingied over time. The sanctuary was dim and smelled of Murphy Oil Soap, but there was an earnest wooden pulpit and the pews were polished to a high shine. Brother Merrill was saving for a stained glass window. Toward this effort, Sala dropped fifty cents into the collection plate at every service. In her pocket were two quarters August had given her that morning. She rubbed her fingers over them as she and her grandparents made their way to a pew near the front. "Well, Little Miss," said one of the congregants, "will you bless us with a song this morning?" Some Sundays after the group hymns and before the sermon, Sala would sing "Amazing Grace" or "His Eye Is on the Sparrow." She sang a cappella, with her hands clasped in front of her, knees shaking. During her solos, the church was utterly silent, and when she finished, the parishioners shouted "Praise Jesus" and kept on shouting even after she'd reached her seat. Brother Merrill told her that singing was its own kind of worship, though Sala felt something closer to pride than reverence. There would be no singing that Sunday.

After the announcements and the opening hymns, Brother Merrill began his sermon: " 'Yet man is born unto trouble, as the sparks fly upward.' Brothers and sisters, I want to talk to you about the book of Job this Sunday. The Lord tells us in Job, chapter five, verse seven, that man and the sons of man are born into suffering. Now, Job was a righteous man, but the Lord saw fit to test him. He lost his house, he lost his camels, his sheep, his oxen. And just when he thought he had reached the darkest hour, he lost his sons and his daughters. He was covered with boils from the crown of his head to the soles of his feet. He rubbed himself with ashes, and his wife said to him, 'Job,' she said. 'Curse God and die.' "

Sala's grandparents sat in rapt attention. Hattie's face was expressionless—placid lake, silvered ice—but her hand grasped the top of the pew in front of her so hard that her knuckles whitened and the tendons showed through her skin. August's finger rested on the verse Brother Merrill read. Sala read it too. Curse God. She had heard the quick, nasty words some of the kids used on the playground at school. They formed now in her mind. Fuck and damn and shit. How could my mother allow herself to be taken away? Sala thought. And if she would just be normal, just normal, none of this would have happened. She did this to us. Sala wanted to put the words together: Fuck and God, Fuck and Mom, but when she tried, a fearful place within her would not allow it.

Sala had seen them take Cassie away. She got home early that afternoon. No one had remembered there was a half day at school. She walked from the school bus stop through the sparse pine forest along the highway's shoulder. Her house came into view through the trees. She was thinking about what her mother had done to the yard two days earlier. Most of the holes were filled, though the white wire fences around Hattie's flowerbeds were still bent. If she hadn't been looking at those fences, Sala would have seen her mother and grandparents walking to the driveway. She would have seen August struggling to carry Cassie's small suitcase. She would have seen all of that, but she didn't because she was looking at those stupid little fences, and by the time she saw her grandfather lift Cassie's case into the trunk, it was too late. Cassie jumped when August slammed the trunk closed. Hattie stood beside the passenger door leaning toward Cassie as if she might have to pounce on her like one does an escaping animal. "Mom!" Sala shouted and ran toward the car. But in that moment Cassie opened the back door and got in. August backed out of the driveway, pulled onto the road, and they were gone.

Brother Merrill continued, "Job wouldn't curse his God. He remembered his children and his house and his barn. The Lord had blessed him so much, Amen, so long, Amen, so bountifully—Amen!—that if He never saw fit to give Job a single blessing more He had already given him enough for a thousand lifetimes. Now, we struggle, brothers and sisters, and we strive. We have our trials and our tribulations but we are blessed. We go to bed, praise Jesus, and we rise again in the morning. And if that's not a blessing, I don't know what is."

"And on top of all of that, the Lord gives us more. He gave Job more. Yes, He did. 'For He maketh sore.' Stay with me now. 'For He bindeth up; He woundeth.' But I am here to tell you today that 'He maketh whole.' Glory be to God."

The preacher's hands were balled into fists. August's Bible slid from his lap. Hattie cried "Amen!" The sermon crescendoed to such a volume that Sala found herself tapping her foot to the rhythm of the reverend's words. The pastor pushed up his sleeve, and before it slid back down, Sala caught a glimpse of the faded tattoo on his forearm. Grandpop said that Brother Merrill had been in a bad way, that the Lord had saved him from something terrible and that was why he was such a good preacher. Sala looked up at him from her pew and saw that her grandfather was right: the preacher was wild eyed, dark circles of perspiration spread beneath his arms and across his back. He pounded the podium with his fist.

If Cassie were with Sala now, she would nod her head slightly, and smile and her eyes would glisten. Sala listened closely; she tried to commit Brother Merrill's words to memory so she could repeat them to her mother if she called.

It was the groaning hour. The congregation swayed on its heels.

"His arms are ever open. His grace is right on time," Brother Merrill said. "All we have to do is say yes to Him. Yes to glory. Yes to joy."

The spirit of the Lord came down, and the parishioners closed their eyes and raised their arms to heaven. Hattie bowed her head, but she did not close her eyes. She watched the congregation. It seemed to Sala that she and her grandmother were the only ones who were not lifted out of themselves.

"Is there anyone here this afternoon who would like to give his soul to Christ?"

Once Sala asked her grandfather how big God was, and he'd said he was smaller than a grain of salt and bigger than the ocean. When Grandpop prayed, he could hear His voice like a soft white bird cooing in his ear. "I hope you hear it one day," he'd said. Sala heard only organ murmur and someone crying softly in the back pew. Tears ached in her throat. She raised her hand like the ladies in the congregation had done—just to see how it would feel, just to see if something divine would flow into her.

"The Lord doesn't care what you've done," Brother Merrill said. "He'll take your sorrow and your suffering and He will wash it clean. Accept Him as your savior. Come on up. Come on up to the mercy seat."

A man made his way toward the altar. Brother Merrill said, "Praise Jesus. Brother, come on up."

The man took small wavering steps, as though he had just learned to walk. The preacher came down from the pulpit and put his arm around the weeping man's shoulders. Sunday after Sunday Sala had seen the people walk sobbing down the aisle; she had seen them fall to their knees. Sala's mother and grandparents had come to God in this same way, and they had been saved.

"Is there anyone else?"

Sala felt a stab of mother-want so strong it winded her. She stepped out into the center aisle. The preacher stretched out his hand to her. Someone said, "Praise God, He's bringing the babies back to his fold." Sala was swept forward on the current of the congregation's fervor. The ladies wept in the pews behind her. Sala would become a child of God, and all of those women would be her mothers in Christ. She arrived at the altar, and the pastor took her hand.

"Do you understand what it means to take Jesus into your heart?" he asked.

Sala understood nothing. She didn't feel the way the other parishioners seemed to feel. She had only the slightest inkling of their devotion, as though it were an image in a mirror glimpsed through a half-open door. But she nodded in response to Brother Merrill's question—because the organ thrum compelled her, and the preacher had extended the promise of love.

"Do you accept Jesus as your Lord and savior?" Brother Merrill asked.

The congregation began to hum. They did this every Sunday during the altar call. Sala was always amazed that they knew exactly when to begin and which tune to hum. Now they hummed for her. She felt a tingling at the top of her head. She let her body relax into the preacher's arms.

"Do you accept Jesus as your savior?" Brother Merrill asked again.

"I do," said Sala.

She closed her eyes and waited for the spirit. It would surround her, gather her in its embrace. She felt a hand on her shoulder, hot and urgent and tightening. She opened her eyes. Her grandmother stood next to her.

"No," Hattie said.

"Sister Shepherd?" said the preacher. "What's the matter, sister?"

"No," Hattie said again and pulled Sala away from him.

The organ thrum stopped, the congregation's hum as well. The sanctuary was silent. Hattie pulled her granddaughter down the center aisle. She couldn't allow it. She had lost Six to the altar. She sent him off to Alabama with nothing but a Bible, and he had become a womanizer and an imposter. By the time she understood the depth of his unhappiness, it had been too late to save him.

Her twins were dead. She had given Ella back to Georgia. It was too late for Cassie, whom Hattie had also sent away. And it was too late for Hattie, who was a fraud in Christ and had shown Sala the ways of fraudulence. She couldn't bear that the child was already so broken she was driven to the mercy seat. There was time for Sala. Hattie didn't know how to save her granddaughter. She felt as overwhelmed and unprepared as she had when she was a young mother at seventeen. Here we are sixty years out of Georgia, she thought, a new generation has been born, and there's still the same wounding and the same pain. I can't allow it. She shook her head. I can't allow it.

They arrived at the pew, where August was waiting. "I don't know why you done that, Hattie," he whispered. Of course he didn't. August's faith was simple and absolute. He had aged into a sickly old man who prayed and loved the Lord. And if he understood more than he let on, if he was wiser than he acted, he kept it to himself. It's easier to play the fool, Hattie thought, and August always did what was easy. She felt a spark of her old anger. But they were past all of that—it hadn't served her when she was young and wouldn't serve her now.

Hattie looked around at the disapproving faces of the congregation. Their indignation would pass—everything passed sooner or later—and if it didn't, she would give up the church too, this dear comfort of her old age. She was not too old to weather another sacrifice. Hattie put her arm around Sala and pulled her close; she patted her granddaughter's back roughly, unaccustomed as she was to tenderness.

Acknowledgments

It is my great honor to express my gratitude to those who, in ways direct and indirect, made this work possible.

Many thanks to the James Michener and Copernicus Society of America, to the Maytag Fellowship and the Flannery O'Connor Fellowship. To the Iowa Writers' Workshop to which I owe a great debt. To the Philadelphia High School for Girls, for being a light in the darkest part of my life and for preparing me to meet the world in ways I am still discovering.

To my agent Ellen Levine, the best advocate and guide I could ever have hoped for.

To my editor Jordan Pavlin, for her elegance and subtlety, her unwavering belief in this novel, and for seeing all the things I couldn't.

ACKNOWLEDGMENTS

To the teachers who set the highest standards and demanded I meet them: my high school English teacher Sandra Johnson, who refused to let me fail, in any way—ever. Jackson Taylor, who inspired and coaxed and persisted until I found what I feared was lost. Thank you, Edward Carey; Alexander Chee; Allan Gurganus, who leads by example; and Michelle Huneven. Paul Harding for his support and unflagging encouragement.

To Lan Samantha Chang and Connie Brothers: to the former for being a superb teacher, to the latter for her wisdom, and to both for taking a chance on me.

To Marilynne Robinson for her friendship, for the example of her life and belief, and for the rigor of her standards, which urges me forward even when I have reached my limits.

To the novels and essays of Toni Morrison, whose words are both lighthouse and anchor, and whose work has made a way for all of us. Also to Rita Dove's beautiful collection Thomas and Beulah, which never ceases to teach and astound me. And to Isabel Wilkerson's The Warmth of Other Suns, a more necessary work I could not imagine.

To Robert Hayden's poem "Those Winter Sundays," quoted in the novel. And to Emily Dickinson's "After Great Pain, A Formal Feeling Comes," also quoted.

Thanks also to Sally Dorst, Ames Giganous, Jill

Herzig, my red-headed friend Jenna Johnson, William Johnson, Tanya McKinnon, Cassandra Richmond, Victoria Sanders, and A Public Space. To Emma Borges-Scott, Angela Flournoy, and Alexander Maksik for being insightful readers and for their big, beautiful brains.

Through thick and thin all of these years: Ayana Byrd, Karin Kissiah, and Laurence Vagassky.

To my dearest Justin Torres, without whom this book would not be and without whose friendship I could never have done what needed doing. My thanks and my love, for everything and forever.

With love, to Nikki Terry for the depths and reaches of her generous heart, and for her patience and her indefatigable spirit.

Finally, and especially, to my grandparents Leroy and Lucille Hundley, in respect and in homage. And to my mother, Norma Hundley, a woman of extraordinary gifts, extraordinary struggles, and extraordinary love.

A Note About the Author

AYANA MATHIS is a graduate of the Iowa Writers' Workshop and is a recipient of the Michener-Copernicus Fellowship. **The Twelve Tribes of Hattie** is her first novel.